The Theta Syndrome

Elleston Trevor

The Theta Syndrome

DOUBLEDAY & COMPANY, INC.
Garden City, New York
1977

ISBN: 0-385-07463-8
Library of Congress Catalog Card Number 76-55904

FOR

GERTRUDE AND GERSON MARKS

Chapter 1

The blue water burst against her hands and she felt the tug at her breasts as she went under, the roaring dying away and the silence coming, someone's quick laugh breaking it from up there in the sunshine. For a moment she drifted, then rose through the half-light until the high noon sun exploded against her eyes and she turned away from it, kicking in a slow sidestroke toward the edge of the pool and pulling herself out as the water streamed from her body and the sun's heat began warming her skin again.

The breeze had made a fold in her towel and she straightened it and lay face down, shutting her eyes. A trickle filled the whorls of her left ear and spilled over, running down her cheek; the nape of her neck was numbing cold under the mass of her wet hair. Her breath was coming back and she consciously felt the flexing of her ribs against the hard flat cool-deck beneath the towel.

She was vaguely aware that she ought to rejoice in some way, or feel impressed by the fact that this particular creature had just reached back across the uncountable millennia of evolution to wallow for a few minutes in the element that once had been its home; but she was aware also that the idea was an attempt to divert her from a more immediate truth: that nothing had really changed. She could dive into the pool a hundred times and nothing would change: the problem on her mind would still be there.

"Claudia."

Don't answer, she thought.

A shadow fell across her: she felt it as a coolness along the back of her legs. It had been Rick's voice, or Peter's; she wasn't sure which. She supposed he was crouching beside her, waiting for her to answer; but she wasn't going to. He'd said her name from a distance as he'd approached, and wouldn't be certain she'd heard him. The younger men at the club had begun seeking her out, recently, because they assumed she was now "available" again, though the divorce wasn't yet through. She tried to avoid them.

"Claudia?"

I can't hear you. I'm asleep. I am a monster lying here on the baking rock, evolving, having dragged my fins-becoming-legs from the primeval pool. And I am not available.

He didn't say her name again. She heard nothing, but the warmth was coming back along her legs where the cool of his shadow had been, and she lay listening to the voices of the others, their tone oddly changed because her ears were so close to the ground. She hoped nobody else would come over, wanting to talk to her; because she needed to lie here and try to think what to do about this thing that was on her mind; because she knew that some time soon she would have to take some kind of action.

Sounds came in waves: the lightness of voices and Diane's quick laugh again, the soft explosion as somebody dived, the faraway rhythmic *throp* of the balls in the tennis courts where people were still playing, even in this heat.

"Claudie?" It was Kim's voice, gentle and inquiring. "Are you okay?"

Claudia rolled over and squinted upward against the glare.

"Yes."

"D'you want to talk about it?"

"No."

2

"Oh." Then with a nervous little laugh, "You don't have to, I guess!"

Claudia waited three seconds and rolled over again onto her front.

Kim was a very sweet person and was only wanting her to know she was always available for in-depth broken-heart sessions at any time of the day or night; but Claudia suspected she was also eager to vicariously wallow in the hot salt tears that had to be shed in order to blur the image of a wrecked marriage, and for Claudia the time for tears was already over. She had got rid of them, she remembered clearly, between a quarter after two and five-fifteen on the morning of May 6; because it was at a quarter after two when she'd put the phone down after listening to the strange and slightly scared and slightly defiant little voice that had talked about "me and Patrick," and it had been five-fifteen when she had noticed the first crack of light along the horizon and picked herself up from the weeds and beer cans and other junk in the patch of waste ground at the end of the street where she'd gone to be alone because there seemed nowhere else—the apartment had been blown sky high and the debris was mostly their wedding gifts.

But she had walked back to it, in the first inconsequential light of the new day, and by that time the tears were over and they'd never come again.

If Kim was so eager to feel them she'd have to go through the same thing for herself: there were plenty of Patricks around. And the silly thing was that Kim had got it wrong anyway; it was more than seven weeks now and life had started up again and she was still a part of it and there were whole hours in every day when she didn't think about him at all. People thought she was lying here feeling bitter or numbed or abandoned, but she wasn't worried about Patrick any more.

She was worried about the rats.

3

Brian watched from the bench.

His thumb still tingled a little, and he'd glanced at it a couple of times to see how the bruise was coming.

As his head moved from side to side he thought more than once that Bob Anders was being rather showy today, sending the balls back with a slight flick of the wrist, a flourish intended to convey that he wasn't really having to try. He looked, Brian thought, a degree more godlike than usual this afternoon, his tan-and-white figure flexing and turning in calculated ellipses that carried his swing a fraction farther than was needed to drive the ball, his bronze hair flying in a sudden wave as he leapt and descended, contracting again into his correctly composed muscular postures before dancing obliquely to control a wide ball and drop it casually across the net.

Sitting quietly on the worn bleached slats of the bench, Brian didn't think Claudia was looking all that impressed, and in this opinion he allowed for the fact that he didn't want her to be, and might therefore be deceiving himself.

Claudia wasn't performing with her usual deft style today, but looked ready to drop out after only two sets. She'd become erratic in the last ten minutes or so, and Brian dodged instinctively as she sent another wild ball like the one that had made a ricochet off the net post not long ago, hitting his thumb. This one curved well above his head and glanced off the wire mesh behind him.

He went on watching until she was bored with being bad and left the court, apologizing to Bob Anders. Brian left soon afterwards, since he'd come here to watch Claudia, just as he had sat watching her by the pool this morning, though from a much greater distance. For almost a year now he had also watched her at work, when there was a chance, and it had occurred to him that this amounted to voyeurism, however innocent; but there was no thinkable alternative. There'd be no point in talking to her or trying

4

to get acquainted, because she went for men like Patrick Terman—however disastrously—and was unimpressed even by the gold and godlike Anders at the top of his form.

Brian Newby would claim for himself at least one attribute: that he knew his limitations. The other alternative, even less thinkable, was to give up watching her, even from a distance. But the way she walked, the way she turned her head, the quickness of her smile, her stillness when she listened and so many other things had for almost a year now become part of his day, part of his life; and the only thing he could think of more foolish than this would be his not admitting it.

He walked between the hedges of oleander, away from the courts and toward the clubhouse, where she had gone, amused—or trying, against the tug of other and different feelings, to be amused—by the fact that today Claudia had made contact with him more intimately than on any other day for almost a year, if only by hitting his thumb with a tennis ball.

She took the call in the lobby.

"This is me."

"Who?"

She knew, of course, who it was; but he couldn't go on calling her up with only his voice as an identification; it made a claim on her. He was a stranger now.

"Paddy."

"Oh, hello Patrick."

"Paddy" had been "her" name for him. That too was over.

She could hear him being patient.

"Did you decide?" he asked her.

"No."

Jennifer went past, a racquet under her arm. "Hi!"

"Hi!"

5

Patrick was trying to keep silent, so she'd have to say why she hadn't decided. She didn't say anything. She won.

"Listen, baby. You—"

"Don't call me that."

Love–thirty.

"Oh for Christ's sake, Claudia, why don't you make up your mind and get the whole thing over with?"

He was quick to anger. He'd said it so many times: "I'm fast-burn, baby." Said it so proudly.

But the "whole thing" had been gotten over with among the weeds and the beer cans. All he was talking about was the divorce, and that didn't seem very important. They hadn't seen each other since two days after she'd known, and she hoped never to see him again. When they finally got around to it, they wouldn't both have to go to the court; either one would do.

"Baby?"

She was putting the phone down when he said with a great show of articulation: "Claudia?"

"Yes?"

"I just want to know how long you're going to keep me on the hook."

His mouth sounded tight.

It hadn't always sounded like this.

I'll love you forever, baby. Forever, believe me.

But of course one said these things and it wasn't any use looking back at them and trying to understand how so much change could have come, and so fast. It just happened. It was like walking in front of a truck.

"Listen," he said, with a tone of righteous bewilderment that didn't quite come off, "you're not a vindictive person, I know that. We said—"

"You don't know me. I'm a complete—"

"Oh Jesus Christ, okay, okay, we're complete strangers and I don't have to call you 'baby' and I've no idea whether

6

you're vindictive or not, okay? But the fact is I want to marry Teresa and you know that and you're just keeping me hanging around like I was a goddam—"

Now she really put it down and walked back into the club room and finished her juice and tried not to notice the way her hands were shaking. At the back of her mind there was an idea that she ought to warn Teresa in some way. Teresa was eighteen and she was going to walk under the same truck and it didn't seem human to stand by and watch her do it. But of course any kind of warning would be misunderstood.

The end of the straw gurgled at the bottom of the empty glass.

She wouldn't take his call the next time. He called every day from wherever he was, and tomorrow she'd tell them to say she was busy and couldn't come to the phone.

Forever, baby.

I just want to know how long you're going to keep me on the hook.

But the sex had been fantastic. Even by twenty-eight she hadn't had many experiences, but she'd had enough to know Patrick was exceptional. At first it had been one long roller-coaster ride through the rainbow, dizzying and body-blowing; but finally it became exhausting, and she'd begun making excuses. His energy was an unrestrained force, and once she'd bitten him hard, on purpose, drawing blood and making him stop, because she knew blood scared him.

It had been during the sex that she'd really come to know what he was. In the beginning she'd believed it was passion, even that she turned him on so effectively that he couldn't think of anything else; then she'd realized there was nothing abandoned about it, nothing animal, nothing spontaneous. He was doing exactly what he did so successfully on the baseball field: he was performing. His performance was all that mattered to him, and he worked at it, showing her new

7

positions and keeping her waiting long after she was ready, parading his erection and even timing its endurance—*you know something, baby, it's been a whole hour already and just look at this*—till the time came when she had to use her own fingers because she couldn't bear to wait any more. And he didn't even notice. Didn't even know.

That was Patrick. He was a baseball player, Triple A. He played it on the baseball field and he played it in bed and all over the living-room floor and in the back of the car and wherever they could find a place and take the time. And his performances were so consistently successful that she came to know, finally, what she was too. The crowd.

"Feeling down, honey?"

Jennifer stood over her, the racquet clasped in her thin brown arms. She took it wherever she went; she played terrible tennis but was in love with the image, and it suited her looks.

"It's just the heat," Claudia said.

"Sure." She rested her small chin on the frame of the racquet, looking down pensively. "Did he call you again?"

"Who?"

"Well, him! That stud."

Claudia got up, taking her glass back to the bar. "No."

In a moment Jennifer called out: "Are you coming along with us tonight? Marge and me?"

"Could be."

"Uh-huh."

She was alone again, and scared for a moment because now she'd have to start thinking. Not about Patrick; there wasn't anything more to think about him, except to remind herself that if it hadn't been for Teresa she would have left him anyway, because all he'd had for her was an intense sexuality that he'd never learned how to share.

There were only a few people in the room—Marge and

Jennifer over by the television, Brian in the far corner with a magazine, Jim Thorpe repairing his racquet cover—and she found somewhere secluded to sit on the far side of the doors where no one would notice her. Then, because she couldn't avoid it any longer, she began thinking.

Not about Patrick. About the rats.

By midnight she had been lying awake for two hours, going over the whole thing until she began doubting her own senses. An hour ago she'd been on the point of calling Lee Telfer, then had changed her mind; Lee was a curiously withdrawn person, and so sure of what he was doing that he'd probably suggest she was in need of a vacation.

Sometime before one o'clock she got out of bed and put on some pants and a tee shirt and went down to the apartment carport, to pull open the top of the dark green TR-2 and drive through the warm air, heading north along Harbor Boulevard. She didn't have any specific plan; there was no kind of test she could make that would give her the answer; she just had to get there, and be there, and go on thinking. Better than doing it in bed, without a hope of sleep.

Soon she turned left onto the freeway and headed west with the warm humid air of the city blowing against her face, smelling of smog after the heat of the long summer day. At West Coast she found Mac on duty when she let herself in with her key; he seemed surprised to see her but they didn't talk much because neither wanted to; he was hunched in a chair under the main lights of the reception lobby, reading for his thesis, his long legs drawn up at all angles and his red hair burning in the glare.

"Do you need anything?"

"No," she said. "I just want to catch up a little."

In the main laboratory there were only the pilot lamps going, but she didn't switch any more on; she could read the

9

charts in this light and it was a firm principle never to change the night-day environment unless absolutely necessary. In some of the mammals the metabolic cycle was sensitive to disorientation and you could affect the findings of any given trial beyond the margin of error.

Their smell came to her as she walked down the long room, acid and pervading, with the musky scent of the Marsumas giving it an over-sweet perfume that she hardly noticed because she was so used to it. In some of the cages their shapes moved, disturbed, and settled again as she passed. Somewhere in Row 11 a fight was going on, the shrill squeals of the adversaries only just this side of the supersonic pitch; it was where Dr. Montabon was running his own proximity-stress project.

Claudia took one of the high stools and moved it in front of the Marsumas and went through the current charts one by one, taking her time. These toxicity trials had been running for a month, with a control and seven test groups under precisely increasing dosages of the new X5-79 adrenyl-phenox derivative against a broad range of tropozite and cyst states. It was the final clearance project for Fiorenzo Pharmaceutical, a routine requirement of the FDA, and so far Lee Telfer was satisfied.

This was one of the things she knew she had to forget: that Lee was satisfied. They were colleagues of equal status, but he was senior in experience and she trusted his judgment without question. But he wasn't infallible; no human mind at work at West Coast Research Laboratories was infallible, and this was so well recognized that a team of two observers had been allocated to the X5-79 trials when one could easily have done the work: it was a parallel-series project with no cross-analyses and the main task was to write up the charts. Until a week ago Claudia had been equally satisfied; then for three days the full-dose rat in Cage 2 had started showing progressive sensitivity to the

10

adrenyl-phenox derivative, with tissue morbidity setting in on the third day. The condition had cleared gradually over the next four days and Lee Telfer had noted it in the charts as "other-induced reactions" because no one had been able to work out a drug-derived model for the causative agent.

It had been the fourth day when the rats in the three end cages had started their behavioral changes. They were barely noticeable and Lee had dismissed them as "day-to-day differentials," asking Claudia do *you* always feel and behave the same way, *every* day? It was true that these white-pelt Marsumas were sensitive to a variety of random stimuli, and expressed discomfort or disorientation to a marked degree. Last year the Series 1 trials in X5 had to be rerun and reassessed because one of the lab assistants had been given a foxhound for her birthday and its scent on her clothes had induced an alarm syndrome in seventeen of the rats, and it had taken almost two months and a thousand dollars' worth of fresh animals to find the cause and produce error-free patterns.

All the same, Claudia didn't feel easy. Lee Telfer was practical, clinical and highly experienced; but he wasn't a computer, or above making a mistake. She had decided to agree with him formally and keep her reservations to herself, for further examination. If the slight behavioral changes had settled down to the prescribed norms she would have got the whole thing out of her mind. But they hadn't settled down. That was why she was here now.

Tonight, admittedly, there was nothing wrong with the charts. At the current stage of the work (Phase C and Biopsy), death typically occurred in the region of a 200 mg/kg of body-weight dosage at the fifth-day period, and this matched perfectly with the background scenario. In the glow of the pilot lamps she filed the charts and began studying the rats, knowing it was wrong to do it, but knowing she had to. Mr. Heideker was precise on this point: *We have to*

11

rely on the evidence and the evidence alone. We have to forget about intuition and instinct; we are pursuing an exact science. We have to examine what happens, and not what we think ought to happen.

At West Coast some of the staff didn't agree, and even Mr. Heideker wouldn't argue that Einstein himself hadn't functioned significantly on the right hemisphere of his brain, to arrive at cosmic truths by pure intuition. But in this laboratory the chemical and the computer were the two major tools, and West Coast had an outstanding reputation with the FDA and the top pharmaceutical firms across the country; and if anyone disagreed with Mr. Heideker he did it in private.

Claudia sat perfectly still, watching the rats.

They were aware of her presence, of course; in the primitive brain stem they'd become aware of her the instant she'd walked in here. They were now reacting consciously, in the tiniest of movements, their sharp heads turning to catch any sound she might make, their snouts lifted slightly as they analyzed her smell and found it unalarming. Two of them had come to the front of their cages to watch her, the pilot lamps reflected in their bright black eyes.

These two would be dead tomorrow, but she had long ago tackled that problem and licked it, with the help of a friend who was an intern at a cancer hospital. He'd said without any wish to impress her: "I'd estimate that research using animals has cut the overall mortality rate for the major diseases by half."

So these two rats would die tomorrow, and somewhere a human life would go on, perhaps a child's. The thought was no less valid for its simplification, and she'd learned to accept it and work with it. Tonight they stared back at her, their fur ghost-white in the lowered light, their noses wrinkling in small spasms as they scented, the black beads of

12

their eyes winking steadily, examining her image and finding that, too, unalarming.

Hello, Sam.

Hello, Charlie.

They were the permanent names for the rats in the two end cages, whichever rats they might be. It was a means of identifying them in discussions, easier than using their lab series numbers.

They watched her, their silence intense. Sam had moved slightly, grasping one of the cage wires in his pink sinewy paw and rising a little on his haunches to see her better. Charlie was on the straw, watching her in utter stillness. In Cage 3 Rufus was on the prowl, loping from one side of the cage to the other and back, the straw rustling under his feet but with a sound so slight that she hardly caught it.

Hello, Rufus.

Rufus was to live two more days: he would be sacrificed first thing on Wednesday. The fourteen others would be allowed to die progressively of the drug's toxicity, at an overdose of two thousand pharmacological units.

She watched them for thirty minutes, twice getting off the stool to stretch her legs, once looking again at the charts. But when she moved she went on observing their reactions: she was making movements they had seen for a month, a dozen times a day, but they still reacted, each in his own way.

Her eyes were tired from the strain of observing in a poor light, and she decided that if she went back to the apartment and got into bed she would sleep. But something bothered her, something quite new. Nothing had changed in the charts; nothing had changed in the rats' behavior: each was reacting in the same familiar pattern. Her movements were—

Stop.

Stop right there. And think.

13

It didn't take long. Perhaps a minute.

Okay. Each was reacting in the same familiar pattern. *But not each in his own way*.

There *was* a change—a big one. A personality change. Sam was behaving like Rufus, and Rufus was behaving like Charlie, and Charlie was behaving like Sam.

Impossible. X5-79 adrenyl-phenox was a broad-spectrum antidote for the basic organic toxins in the Western Hemisphere group, and there was just no way it could affect behavior. She'd seen ninety of these Marsumas die in the prelim trials and there'd been no sign of any psychological effects. A biochemist wouldn't be able to suggest how it could possibly occur; nor could a behavioral psychologist. But it was happening, and she was watching it.

She didn't move from the stool until her legs were cramped, but by that time she'd got it. It had taken a little time because the only possible explanation didn't have anything to do with biochemistry or behavioral psychology, and every time it had occurred to her she'd dismissed it; and that was why it had taken her so long—she'd refused again and again to admit this one possibility. Because in a word it was sabotage.

Sam and Rufus and Charlie hadn't started to behave like each other. They were still behaving like themselves, each in his own way; but in the wrong place. In the wrong cage.

Not quite. But she was halfway there and couldn't miss it now. Not in the wrong cage, because their pelts were branded to avoid a mistake when they were taken out for treatment or examination. These three rats were still in their right cages and their brands tallied. The cages themselves had been switched around.

Sam watched her, his paw clenched around the wire upright, his black eyes directed at her own in the silence. His nose was wrinkling again as he scented her, perhaps detect-

14

ing the change in her odor as her system absorbed the shock and expelled new secretions through the skin.

Get Mac.

Mac wouldn't know what she was talking about; he was in his initial term as a computer analyst.

Call Lee.

Lee was already "satisfied" and had said that any behavioral changes weren't "critical." He'd suggest she take a vacation.

Call Mr. Heideker.

At one-thirty in the morning? Yes, because of what the notice said, above the door of the laboratory. IF ANYONE LEAVES ANYTHING TO CHANCE IT'S THE LAST ONE THEY'LL GET AT WEST COAST RESEARCH. And because of what happened last year when an observer had worked late under the pilot lamps and noticed a spontaneous light-stimulus reaction in one of the Liberian mice when he'd used a flashlight to find a chart. He'd left a note about it, but by next morning there was an epidemic already beginning to wipe out half the North African mammals in the laboratory, the virus attacking the retinal cones and moving through the optic nerve to the brain. There hadn't been time to combat it, and its virulence had trebled the mortality rate within six hours.

Five trials had to be abandoned, three hundred mammals were slammed into quarantine and the observer was fired. And there was another notice on the wall, over the telephone: IF IN DOUBT CALL ME. I DON'T CARE WHEN. Carl Heideker had signed it himself with a thick felt pen.

The big clock read 1:33 A.M. when Claudia made the call.

The phone rang seven times. She counted them.

"Yes?"

"Mr. Heideker?"

"Yes."

He sounded heavy with sleep.

15

"This is Claudia Terman, Trial Finals and Biopsy. I'm sorry to call you so late."

In the next two or three seconds she found herself going through an automatic review of the whole situation in her mind, surprising herself. She didn't want to look a fool: her reputation was pretty high at West Coast and if she were wrong about this thing it could involve quite a lot of people in an unnecessary inquiry and Carl Heideker wouldn't thank her for that.

The line was silent; he was waiting for her to go on. She could hear Mac out there in the lobby, turning a page of his book, and one of the rats squealing again in the proximity-stress unit at the end of Row 11. She drew a quick breath.

"I'm still worried about the trials we're running in X5—you remember I mentioned it a couple of times before?"

"Yes. But we agreed to go along with Lee Telfer's thinking."

She paused a moment, hoping to find courage. "That's right, Mr. Heideker, we did. But I'm still finding behavioral changes, and I'm finding them immediately subsequent to the tissue reactions we began getting last week. The thing that worries me is that these behavioral changes are only apparent, not real. At first I thought they'd been put back in the wrong cages by mistake, but—"

"That couldn't happen."

The sleep had gone out of Heideker's voice.

"I know. It was just my first thinking."

"Go on," he said in a moment.

"Well, I—" she hesitated, sensing new dimensions to this thing that hadn't occurred to her before. "I couldn't sleep tonight, with it all on my mind, so I came on down here. I've—"

"To the laboratory?"

"Yes. That's where I'm calling from."

16

"Go on."

She wished she hadn't started this, at least not tonight. She wanted more time to think, more time to observe the Marsumas. It was late and she'd lost sleep and maybe there were things she'd missed, some other explanation for what was happening in those cages. Carl Heideker's voice should have calmed her, but it hadn't; his very attentiveness was driving her to say things she might regret.

"Mr. Heideker, could—could you possibly come down here and let me show you what I mean?"

There was a short silence.

"Perhaps. But tell me a little more."

It wasn't going to be easy. West Coast was an establishment run on the lines of a clinic, with every precaution taken against the risk of error or clumsiness on the part of the highly trained staff. To suggest actual sabotage was almost unthinkable. But then, on a vaster scale, there'd been Watergate, and its beginnings had been as simple as these.

"I've thought about this for days, Mr. Heideker, and tonight I've spent almost an hour here, trying to find out what's going on. And I think I've done that. I think there's only one possible explanation."

In a moment he asked tonelessly: "And that is?"

She drew a breath. "I believe the drug we're testing began proving toxic in low doses. I believe someone wanted to hide that fact—so they switched three of the cages around. At least three. There could be more."

She could feel the slight thudding of her heart.

A rat squealed again in Row 11.

The line was silent.

Then she heard Mr. Heideker clearing his throat. "You suggest the drug is beginning to prove unsafe?"

"Yes."

"And that some person is trying to cover it up?"

"Yes."

17

The line was quiet again.

"Mr. Heideker, I know I'm—"

"Please wait for me there. I'll be along as soon as possible."

The line clicked and went dead.

At 2:15 Claudia called Heideker's home again and waited till the phone had rung more than a dozen times. It probably meant he was already on his way here, but it was only a ten-mile ride along the freeways and she'd waited almost forty-five minutes and she was now more tired than she'd realized. The shock of finding out and the strain of telling him had used up the last of her energies, and she was desperate at last for sleep.

"Mac."

He looked up vacantly, his mind still on his studies.

"If Mr. Heideker comes, tell him I've gone home. Tell him I waited till now."

"Okay." Her face began registering on him. "Is everything all right?"

"Sort of."

She left him quickly, going out and letting the doorlock snap behind her. The moon was up as she crossed the parking lot, and the air was cooler; she breathed deeply, trying to relax. She had done all she could be expected to do; she hadn't left anything to chance and she'd called Mr. Heideker and told him all she knew. Now she wanted to sleep, and go on sleeping.

The headlights of the little sports car swung across the almost empty parking lot as she turned onto the roadway without seeing the Pontiac, and headed for the Garden Grove Freeway with the exhaust note echoing among the buildings.

It was the only explanation, the only way it could have

happened. Their pelts were branded, so there couldn't have been any mistake. If Lee had—

Stop thinking. Just stop thinking.

Along the freeway the cool air slapped at her face, and her dark hair blew sometimes across her eyes. Near the exit for Brookhurst she saw the gas warning light come on: the boy at the service station had forgotten to fill up with gas when she had the oil changed this morning. She slowed for a moment, but there was more than enough to get her home and take her to the gas station tomorrow, and she sped up again and kept on driving.

Could be Mr. Heideker wouldn't mention it to anyone, even Lee Telfer, until he'd talked to her in private. It was a crazy thing to say, that someone had been switching the cages around; but she wasn't crazy and she'd said it and Mr. Heideker would have to believe it. He wasn't a man to—

To anything. Nothing. Stop thinking.

Light came into the mirror and went out again. There was hardly any traffic at this hour and in the small humming sports car she felt strangely isolated, aware for an instant that she was a creature sliding across the surface of the planet, alone except for the moon above her head and closer to it than to the glimmer of streetlights below the freeway where people slept.

Five minutes ago she'd let a truck go past, wanting to keep out of its way and wanting to feel alone again under the vastness of the night sky, beginning to enjoy the thought that at this moment nobody knew where she was, nobody could reach her and pin her down with obligations.

Driving due east she had the moon directly over the frame of the windshield, the dark line sometimes touching the globe of light as the pavement undulated. The suburbs on either side seemed darkened by contrast, their streets half lost among the trees. The gas warning light made a small red glow on the instrument panel, and she must knot the duster round the gear shift tonight, as she always did, to remind her to fill up tomorrow.

The Pontiac was on her very fast and its headlights blinded her in the mirror, making her flinch. It must have been using only its parking lights for a time, otherwise she'd have seen it following. It seemed very close and she could see the shadow of her own car slipping along the guardrail as the wash of light flooded the roadway from the left side.

She could hear the other car now and it sounded awfully close, a heavy rushing of tires right beside her. She felt she'd got suddenly caught in something and it scared her and she jerked a look over her shoulder and saw the car and the driver alone in it, his head turned this way and the backwash of light showing his face. In the last instant she was aware of not recognizing him: he was a stranger. But what made her frightened was that he was watching her, as if they had something to do with each other; and she turned away and looked through the windshield again, not understanding but just feeling the fright come into her as the first bump sent her swerving with a sudden squeal from the tires.

Reflected light from the windshield hurt her eyes but she couldn't make it go, then the second bump came and the wheel jerked in her hands and she tried to wrench it back but the car was slewing badly from side to side in the glare of the lights, its movement sickening her. She tried all the time to get the wheel straight but there wasn't any control left and then it happened, the rushing of the guardrail across her eyes and the racketing of metal and the smell of rubber, with the other lights blinding her, right in her face as the sky swung over and the moon sped like a ball, over and over, down and down, her voice crying out above the noise.

Chapter 2

They used the siren coming off Brockhurst onto the freeway but there wasn't any traffic and they put on speed, picking up the accident a half mile farther on: a small car upside down against the guardrail, its lights still on and shining low across the pavement.

When the ambulance stopped they saw the driver in a heap not far from the car, a young woman with one arm across her face like she'd been trying to protect herself; but she'd just finished up that way, that was all; she must have come out of that car at all angles and landed like a doll someone had thrown.

One of the paramedics tilted the big chrome lamp on its swivel and went to the victim, looking for blood and noting the set of the limbs, while the driver put some flares out behind the vehicle as an extra precaution: they were blocking the inside lane.

"Jim!"

"Yeah?"

"Get the bag. She's not breathing."

They began working together, one of them giving the woman mouth-to-mouth resuscitation while the other brought the ambu bag and set it up, shining the tracheal light to check the vocal cords and then passing the tube into the trachea, his hand a little shaky because it was only the second time he'd done it on the crash scene and the first time at night.

"Okay?"

He thought he was taking too much time. It had to be done fast.

"Jim—okay?"

The light kept moving.

"Yeah. Okay now."

He started squeezing the bag.

"Keep her head still."

"Right."

A cool wind was blowing from the ocean, drying their sweat.

Squeeze. Squeeze. Squeeze.

"She's taking it."

"Yeah."

The vehicle's emergency light swung rhythmically, its reflection in the smashed windshield of the TR-2 going bright and dark again, bright and dark as the minutes went by.

"One hundred over seventy."

"Okay."

She looked quite pretty, even with the tube in. Dirt on her face.

"A hundred ten bpm."

"Okay."

Squeeze. Squeeze. Squeeze.

Not much bleeding. No limbs broken. Wasn't so bad. It wasn't ever so bad as you thought when you first came on the scene, except maybe that one on the San Diego a month back. Christ.

"Doing okay now, Chuck."

"I guess."

They put in the IV catheter and rigged up the bottle, setting the measure at 32. Jim never stopped squeezing the bag. A siren was sounding from somewhere north.

"'Bout time."

"I guess."

He sat on his heels, wiping the sweat off his face and shutting his eyes for a second. He'd done it again, got the damned thing in, second time, first time in the dark, and done it fast enough. The heap on the ground was breathing again, or at least being breathed for; they'd got something still alive.

"You okay, Jim?"

"Sure." He opened his eyes. "Better get started."

The siren was louder now, and from the west: the police car was on the freeway. And there was another one somewhere, fainter. They got the woman onto the stretcher and into the ambulance with the bag and the IV still going. Jim pulled one of her shoes off and cut the stocking away, scratching the sole of her foot and seeing the toes splay out; he'd already seen the pupil fixation. It figured: the only real bleeding was from the back of the neck.

They were turning around when the first police car came in fast under the brakes but Chuck didn't stop to say anything: they'd get it on the radio. He began calling as soon as he'd put on some speed.

We're coming in with a Caucasian female, age around twenty-eight, weight around a hundred twenty pounds, height five feet, a bit more. Severe contusion and laceration in the suboccipital area, minor contusion on forehead. Babinski bilaterally, pupils fixed, comatose state.

The second police patrol had got to the scene: he picked up its lights in the mirror. What had she been doing, then, all alone on the freeway this hour, turning the thing over? She been high on something?

She was high now, all right: the tests showed brain damage.

We're currently running a D5 and W at thirty-two drops per minute and she's breathing on the ambu bag. Blood

23

pressure is one hundred over seventy and heart rate is a hundred ten bpm.

In five minutes they swung off the freeway at Harbor Boulevard and turned west again, taking the fast lane back. Chuck saw the two patrol cars at the crash scene as he went by. They'd switched off the headlights of the sports car and it just looked like a lump of metal now.

In the back of the ambulance the paramedic sat watching the young woman, squeezing the bag to keep her alive. She was still in coma, and in the glow from the roof lamp her face was calm.

At this hour the lights burned low in the windows of Garden Grove Hospital, and only a dozen or so cars stood in the moonlit parking lot. Inside the building voices were quiet, and only a few of the three hundred patients were awake.

Even the paging system sounded muted by the night.

Dr. Gomez, please—Code 1. Dr. Gomez.

The coffee shop on the ground floor was still open, its single waitress talking to its single customer, one of the night guards.

In the children's ward, higher in the building, a small boy was whimpering in his sleep, and a nurse went across to him.

Dr. Rand, please—Code 1. Dr. Rand.

In the Cardiac Care Unit on the fifth floor a patient wandered from his room and along the corridor, keeping his hand on the rail until he reached the bathroom. On a screen at the nurses' station the electrocardiogram displayed his heartbeat.

A siren sounded from outside the building, half a mile away.

On the sixth floor a young intern rechecked the patient, nodding to the nurse. In a moment she went to the tele-

24

phone and made the required call, bringing a screen back with her to put around the bed.

Most of the crew had now arrived in the Emergency Room, in answer to the Code 1 calls. They could hear the siren now, coming closer.

"Hi, Mary. When did you get back?"

"Saturday."

"How was it?"

"Fantastic! We did Grand Canyon and everything."

"Wow!"

A nurse was washing her hands again at the basin.

Dr. Rand, please. Dr. Rand—Code 1.

An orderly stood at the water fountain, gulping.

"Who left these gloves here?"

Nobody knew.

Dr. Gomez came in quickly, blinking in the light, smelling of cigarette smoke.

"Hi, Doc."

"I was just going home!"

Someone laughed.

The siren howled low, dying away outside.

They could hear doors slamming.

The nurse shut the faucet off and dried her hands.

At the end of the passage the Emergency entrance doors banged open and the cool smell of the night air came in, something of the ocean in it.

Gomez went along to meet the ambulance crew.

Everyone had read the report radioed from the crash scene and knew approximately what to expect.

Dr. Rand arrived as the stretcher was being wheeled into the Emergency Room. Gomez was noting the skin color of the patient and checking her breathing sounds, particularly the left lung. Sometimes a paramedic would let the tube slip down past the carina into the right bronchial, and the patient would breathe only with the right lung.

25

Inside the room he passed a new tube and hooked up to the mechanical respirator, checking to see if the patient was assisting on it. She wasn't.

"Did I do it okay?"

One of the nurses began cleaning the injuries, picking out chips of tarmacadam. Someone adjusted the main lamp overhead. Everybody was moving a little faster now.

"Was it okay, Doc?"

"Uh?"

"The tube."

"Oh, sure. Right on."

The young paramedic went out of the room, his face losing its worry.

Dr. Rand was looking at the main injury as the nurse's swabs eased the dirt and the drying blood away from the suboccipital area below the back of the head. It was a simple laceration but quite deep, extending three or four centimeters into the galea aponeurotica. The area was cleaned and debrided, and the laceration repaired with interrupted sutures.

The patient was now stabilized but still not assisting the respirator, and Rand thought the problem was most likely neurological, a result of the trauma.

"Can you squeeze your hand?"

There was no response.

Rand looked across at the nurse.

"What's her name?"

She tilted the chart.

"Claudia Marianne Terman, Doctor."

He said more loudly: "Claudia, can you squeeze your hand for me?"

Her pale fingers lay still.

"Claudia, can you hear me?"

He pinched the skin of her throat, twisting it gently, doing it twice. She didn't respond.

26

The respirator pulsed softly beside her. If they switched off the respirator they would switch off Claudia Marianne Terman; but Dr. Rand didn't quite know why. The trauma hadn't penetrated the skull and there was no other major injury.

He lifted her eyelids again. Her stare was fixed, the pupils dilated.

"How's it with you, Ramon?"

"I'm through till we move her." Dr. Gomez felt for the cigarettes in his pocket, an unconscious habit, bringing his hand away empty. "It must be deeper than it looks."

"Could be."

Rand ordered arterial blood gas studies, a complete blood count, urine analysis and a skull series. The radiologist began work on the pictures right away.

Rand tried a final pain stimulus test and got no response.

"Was it a crash?"

"Yes, Doctor."

"She alone?"

"As far as we know."

He went over to the basin, nudging the faucet lever with his elbow. "As soon as you're ready to move her, give me a call."

"Yes, Doctor."

"If I'm not in my office, put out a Code 2."

Soon after 4 A.M. Dr. Rand performed a tracheotomy on the patient in Room 6 of the Intensive Care Unit and she was hooked up to the MA1 ventilator, which continued to breathe for her. The screen of the electrocardiograph above the bed was giving satisfactory readings but the resident still had his doubts about this case and had ordered pulmonary and neurological consults.

At this stage he didn't know for certain whether the brain was still alive. It could be dying. The skull films were thorough but they didn't show any critical trauma, and Rand had ordered a further series. The human brain died gradually, from the upper part of the brain stem to the deeper regions, and tests were difficult to make without specialized equipment. Twenty minutes ago he had called for an electroencephalograph hookup and the technician was working on it now.

The respiratory therapist had set up the MA1 according to the blood gas report and adjusted the delivery appropriate to the PH, PCO_2, PO_2 and the base excess levels, and would check back in half an hour unless anyone called him sooner.

The IV catheter was now providing essential fluids and vitamins direct into the bloodstream and the EKG monitor was showing a heart rate of 76 bpm, only a little above normal.

Until the pulmonary and neurological consults were made and the new series of skull films processed there was nothing more for the attending physician to do, but Rand stayed until after five o'clock, when the daylight was strengthening in the windows and the banging of the garbage truck in the yard below was waking everyone up.

He had been working most of the night and ought to get off home but didn't feel ready yet. He didn't question this. Cases varied and his mood varied and a whole lot of things varied in the context of his work at Garden Grove, and he liked to keep flexible. As a long-established policy, though, he didn't let himself become too involved with his patients except on the clinical level: it was wearing, often harrowing and potentially dangerous, because a physician whose nerves were stressed by his concern for those he was trying to heal could start making mistakes and they could be critical.

A coronary was a coronary, and all you could do was get the crash cart into action and go on defibrillating till you saw you were wasting your time. That was all you had to think about. It didn't have to matter if the patient lying there on the bed with his face gray and his mouth open had been the greatest guy in the world to his five kids a few minutes ago. You did your best and now you had to forget it. Cancer was cancer, and all you could do was dole out the routine useless chemotherapy and shoot the X rays in until you inevitably failed. It didn't have to make any difference that only last week she'd been writing to Santa Claus and asking him for her first ballet lessons. You did everything the book said and there'd been no hope anyway, and now you had to forget it.

If you didn't, you'd go the way Dan Taylor was going, working a regular fourteen-hour day and knocking himself out with scotch and Valium betweentimes. And no one could talk him out of it: he'd just ask you what the hell you were trying to say. But they'd have to report him sooner or later, for everyone's sake, before he followed the typical pattern of divorce, loss of license and the final overdose.

"Dr. Rand?"

"Yes?"

"We have a request from the police. They're trying to find out what happened to Mrs. Terman and they'd like to know if any traces of alcohol or drugs were noticed in the system."

"You could ask the lab."

The new skull series came in soon after five-fifteen and he looked at them with the radiologist. They weren't any different from the first batch; a little clearer, maybe.

"Would you say these are conclusive?"

The radiologist put his head on one side. "Depends what you mean, really. I don't think we could take any better ones, or use any different angles."

"There just isn't any damage to the skull."

"Not that I can see."

29

Rand went back to his office and drank some coffee.

"Dr. Rand?"

"Yes?"

"I have the EEG running now."

He went into the Intensive Care Unit.

The contacts had been taped to the patient's temples and the technician was tying the wires out of the way beneath the monitor. The rhythm of brain waves crossing the screen was slow, right down in the theta region at fewer than 5 cycles per second, the twilight area of consciousness between meditation and dreaming.

"Claudia."

Rand watched the screen.

"Claudia."

The brain rhythm was constant.

He pinched an earlobe, watching the screen.

Pinched it again.

The rhythm was constant.

He looked at the EKG and the chart and turned away. "It's time I went home. Call me if there's any significant change."

"Yes, Doctor."

He looked back once at the patient. She was lying perfectly still, the tube in her neck and the bellows of the ventilator pulsing softly, keeping her alive. They were doing all that could be done. That didn't mean, of course, that it would be enough.

Eve woke him at two in the afternoon, as he'd asked her to, and had a salad with him at the counter in the kitchen, her slender body poised on the high stool, her long hands using her fork deftly and sometimes passing him things, tempting him.

"Egg-avocado. I made it."

"It's fattening."

30

"You need fattening," she said.

Their talking was desultory; Scott hadn't long been up, and needed a while to pull his thoughts back in shape. He was already thinking about the patient in the Intensive Care Unit, but consciously put her out of his mind; there hadn't been a call from Garden Grove, so there couldn't have been any significant change.

Eve was never talkative anyway, though she knew how to listen, and sometimes remembered things people had long ago forgotten they'd ever said.

"You're also overworking."

"We had an emergency come in."

She forked an anchovy.

"Not until two in the morning."

"How did you know?"

"You told me."

"I was on call last night anyway."

"That doesn't mean you have to hang around the place."

It was true. He could have come home as usual and slept.

"The Thompson kid threw a reaction to the antibiotic, and then Mrs. Alvera went into adrenal failure, and by that time—" He shrugged.

Eve said nothing. The pattern of the conversation was familiar and she was satisfied with it: Scott was getting the message but putting up a defense to protect his ego and that was okay; in a day or two he'd start letting himself think about what she'd said and then it was up to him: either he'd feel she was wrong or he'd realize he was coming to believe he was indispensable and had to drive himself. Hopefully he'd then relax and leave a few more things to others at the Grove. The other route was the one Dan Taylor was taking.

"It's fantastic."

She looked up. "What is?"

"The egg-avocado."

"I told you."

31

She slipped off the stool and went across to the fridge for the dessert, and he watched her for a moment as he sometimes did, because she taught Yoga and Tai Chi at the Community College and moved beautifully, wherever she was. He sometimes wondered why this still young and willowy woman with her pale Renaissance face and her grape-green eyes aroused him so little sexually; but he never really wondered long enough to find an answer, possibly because he might not like it if he did.

"Chinese figs." She came gracefully back to the counter, handing him a long three-pronged fork. "Organic."

"And fattening."

"I'm telling you, darling, you need ten more pounds. A bit more sleep would do it."

"I didn't know you cared."

"But you know I nag. Who was the emergency?"

He'd want her to ask.

"A girl in a car crash."

He wanted to feel they were human beings, not just cases, so he liked her to ask about them; but that was all, just ask about them; they didn't have to go into it deeper than that. The pattern here was familiar too, worked out thread by thread over the seventeen years of their marriage. Once he'd put it into actual words, all at one go, at a very late party last year at the hospital when most people had gone home. "Sometimes I feel like a middle-aged medical student running around trying to patch up people who get sick because they don't know how to stop worrying or eating a diet of unadulterated crud. Is that what I am?"

Eve had said no, it wasn't. She'd driven him slowly home from the party and told him on the way that people would go on worrying themselves to death and eating a diet of unadulterated crud and that someone was urgently needed to comfort them and give them ease and maybe even make

32

them well again, and that she admired the people who did that, above all others.

They'd never talked about it since then. With Scott Rand, a little praise went a long way.

"Caroline wrote," she said.

"*Wrote?*"

She laughed gently. "Yes. I told her any more collect calls were going to be taken out of her allowance."

"How is she?"

"Fine. Broke."

He left the last fig on his plate.

"How much are you going to send her?"

"As little as the humanities will allow."

He poured himself another cup of coffee. "That sounds like a hundred dollars."

"No." She began taking their things to the dishwasher. "I know how hard you work."

He realized he was waiting for the phone to ring. At the hospital they knew he didn't want them to call unless there was something really urgent that nobody else could handle, providing he wasn't on call anyway. But he felt himself waiting.

"I've got a couple of tickets," he said, stirring his coffee, "for the Hollywood Bowl."

"When?"

"Tonight. Mozart."

"Oh, darling, you didn't *buy* them?"

"No. Grateful patient."

Eve rolled the bottom tray of the dishwasher in and reached for the soap powder and poured some and put it back and swung the door shut and slid the lever and switched on, all in a series of graceful movements that looked as if they'd been rehearsed for hours.

"The photographer's coming tonight," she said above the noise of the machine. "To the studio."

33

"I'll give them to someone else."

"It's a shame—I love Mozart."

And photographs. They were all over the place: Eve in a ballet dress, Eve in a track suit, Eve in leotards. Everyone admired them, and so did he. They all said how graceful she was, and he agreed.

He fetched his briefcase.

"Why don't you go, Scott? Isn't there anyone you could take?"

"I'll ask around."

They both knew he wouldn't.

He was on his way to the garage when the phone rang and Eve picked it up.

"Yes, he's here." She gave it to him.

It was the hospital. They said Dr. Kistner was interested in the Terman case, and wanted to operate immediately. Scott told them he was just leaving.

Chapter 3

The Intensive Care Unit at Garden Grove had just been done over, and two workmen were finishing the ceiling light panels, creeping up and down their ladders in borrowed operating-room slippers and trying not to make a noise with their tools.

Viewed from above, the unit had the shape of a keyhole: the nurses' station was in the center of the round area, with the eight rooms in a circle at the perimeter, so that the staff could see the big screened windows and hear the pulsing of the artificial ventilators at all times. The other rooms, down the sides of the oblong, were for patients under recuperative observation.

The alterations had made more space around the central nurses' station and there was now more light coming in from the patients' rooms when the screens were open. The EKG and EEG monitor displays were grouped at one end of the station, with the filing cabinets and telephones at the other. The crash cart stood on the far side of the station from the observation rooms, near the emergency exit.

Candystriper to the Pharmacy, please.

The two men worked quietly at the top of their ladders, sometimes throwing the box of screws to each other and missing only once. After that they put some of the screws into a spare box so they didn't have to share.

At this time, three-thirty in the afternoon, four nurses

and two nurses' aides were in the unit and six of the beds were occupied.

Dr. Matheson to Operating Room 1, please.

The wall speakers were not switched on in the Intensive and Cardiac Care units but the calls could be heard from the corridors outside; the soft and unceasing music was similarly only half audible in the units, where the sound background was important: the ears of the staff were tuned to it by habit, and if a warning buzzer went off or the pulsing of a ventilator stopped they would hear it immediately.

Candystriper to Outpatients, please.

A half hour ago Denise Ross had taken over the afternoon shift and the patient-condition reports had been discussed. She was responsible for two patients, one of them Mrs. Terman in Room 6.

During the morning there had been several calls from friends of the new patient but permission to visit her had not been granted, since her condition was critical. One of the callers had not given his name, though the ward clerk had asked for it.

Soon after Denise had begun her shift the electricians got the last ceiling panel fitted and the main lights were turned on.

"That's nice," one of the girls said. "I was beginning to think I was a mole."

Nurse Wyatt to Pathology, please.

A young man had come in through the main doors and stood looking around him.

"Can I help you?" a nurse asked him.

"I'd like to see Claudia Terman. I was told she was here."

She led him to the desk. "Is it her brother?" She was checking a list.

"No."

She looked up at him. He was holding himself in, she saw, as some of the visitors did.

36

"May I have your name?"

"Brian Newby."

She checked the list again.

"I'm sorry, Mr. Newby, but Mrs. Terman isn't permitted any visitors today."

In a moment he said absently: "Isn't she?"

He went on standing there, a young man with brown hair and brown eyes and nothing exceptional about him but for the way he was keeping control of himself, with an effort that she sensed rather than saw.

"I'd like to see her," he said simply.

"Are you a relative of this patient?"

"No. But I'd like to see her."

"I'm really very sorry, but that isn't permitted. Would you—"

"Just for a minute. Just see her."

Miss Stein to Central Supply, please.

He stood perfectly still, looking steadily at the nurse without any expression at all.

"Tracy, did the needles arrive?"

"What? Yes."

"Where are they?"

"In that drawer."

"Just for a minute," the young man said quietly.

"I'll see what I can do, Mr. Newby. Please wait here."

While she was talking to another woman he looked around him at the circle of big screened windows, some of them with vague shapes moving on the other side of the slats. He could hear some kind of equipment pulsing, and could see the green jagged lines crossing the row of little screens. He waited quietly.

Scott Rand got in soon after 3:45 and shut himself in Room 6 of the ICU with the reports of the pulmonary and neurological consults on the Terman case that had come in for him. He didn't want to see anyone yet, least of all Kistner.

There had been further radiological work-up during the day, including computerized axial tomography, but there was still no explanation for the continuing state of coma in the patient. Nuclear Pathology had done a cerebral imaging study and brain scan, beginning at ten o'clock this morning, using an IV of 15 mCi 99 mTc DTPA with apparent adequate perfusion through the left internal carotid artery of the neck. A bilaterally symmetrical "blush" was noted in the cerebral artery, and filling of the anterior arteries also appeared symmetrical. The anterior brain scan had followed the imaging study an hour later, with subsequent posterior, vertex, and left and right lateral views.

Halfway through reading the reports Scott became aware of the young woman lying near him, and glanced down. You got used to being near people who were unaware of your presence or even of your existence, though you might be involved with them so intimately that their life itself rested sometimes in your hands. But they were still there, however dead-looking, however fish-on-a-slab, and it was a good thing to remember that they still possessed, somewhere within themselves, an identity.

Looking down at this patient, he was able for the first time to study her, undistracted by the pressures of emergency. It was a young face with a firm mouth and well-defined cheekbones, the lashes and eyebrows silky and black, the eyelids hollowed and the skin pallid, revealing a scattering of pockmarks—the healed scars of adolescent acne. But these were just features: she looked attractive but that was all; without the eyes or any movement of the mouth he couldn't tell what she really looked like.

The monitor screens above the bed were displaying the same rhythms he had seen when he'd left here this morning to go home: the heart rate was near normal and the brain was functioning in theta, the region of deep meditation. The artificial respirator was still breathing for her and according to the reports she had made no effort to assist.

He took one of her hands, squeezing the long fingers a little, watching the screen of the electroencephalograph.

"Claudia."

He tried three times, pressing harder, saying her name louder.

There was no slightest change in the brain's awareness. There should be. According to all these reports, there should be. And that was what Neil Kistner was talking about.

Scott went into his office and telephoned the neurosurgeon at four o'clock, giving him a few minutes out of professional courtesy.

"Good of you to call." Kistner's measured tones came over the line. "Shall we meet?"

"There's really no point. I want to give this patient a few days to get over the worst." He gazed at the photograph of Eve on his desk, gazelle-like in her leotards. It was one of her favorites.

Kistner began talking, steadily and unhurriedly in the didactic tones he used at his lectures, and Scott listened until he began getting bored. The surgeon's point was that the axial tomography revealed bilateral subdural hematomas, and that this was confirmed by cerebral angiography, the hematomas being shown as approximately one millimeter in size.

"I submit," the heavy voice went on, "that this is ample justification for my going in there and finding out what the situation really is."

Scott was now looking around the little office at the picture of Caroline on the wall, the two dried corn husks mounted on a varnished board, the rows of framed diplomas. They were the things he saw most, and least, in his life.

"The condition could resolve itself," he told Kistner. "It often does, as you know."

They spent two minutes arguing this point, then the surgeon played his familiar last card.

"It's your responsibility, of course."

"Yes. That's why I want to get it right."

"Well, don't leave it too late." A low chuckle, to express knowing camaraderie. "It was good of you to consider my recommendation, Scott. Let's keep in touch."

Kistner always played it slow with him; later, if Scott had a series of setbacks and began thinking he'd been wrong, Kistner would come on strong and start fighting for the patient. And for his four-thousand-dollar fee.

Soon after his call to the surgeon Scott had a talk with Miss Dean, the charge nurse. Among other things she told him that Mr. Oakridge in Room 3 was now hemorrhaging generally and was considered terminal, that young Linda Joachim had been transferred to recuperative observation, that the Arteriosonde had fused out and that the police had sent an officer to exchange information on the case in Room 6, Mrs. Terman.

"They're puzzled about the accident, Dr. Rand. It seems the brakes, tires and steering were all in order, and there weren't any witnesses."

"Did they get anything from the blood lab?"

"Yes, we phoned it through earlier. No trace of drugs or alcohol in the system."

"What else did the police say?"

She had it written down in her small backward-sloping handwriting on the long scratch pad she kept in her linen coat. Miss Dean was nearing sixty and retirement and when she left Garden Grove she was going to take the principles of

40

a whole generation with her, and they wouldn't be practiced here again.

"We are told that Mrs. Terman's husband is on his way to see her; apparently they're estranged and a divorce is pending. Her brother is also coming here today—he was out of state when he heard the news. She has no parents surviving."

She put away her notes.

"Oh Miss Dean, could you—"

"I'm talking to Dr. Rand."

The candystriper crept away.

"All right, Amy, is there anything else?"

He was the only man in Garden Grove who called her that, and it had been seven years before she'd allowed it, as a matter of grace and favor.

"Only small business," she said. "Maria Rodriguez left a dry IV in Room 4. I had her suspended. The new needles have arrived at last and I'm dispensing them by name. That's it."

At 4:25 Patrick Terman came into the Intensive Care Unit and Scott saw him for a few minutes in Room 6 before taking him along to his office. Terman was a pug-faced-handsome young fellow with bushy hair and bright blue unimaginative eyes and a way of standing balanced on the balls of his feet, which were in blue-and-white sneakers. Scott thought he looked very fit, very engaged with life.

He stared down at his wife.

"Okay, Doc. What are her chances?"

"We don't know."

"You don't *know*?"

"Not yet."

"Well for Christ's sake, when are you going to find out?"

Scott looked at him steadily; it was a long time before

41

Terman glanced away. "I mean, this has come at the wrong time."

"There's a right time to have a near-fatal accident?"

"You know what I mean."

"No."

Terman looked down at his wife again, taking a breath and letting it out. "I don't know what she could've been doing. She didn't drive too bad."

"Let's go along to my office."

Scott had to take a call at the nurses' station on their way out of the ICU, and when he found Terman again he was signing an autograph book for one of the orderlies.

"Are you an actor?" Scott asked him.

Terman looked puzzled. "I'm with the Wildcats."

In his office Scott gave him a rundown of his wife's condition, treatment and prospects, deciding it wasn't necessary to break anything gently. "It's early yet. All I can tell you right now is that your wife may live, die or continue to survive in a comatose state."

"Indefinitely?"

"Yes."

"Like a vegetable?"

"If you care to put it that way."

Patrick Terman went on staring at him with shock in his eyes, and it was a while before he said quietly:

"That'd be great. Really."

He got out of the chair and wandered up and down the office, looking everywhere and at nothing, his strong square hands stuck in the pockets of his jeans with his thumbs hooked over the top. Once he turned and looked down at Scott and seemed about to say something but decided against it and turned away, bouncing slightly on his feet. Scott thought of a shadowboxer who didn't know what to hit.

He got up from behind his desk and said: "We'll keep you closely informed of Mrs. Terman's progress."

The young man looked at him with his eyes bright.

"You better, Doc."

He walked out of the office and went a short way along the corridor and stopped, looking at the floor for a moment and then coming back.

"Listen, I guess I sounded kind of upset. You see—"

"I didn't notice," Scott said, and turned along the corridor in the opposite direction.

At 4:47 Mr. Oakridge died in Room 3 with two physicians and four nurses in attendance. Scott Rand was one of the physicians. In the past two weeks this patient had received three complete transfusions and the people who now stood grouped around his bed had the satisfaction of knowing that at least they'd got all the alcohol out of his blood before the end came.

"Get an aide in here, Tracy."

"Sure."

There was a lot of mess.

Nobody, Scott knew, felt any real sympathy; this was the kind of case that came under the heading of slow suicide, when people systematically destroyed their own bodies in the full realization of what they were doing. All the staff of the ICU could do about it was to try making things easier for them and keep up the pretense that they were dying of some disease, and not of the death wish that at some time in their lives had crept like a worm into their heads and begun eating.

A telephone call was going out to Mrs. Oakridge at five o'clock when David Pryor, a solar-heating engineer, came through the double doors of the ICU and stopped halfway across to the nurses' station, tense, tousle-haired and red-

43

eyed, stubble on his face and dust on his shoes, nothing to say as he stared around him.

"May I help you?"

She was a graying woman in a white coat, looking right into him with her mild eyes, waiting.

"I'm her brother." One hand clawed his hair back in an unconscious gesture. "Claudia Terman—she's here, isn't she?"

"Yes, David. And she's perfectly comfortable."

"Comfortable?"

"She's not in any pain. Let's go and see her, shall we?"

"I was out of state."

"Yes."

He was aware of a lot of faces, white clothes, a phone ringing, some pale green machines with chrome pipes, this woman who knew his name, the end of his journey.

She was talking to him as they went toward one of the open doors.

"We put a small tube in her neck, so that we can do her breathing for her till she's ready to make the effort for herself."

One of the machines was in here, an air pump.

"There wasn't a plane connection," he said quickly, "it would have taken *longer* than by road. I drove all the way."

"It was nothing you could help."

Then he looked down and there was Claudia. For a while the hiss of the machine died almost away and he felt a lightness in the air, a kind of floating; then things came back into focus and the woman took her hand from his arm and he said:

"Claudie?"

"She's in quite a deep sleep, David."

"Look, will you tell me the *exact* situation?"

Then there was someone else in the doorway, a man with a lean face and steady eyes, watching him.

44

"This is Dr. Rand."

"You're Mr. Pryor?"

"I got here as fast as I could. Will somebody tell me how she is? Without any—you know?"

A voice was calling *Miss Dean* and the graying woman went out.

"It's early," Scott said. He nudged one of the collapsible metal chairs with his foot but Pryor didn't want to sit down; he stood looking at his sister with his head at an odd angle and his hands hanging loose by his sides, and Scott had the impression he was asking some kind of forgiveness, but it was just an impression.

Close relatives never seemed quite what they were; sudden hospitalization always caught them on the wrong foot and they tried to cover their shock, sometimes overcorrecting. There'd been a man in here not long ago, saying stiffly: "The kid was a plain damn fool to go climbing that rock on his own," and the next second he hit the floor before anyone could catch him.

Pryor had forgotten Scott Rand was here.

Below in the street an ambulance siren was fading in.

In the quiet of the room the spirometer pulsed.

The young man took a breath, straightening up.

"Okay, will you tell me what's happening? Did she say you were the doctor?"

"Right. Scott Rand."

"I'm her brother." His dark eyes wandered around the room, still trying to place himself.

"As far as the tests show, there's no major damage. But she's in coma and we're having to breathe for her. She—"

"Having to breathe? You mean this thing?"

"Right. Don't worry, it can keep it up forever."

Pryor looked at him, stilled.

"Forever?"

45

"I just mean it's a very reliable machine. Listen, David, why don't we go along to my office, and I'll—"

"I want to stay here."

"That's okay too." Scott took a few paces toward the window, dropping his stethoscope onto the second bed and looking out at the smog that had begun drifting in yesterday, sluggish and pink. When he'd thought out his approach he turned back and looked at Claudia's brother. "I want you to know that we've made exhaustive tests and that I've taken all essential consultations, and as I told you we haven't found any major problem. She picked up a nasty wound at the nape of the neck and a few light bruises—but of course she was lucky; apparently the car turned over and she was thrown out. She's now stabilized and healing is in progress, and I'm expecting her to start assisting the ventilator—breathing for herself—at any time."

The good news first.

"We had a fight," David said.

"Pardon me?"

"We had a fight. Not a bad one. You know, brother and sister. About her marrying that—guy."

"I see." It explained the guilt feelings, earlier: *I got here as fast as I could.*

"Now there's this. Wham." He dragged his thick hair back with hooked fingers. "I mean, we didn't have time to make it up."

"You'll have time, David."

"Will I?"

His gaze was very direct. He really wanted to know.

"Probably."

"Probably. What does that mean? I just want you to tell me. I mean, give it to me straight. Is she going to die?"

Tell me. Help me. *Do* something. You know everything. You're God. This was why Dan Taylor was on scotch and Valium, because being God was strictly nonfattening, and in the end it could kill.

46

"At this stage I'm hopeful, David, but I'll give it to you straight. She might die. She might stay in a coma indefinitely. She might recover completely. But the most difficult thing for you to take is this: *I don't know.*"

David stared at him for a moment, then looked down at his sister. "That's okay. But she wouldn't like it."

"Like what?"

"Being here forever."

"Listen, we don't have to let just one case in New Jersey affect our thinking. People are coming out of coma every day, hundreds of them, okay?"

The young man couldn't seem to look away from the face of the girl on the bed. It occurred to Scott that they looked quite alike: good features, fine-boned, their hair black without relief. This tension would be seen in Claudia, if their roles were reversed, this capacity to feel deeply without breaking up.

"Wham," he said quietly between his teeth. "What the hell was she doing?"

"The police are trying to find out."

"She drove perfectly. Like she did everything."

Scott put a hand on his shoulder. "She *drives* perfectly, like she *does* everything."

"Okay." David looked up at last. "Sure."

"I'm going to catch a cup of coffee. Want to join me?"

"Okay."

"You need to know," Scott told him on their way through the unit, "that surgery has been suggested, on the grounds that if we can't find out why Claudia isn't responding then someone should get inside her head and hope to find whatever it is we're missing."

David's step faltered and Scott slowed for him as they went along the corridor. People still felt scared at the idea of surgery, no matter how easy it was to do these days or how euphoric the patient could be made to feel under sophisticated anesthetics; the image remained stark in the mind: the image of masks, knives and blood.

"Do you advise it?"

"No," Scott said, and showed the young man into his office. "At least not yet."

"Do you think I should check it out?"

"Yes."

"Why?"

"You should check everything out. You're her brother."

Scott indicated the chair but David didn't want to sit down.

"Okay."

"Now we'll go through the reports and later I'll have you meet the pulmonary specialist and the neurologist and then you'll know everything." He opened the file on Claudia Terman. "Or at least you'll know as much as we do."

While the young man stood patiently with his hands hanging at his sides and his head tilted as he listened, Scott went through the reports, quoting as few of the technicalities as he could and explaining where he had to. By the time he'd finished he wasn't sure how much David had really been listening: he had the impression that he was still trying to come out of shock, trying to relate his young vital sister who "did everything perfectly" with the motionless figure in the bed in there that couldn't breathe without a machine, couldn't live without help.

"Now you know it all, David. All we have. It isn't good and it isn't bad, and it's still early. Claudia is young and has an excellent constitution, and that can make all the difference."

He meant what he said but he'd said it so many times it had lost its meaning; the facts were there but they didn't sound real. It mattered terribly to this young man whether the patient in Room 6 of the ICU lived or died, but to Scott and the staff it meant only that they were going to write up a success or a failure: just another success or just another failure in dozens, hundreds. Then how did you manage to heal people when you didn't care about them as people, only as cases? You did it by remembering that medicine was a science, not an art.

Sometimes he felt guilty because he couldn't relate with the visitors who came into his office with their faces drawn and their speech clumsy and the end of the world in their eyes, and he'd devised a gruesome trick he could play on himself: he would look at the picture on the wall, the one of his daughter Caroline, and tell himself *that's not a stranger out there on the ward with the left leg amputated or the carcinoma spreading or the renal failure, it's Caroline, so how do I feel now?*

Often the trick worked and for a while he could share the dread and the hollow heart with the people who expected so much of him. But often, as now, he shied from doing it, and remained remote, a practitioner who dealt with sickness, not with the sick.

Eve's picture was here in the office too, but he never used Eve for the trick; it was always Caroline, though he'd never asked himself why. Perhaps he shied, also, from the answer: that Eve didn't mean enough.

"Okay," David said numbly, "how do I check out the surgery idea?"

"By talking with the surgeon. His name's Kistner, and I'll arrange a meeting and let you know."

"Thank you." He was on his way out when he asked: "Did her husband come here?"

"Yes."

"Did you meet him?"

"Yes."

David gave a little nod. "For any kind of operation, you'd need a form signed, right? Someone's authority."

"Right."

"That might be quite an important decision. I wouldn't

49

be the one to make it. I'm only her brother. Terman would be the one." He looked down at his hands. "That's really funny, but I don't feel like laughing."

Scott said: "He'd want to confer with you, of course."

"Would he?"

"Why, naturally. He—"

"Can I see her again for a minute, before I go?"

"Sure, David." He came from behind his desk. "Tell one of the nurses I said so. And we'll keep in touch."

Soon after ten o'clock Scott Rand closed his office and took a final look at Claudia Terman before he went home. He'd given the tickets for the Hollywood Bowl to Bill Brickman, one of the anesthesiologists, because he wouldn't enjoy the concert on his own and couldn't think of anyone to take.

The condition of the patient in Room 6 was unchanged: the MA1 was sustaining life, the EKG screen was displaying a heart rate of 75 bpm and the EEG monitor showed brain waves in the theta region of twilight sleep.

He told Denise to call him if there were any significant change, and checked with the ward clerk that she had standing instructions that David Pryor was permitted to visit the patient at whatever time.

By eleven o'clock the quiet of night had come to Garden Grove. On the wards and along the corridors voices were low as the late staff came on duty, relieving the afternoon shift. To those few patients still awake, small sounds were reassuring, a reminder that they weren't alone: the tinkle of instruments on a trolley, the ring of a telephone, the soft squeak of sneakers on the polished floor.

In one of the observation rooms young Linda Joachim slept undisturbed, her heartbeat displayed at the nurses' station where Julie Sears sat writing a report.

Three floors below in the dispensary a pharmacologist dug with her thumbnail at the name tab on a bottle, peeling it away and dropping it into the trash can: *J. M. Oakridge— ICU 3.*

In one of the laboratories a faucet dripped, bringing a small note of music to the silence; light from the street was reflected from the ceiling across the biopsy report on the bench, where the last inked word stood out darkly from the print: *Benign.*

On the fifth floor, in Room 6 of the ICU, Claudia Terman lay perfectly still, as she had lain since she was brought here in the early hours of this day. The rough sighing of the spirometer was unceasing as it arranged the exchange of gas between the machine and the lungs of the patient on the bed, and on the wall the cathode hieroglyphs traced their pattern across the screen, indicating that the brain was alive and functioning in theta but telling nothing of its thoughts, if thought were there.

For some minutes the wail of a siren had been loudening insistently, its sound coming to penetrate the walls of the building. For a time it had faded as the vehicle passed below the freeway but now it was back, moaning to silence as headlights swung across the windows.

Dr. Fineman, please—Code 1.

In the communications room the radioed report of the casualty was still being transcribed for onward handling.

An orderly came down the corridor to the Emergency Room, his arms full of linen. A nurse on the night staff swung open the double doors, knocking the bolts down with her heel.

"Where's Johnny?"

"I don't know."

Ann Fowler, please—Code 1.

In the lower windows the headlights went out and a man's voice called something. On the grass alongside the ambulance ramp the night crickets fell silent as a door banged and the stretcher was brought down.

"Steady, Bob."

"Okay."

Standby personnel, please—Code 1.

"Where's Betty?"

"I'm here."

Dr. Fineman was in the Emergency Room, pulling his white coat on as he began reading the report from Communications: *Severe chest pains radiating down left arm, onset of dyspnea, cold sweats.* Over his shoulder he called out: "Is he on oxygen?"

"Yes, Doctor."

The patient had a "keep open" IV going as he was brought into the room. Still conscious, he was given 100 mg of Demerol IM and linked to an electrocardiograph. At this time the rate was less than 9 bpm above normal.

"You'll be all right."

"Will I?"

The eyes frightened, the voice a whisper in case any effort might prove too much.

"Sure. Keep still and don't worry."

At 11:19 the patient was transferred to the Cardiac Care Unit on the fifth floor with oxygen and the IV still running and a cardiac monitor taped to his chest. His name was Mario Mancini.

Sometime before midnight an odd little incident occurred in a distant wing of the hospital; it was without explanation and no immediate notice was taken of it. One of the staff on duty in Recovery, near the operating room on the first floor, came upon a message scribbled across a scratch pad at the nurses' station. It read:

For God's sake help me.

Chapter 4

"It isn't that I mind dying," said the woman in the bed. "It's just that I never lived."

Squares of light swung across the wall as a car took the off ramp from the freeway a half mile to the north. Somewhere a big truck was on the move, like something that had got loose in the sleeping city. Nearer, sharper, the traveling clock on the bedside table ticked quickly, hurrying the night along.

"A lot of people feel like that," said the man. "Life's there for them, but they're just too busy to live it." He was kneeling on the floor, because he couldn't sit on the edge of the bed without disturbing the array of tubes and pillows. She had to lie half on one side, and not move. Whenever she tried to move, she screamed.

In the low light he watched her face, a shapeless blob against the linen half turned away from him, so that he saw only one of her eyes, less like an eye than a lump of translucent gristle, an onion, not like an eye at all. The thought came to him, as it had come to him before, that the dying lost their identity by degrees.

"Jim's coming to see you in the morning," he said.

"What for?"

It was a good question, and there wasn't an answer that made any sense. Jim was coming to see her because she was dying; but she didn't want him to come; he didn't mean anything any more because this thing had been spreading for three years, starting small and growing bigger, taking its time but never pausing, never giving ground to the surgery, to the chemotherapy, to the bombardment of electrons. It had pushed through her body like a slow blind rage, taking its time, taking three years. And now she didn't want to be seen any more, even by her children. Nor did young Jim want to see her any more; she had lost most of her resemblance to the mother he'd known: she was now a stranger with a name he knew, a living, dying reminder that terrible things could come to you in your lifetime, to anyone, to Jim, even. He didn't want to be reminded.

She was so right to ask why he was coming.

The man shifted his position to ease the ache in his knees, while the sweat from her hand ran into his, and he felt the fever burning in her bed. His name was Donald Glezen and he was a clinical psychologist.

Outside the building the big truck battered at the night.

He thought of telling her that Betsy would be coming to see her too, tomorrow; but there was no point; she'd only ask why. She had told him about the others, about her family. Her husband had left her four years ago for a girl half his age, one of the welfare workers who had been sent to help the family with good counseling and had successfully wrecked it. Of the five children one was in jail for rape, another up on a drug charge and a third working in a massage parlor on Hollywood Boulevard. That was the seventeen-year-old, Betsy.

"I want to go," the woman said.

"I know." She had told him many times.

She moved her head and stopped and kept so still that he felt her stillness in the locking of her fingers. They both waited. Earlier she had simply screamed and then had learned to bite on a washcloth and go on biting till the spasm was over, for the sake of the others on the ward. Now she was quite practiced, and knew how to stop moving in

54

time, before the worst came. It was not only the breakup of the diseased tissue that was causing the agony; the Xylocaine, the two sternum biopsies and then the six marrow extractions from the hips had left the aspiration entry sites and the full biopsy probe site as foci of pain that would continue for as long as she would live.

Her name was Grace Kohler and she had worked in a factory, making hair curlers and surgical corsets. She was thirty-eight.

"It didn't add up to much, did it?"

"What didn't?"

Don Glezen leaned closer to catch what she said.

"My life."

The other eleven patients were asleep, the curtains drawn between their beds. He kept his voice low.

"Life doesn't have to add up, Grace. It's people who have to add up. I think you do that pretty well."

She said something again, and again he leaned closer.

"I never really lived."

"You lived for others."

Her eye, the one he could see from where he kneeled, stared upwards from her shapeless face.

"For those kids, you mean? Big deal."

Many were like this. They wanted to go out the hard way, refusing any kind of consolation; but he had never learned the ability of not giving it, or trying. Others went out clinging to his hands, telling him things he would never repeat.

Don had put up his shingle nineteen years ago as a young psychologist and later became a resident, attracted to the organized life of a big hospital. Within a year he discovered where his interest lay, and began devoting his energies to the one type of patient that had come to claim the whole of his attention: the terminal case.

"Can't you do something?"

She'd asked him before.

She would ask him again. She'd go on asking him till there was suddenly no longer any need, in a day from now, in a week; and till then he'd come here when he could and kneel in the half dark beside her and hold her wet hand and pay off his conscience with the false coin of the consolation she refused to take from him. In the long day they'd minister to their patient, taking away her urine and her excrement and some of her pain but not all, because bone pain was tough to subdue; they would put fluids in and take fluids out, rearranging the tubes and the catheters and the instruments while she remembered to bite on the washrag and bite hard, for the sake of the others and because her throat was still sore from the screaming. Then one day it would end and there'd be peace for her. How would he feel then: that he'd done some good, some harm, anything? Anything, rather than nothing?

"Doctor."

"Yes, Grace?"

"For God's sake, can't you do something for me?"

"You mustn't talk." You mustn't say the things I don't want to hear.

Her eye stared upwards, fishy in the pale light from the street outside, a hemispherical organ that had lost its meaning. But he saw it was changing, as he watched, beginning to glisten, to brighten, until from it there ran the first of tears, a single drop that stayed poised, gleaming, at the edge of her eye, until its volume gathered and it fell, tracing soft light down the shadows of her face.

"Don't you even care?"

He caught the whisper; his head was low, near hers.

"You must sleep, now."

Light flooded across the wall again from the freeway, and slid to the shadows.

56

A nurse sat at her station near the far end of the ward, talking quietly on the phone.

"You must sleep," he said softly. "You must sleep now."

"Yes."

"Don't talk any more. Don't think any more. Just sleep."

The big truck had gone, and the only sound from outside the building was the trilling of crickets. Close by, the clock ticked on the table.

"Sleep now," he said, and despite the softness of his voice he heard the strength in it. "Sleep deeply now, deeply." His knees were aching but he didn't move. "You are sleeping now, sleeping deeply . . . deeply." Her hand in his, her fever throbbing in his fingers. "Sleeping, sleeping so deeply now."

In the gloom he saw that the lid of flesh had drawn down over the eye. She seemed asleep, and perhaps was so, but he went on talking to her softly, knowing that the ear never sleeps.

Far away the crickets sang.

"You are going now, Grace. You are slipping quietly away. You are leaving us, going peacefully your own way, away from us, away . . . floating away, drifting away in peace and with no more pain."

Her hand in his, he felt the heaviness coming into her, the little by little weighing down of her hand in his, the sighing within the body that he could not hear, but felt, and knew was there.

"Take our love with you as you drift away, and go in peace, further and further with every breath, softly away forever, leaving your life behind you, leaving all your pain. Sleep deeply, deeply forever, forever."

He wanted to move but remained still, his whole body aching. At the back of his mind he realized that the intimacy of their communion was causing some of her pain to flow into him; but it would go before long: it was in his mind, not his body.

He went on talking to her until most of his strength was spent; then, when he felt the coldness coming into her hand he took his own away, putting it for a moment over her heart, then getting up stiffly and going to one of the windows, where he stood for a while, looking upwards to where a few pale stars were caught among wisps of cloud.

Julie filed the report and glanced across the array of screens, noting the pattern of the fluctuating green bands without really seeing them. She would see them if they changed.

Dr. Fineman, please—Code 2. Dr. Fineman.

She heard the call faintly from the corridor, taking only momentary notice. The paging system was silent for most of the night at Garden Grove, the only calls being of code status. This one didn't concern her: she was on duty in a critical care unit and would on no account leave it; the only call that might concern her was a Code 1, when a patient was brought in to the Emergency Room: a patient who might be transferred to the ICU. At night they were mostly crash victims, coronaries, knife-wound cases from family fights and drunks who'd walked into things.

Code 4 was their own signal within Cardio-Pulmonary: the panic button was on the desk here alongside the microphone and before the call was finished there'd be someone on the crash cart and someone else at the bedside while the others came running—the interns, nurses, respiratory therapists, electrocardiograph technicians, laboratory technicians, nurses' supervisors, aides, orderlies and anyone who could do something toward saving a life.

That was in the daytime. At night there would only be a few specialists on call.

"Julie?"

"Yes?"

"Did you see this edema on Mr. McCloud?"

"No."

Fran Engel was going her rounds on the other side, over-concerned as usual about edemas; they were best looked for when the patient was turned or when the shift was changed. Fran mothered them too much, especially at night, when they slept more than by day, and didn't want to be disturbed.

Dr. Fineman, please. Dr. Fineman—Code 2.

He was probably in the cancer ward.

Julie went to check the patient in Room 6, wondering again if she should have called Dr. Rand at his home, earlier, when Mrs. Terman's condition had changed slightly. The heart rate had increased to 103 and the brain rhythm had accelerated from theta into the alpha cycles between 7 and 8 cps for a period of some fifteen minutes. But Julie again decided she wouldn't be expected to call Dr. Rand: for a time it had looked as if the patient might be regaining consciousness but she hadn't assisted the ventilator and was now back to her previous condition. The observation had been noted on the chart.

She refilled the IV and felt the patient's skin; it was cool and dry. Mrs. Terman lay perfectly still, and the only movement in the room was the rise and fall of the bellows as they breathed for her.

Doris Graham woke soon after 3:00 A.M. in the recovery unit.

"Nurse."

But she could barely hear her own voice and she tried again and it was worse because of the effort.

"Nurse."

"I'm coming."

Arlene Wyatt hit the toe of her sneaker on the baseboard

59

as she got off the stool and left the nurses' station, thinking *clumsy, I'm getting tired.*

"Nurse—it hurts. It *hurts.*"

"I'll see to it. Don't—"

Then the thin shoulders sagged and the blood drained from the face and Arlene drew the sheet back and cut away the dressing and covered the abdomen quickly and gave a seven-and-a-half gram vial of sodium bicarb., and put out a Code 2 call for Dr. Fineman. It had to be repeated before he arrived on the ward at 3:14 A.M.

By 4:00 A.M. the patient was intubated and breathing on assisted ventilation in the Intensive Care Unit and Julie Sears was in charge of her.

Arlene Wyatt was writing up her report in Recovery soon afterward. At this time she noticed that the emergency had left her feeling anxious, which was most unusual. Dr. Fineman had been late in reaching the ward because he'd been viewing biopsy slides in the carcinoma laboratory, and she'd had to rally the patient single-handed because the other nurse was helping out in the children's ward at the time; but the emergency was now over and the patient was responding well in the ICU and Arlene was no longer responsible for her. There was nothing to feel anxious about.

A little before 4:30 Kathy came back from the children's ward and found Arlene sitting at the nurses' station doing nothing, her arms folded and her legs drawn up on the rung of the stool. There was in fact nothing to do, but normally when there was nothing to do Arlene tidied the filing cabinet or sat with a patient or checked the drug stock, things like that.

"Okay, Arlene?"

"Sure."

She got down from the stool and went to the filing cabinet, but didn't seem to do anything particular there.

"Where's Mrs. Graham?" Kathy asked her.

"She's been transferred to the ICU. She had a collapse."

"I'm not surprised." No one had thought this patient looked strong enough to take a hysterectomy: no one but Dr. Kistner.

Arlene stood at the filing cabinet without moving, realizing she was holding on to it with both hands now as if she needed to steady herself. Her head had started aching again, and she just stood still and waited till the feeling passed.

"Kathy," she said dully, "would you check Mrs. Simon for me? I used a catheter an hour ago—she's been retaining urine."

"Okay."

Again Kathy felt a strangeness in Arlene's manner, but didn't question anything. After checking the patient she came back to the station and saw Arlene over at the water fountain drinking from a wax cup, refilling it and drinking again as if seized by a sudden thirst.

A pencil was on the floor and Kathy picked it up and put it by the scratch pad, her eye catching some words scribbled on the top sheet. They weren't easy to read but they hadn't been there a few minutes ago and she held the pad under the shaded desk lamp.

He tried — kill — and he'll — again.

There weren't any actual gaps: the words in between were too difficult to read. Kathy felt uneasy; the note had been hastily scrawled but it was still recognizable as Arlene's writing, like the other note Kathy had found here earlier, sometime about midnight.

She looked across at the water fountain, where Arlene was dropping the cup into the waste box and coming away. She seemed more alert now and was tidying her fair hair as she came back to the desk.

"Arlene."

"Yes?"

"Did you write this?"

61

The ward was quiet and the only sounds came from outside: the soft whistling of crickets on the lawns below, a truck on the freeway. Kathy listened to them as she watched Arlene's face, seeing it go suddenly still.

"Yes."

Kathy tried a brief laugh but it didn't sound right. "What does it mean?"

"I don't know." Arlene sounded irritable. "Does it matter?"

Bill Brickman got into Garden Grove at 5:30 A.M., a half hour before he was due in surgery as the senior anesthesiologist. He liked to talk to Arlene Wyatt for a few minutes at this time if she weren't too busy, and their little rendezvous had been established for some weeks now, ever since she'd agreed to spend her evenings with him as a regular thing.

He'd known for a long time that almost a year ago Arlene had lost her husband in a scuba-diving accident and that Roger's death had left her stunned. Don Glezen, the psychologist, had worked on her for a time; then Ernst Stein, a senior psychiatrist attached to the hospital, had taken over and gradually got her back to understanding the salient aspect of death: that when it happens, life goes on. Both these men had given their services for nothing, as most people on the staff usually did for one another when they could find the time.

Arlene was not the same person she'd been when Bill Brickman had known her during her marriage; she would never be. Roger had been a part of her and that part had broken away and she was to a degree changed, though the worst of the shock was over by now and to many she seemed no different. At thirty-five she was still attractive, friendly and competent at her job, and only her close friends missed the sudden laughter at small absurdities, the

62

easy enthusiasm for anything new, the willingness to be known for what she was and what she believed in, whether people liked it or not.

These days she laughed less and found new things unappealing, since Roger was not here to share them; and anyone seeking to know her now for what she was and for what she believed in had to go slow and take care, for the void that Roger had left had been filled with a sense of privacy.

At fifty, Bill Brickman had learned patience. Respecting her privacy, tolerant of her moods that sometimes made an evening so quiet as to be a strain, he let her know at every opportunity—without putting it into words—that if ever she felt ready to pick up her life again and share it with someone, he'd like to be considered.

"Bad night?" he asked as he came into the ward.

"Not really."

He leaned at the nurses' station, his arms folded on the counter, his head tilted back to look at her in the direct way he had, the light touching on his thick graying hair. She avoided his gaze, as sometimes she did; it wasn't this that made him think the night had been bad. She looked fatigued, dark under the eyes. And something more than that, though he couldn't define quite what. Disturbed?

He looked along the ward. "What happened to Doris Graham?"

"She had a collapse."

"She in the ICU?"

"Yes."

He looked down at his folded arms, noting his cuff was frayed. Martha would have told him to go buy a new coat, though he liked wearing old ones; but that was in Martha's time.

"How was the concert?" Arlene was asking, and he looked up.

63

"Pretty good. But not really the same without you there."

"More relaxing." She didn't smile.

"Less exciting."

He'd called her last night when Scott Rand had given him the tickets, but she'd said she had some things to do. He would have asked someone else—Betty or Laura—just for the company, but he'd stopped asking other women to go anywhere with him for quite a while now: it was one of the opportunities he took of letting Arlene know how he felt.

"Are you going to take it easy this evening?" he asked her. "Sleep in a little?"

"I might. Why?"

"Do you good."

He didn't tell her she looked tired, though she knew what he was thinking. She moved back a little from the counter, on the pretext of looking up at the wall clock; the light was kinder there.

"Will you call me," he asked nicely, "if you'd like us to meet?"

"All right." She seemed like she was going to add something, and he waited; but that was all she said.

"We could go to Chow's."

"I'll see how I feel."

"Okay. If—"

"I'm not just being—" She gave a little shrug.

"Sure, I know. Get a nice lot of sleep. Today's another day." Her night-shift schedule turned a lot of things topsy-turvy.

"Yes." She gave him a token smile.

"Take real care."

He was on his way out of the ward when she made up her mind to face it.

"Bill."

He went back and found her tearing a page off her

64

scratch pad and putting it beside another one on the desk, her movements impatient. "Bill, during the night I wrote these two notes and I don't know why. I don't even know what they mean. Do you think I'm going crazy or something?"

Chapter 5

The thin boy came into the ward as he always did, looking straight at whoever was on duty at the nurses' station, never glancing around. His hair was a mass of blond bubbles and his face was pink; his pale blue eyes seemed innocent of all thought. He had frayed the bottoms of his jeans himself, using a knife to make them really ragged, and the word SHIT was printed on his tee shirt in curlicued Gay Nineties lettering, inside a circlet of flowers. He was chewing his gum methodically, as if something depended on it.

"Hi, Jim."

"Hi."

It wasn't yet eight o'clock; he was rather early today.

Candystriper to Radiology, please.

"Didn't someone call you?" Laura asked him.

"No." In a moment he added: "I haven't got a phone."

"I see." Laura picked up a chart, though there was no need. "I'm sorry, Jim, but we've got some bad news for you."

His pale blue eyes didn't change.

"Is she dead?"

"Yes."

The name on the chart was Grace Elizabeth Kohler, and a line had been drawn from one edge of the sheet to the other below the final entry.

"Okay," he said, and turned to go.

Laura watched his stooped shoulders for a moment.

"Jim."

He stopped.

"Would you like to go and see her?"

He was feeling for something in his back pants pocket.

"No."

She said in a moment: "You'll be glad to know your mother died peacefully, with no pain."

"Okay."

He turned away again, finding the pack.

"We'll be contacting your elder sister."

"Okay."

"Please don't smoke till you're outside the building."

Scott Rand reached the hospital before nine and saw the two new cases first: Mr. Mancini in Cardiac Care and Mrs. Graham in Intensive.

Mancini was lying down with dark glasses on. The nurse said he had told her he was photosensitive, and she'd found the glasses in his coat pocket. Scott saw from the reports that his CPK and SGOT enzyme levels were still slightly elevated, but all other signs were fair. The patient was on oxygen and had an IV running, and a monitor was taped to his chest.

"Will I be all right?"

He spoke with care.

"Very much so, Mr. Mancini. But we don't need to talk about it now. You're doing fine but you need to rest up for a day or two. I don't want you to have anyone to see you, but you'll be getting messages whenever they arrive."

He saw Mrs. Graham soon afterwards and found her less comfortable. There was right ventricular lift, gallop rhythm, accentuated P2 sound and raised jugular venous pressure. He arranged for early consults and ordered intravenous isoprenaline as an infusion.

On his visit to Claudia Terman in Room 6 he saw in the

67

night report that there'd been a pronounced change in the heart-rhythm and brain-wave cycles at 11:05 P.M., without apparent cause. In Julie Sears's notes it was remarked that the altered state had occurred during an uneventful period between medications and routine attention. The patient's EKG and EEG readings had returned to their previous levels after some fifteen minutes, and since that time only minor fluctuations had been noted.

Scott stayed for a while in Room 6, going over the reports from the last three shifts and trying to believe that the indications at 11:05 last night were to the good. Whatever their cause, the effect was an increase in the vital signs: the accelerated heart rate expressed an excitation within the system, and the higher brain-wave rhythm had taken Claudia nearer the conscious field, if only for fifteen minutes.

The spontaneous change in the patient would at least provide an argument against neurosurgery.

He was still in the ICU when a visitor came in and asked if he could see Mrs. Terman. Tall, quietly dressed in gray alpaca, his white hair carefully groomed, he gave his name as Heideker.

"Mrs. Terman is in my employ at West Coast Research Laboratories."

"I'm Dr. Rand."

Scott took him into Room 6 for a moment, explaining Mrs. Terman's condition as far as it was known. Heideker said very little, inclining his head in response to what was being said, watching the patient's face and sometimes glancing at the two monitor screens.

"Poor young woman," he said at last. "Does anyone know how the accident happened?"

"The police are making inquiries." He took Heideker across to his office, but he stayed only a few minutes.

"I want you to know, Dr. Rand, that Mrs. Terman has been with my company almost four years, and was one of

68

our most reliable employees. Our personnel manager is going into her medical insurance status today, and my instructions are that if funds should prove inadequate to cover prolonged treatment, West Coast Research will augment them as necessary." He allowed the slightest of pauses. "Within reason, of course."

During the morning several friends of Claudia Terman called for news and were told her condition was critical but static. Patrick Terman called but made no visit.

David Pryor came to see his sister just before noon and shortly afterwards saw Dr. Neil Kistner in his office, keeping the appointment that Dr. Rand had made for him.

"Please take a chair, Mr. Tyler."

"Pryor."

The surgeon glanced at a paper on his desk. "I beg your pardon. Mr. Pryor, yes."

David thought the man looked more like a lawyer; it was a large office with a big carved desk and a whole wallful of teak-and-brass diplomas and awards and he walked around in it instead of sitting down, his large hands behind his back, his eyes on the plain royal-blue carpet as he talked, sometimes looking up at David and standing perfectly still for a moment as he drove a point home, never faltering for a word, often throwing in a homely phrase to leaven some of the technicalities he was obliged—with apologies—to use.

"We have a head injury, Mr. Pryor. That is always a great deal more crucial in a patient than a broken leg, as I don't need to point out. Various talented and distinguished colleagues of mine have carried out elaborate tests; an extensive series of pictures have been taken and studied; and both the computerized axial tomography and the cerebral angiography have revealed distinct subdural hematomas." He stopped for a moment and faced David with his level gaze. "The sum total of all these examinations is in my opinion the strongest possible argument for surgery. The very—"

"Dr. Rand doesn't agree."

"Of course not."

David got out of the blue vinyl chair and poked his hair back with his fingers. He found Kistner too dominating and it was partly because he was on his feet and looking down at him.

"Why doesn't he agree?"

"Because he is a physician." Kistner was on the move again, hands behind him as he swung his compact body in half turns at each end of the room. "He is very experienced, clever, dedicated and conscientious. He is also limited, as all physicians are limited. They are scared of surgery because it seems drastic, though that is exaggerated. They are also keen to take the credit for bringing a patient back to full health, as indeed I shall be myself if I'm allowed my part in your sister's recovery. That is why Dr. Rand doesn't agree."

David stood at the window, looking out and seeing Claudia, seeing Rand, seeing a kaleidoscope of images brought to his mind's eye by the circling of his thoughts: a machine with tubes, a nurse's eyes, the wrecked sports car with its windshield ripped away, Claudia serving, reaching high for the ball, a hundred things, his mind swerving and doubling back as he listened to Kistner, following some of his arguments and losing others because they were too technical, until the moment came when he had to shut his eyes and take a breath and face the fact that while Claudia was lying there unconscious, these experienced, clever and dedicated experts who had her life in their hands couldn't agree on the best way to save it.

"It's all very well, you see, to say let's wait a few days and hope the patient will recover on her own."

Kistner stopped pacing again and stood at the window

70

with David, a distant Boeing drifting from one of their reflected faces to the other as it went in to land at the airport.

"She might do that. She might do that. Not perhaps in a few days, but a few weeks or a few months. Wouldn't that be wonderful?" A gold cuff link flashed as he moved his hands in a sudden gesture of impatience. "But she might *not* do that, Mr. Pryor. In fact I'd say it was highly unlikely, judging by the reports on all those tests. What we *might* do, if we wait for 'nature' to bring about a recovery, is to allow time for the condition to worsen, for complications to set in, and for your sister's constitution to weaken progressively. It would then be too late for surgery. I don't wish to sound dramatic; I want to be sure you know the risk we could all be taking as we stand around doing nothing."

David didn't move. Somewhere deep inside him he could feel slow panic beginning.

"I have seen too many cases of everyone waiting around, Mr. Pryor, too many tragedies, to leave you in ignorance of what we are faced with. If we—"

"What's the risk if you operate?"

"I'm afraid I can't answer that. It depends on what we find when we go in there, on what has to be done—if anything can be done. But let me say this: on the evidence of the examinations I would *think* the risk is very small, simply because the trauma is not extensive. It may well be *critical,* but its limited field would necessitate only minor probing. The point is this: at the moment we are working almost totally in the dark, relying on pictures, readings and secondhand evaluations, any of which can be inaccurate. But once I am allowed to go in there physically we shall see *exactly and precisely* what is going on and what we have to do to set it right. You follow?"

"Yes." David came away from the window, wanting to move, wanting to throw off the feeling of panic that was get-

71

ting worse every minute. "You mean you'll kind of explore."

"That is the exact term, Mr. Pryor: exploratory surgery. We would be working on the actual site of the injury, and dealing with it on the spot—where the action is. It may be simply a need to relieve cranial pressure, nothing more. It may call for more extensive work, the deeper we go in. We may find nothing at all, and in *that* case we can leave your sister in the capable care of Dr. Rand while the healing progresses toward complete recovery, and we won't have done any harm. We shall at least have got rid of our *worries* and our *doubts*."

One of the telephones on the desk began ringing and Kistner ignored it and it stopped. A light began flashing and he ignored that too.

"So I'm going to ask you," David said wearily, "the same thing they all ask you."

Kistner turned away from the window, thrusting his big hands into his pockets and standing squarely to face him. "If she were *my* sister . . . ?"

"Right."

"I wouldn't hesitate. Not for one second."

David stood still, looking down at his shoes. They seemed a long way below him, and somehow not his own; he felt if he went on looking down at them he'd begin falling.

He brought his head up quickly. "All right. But it's not for me to decide." His voice, too, seemed to come from a long way off, and he raised it a little. "It's for her husband. Did you know she has a husband?"

"Yes," Kistner said, "all the details are on—"

"Patrick Terman. Patrick L. Terman." He was still raising his voice, and could hear it better now. "He's a baseball player. Did you know?" He was standing closer to the other man, much closer, suddenly. "Did you know?"

"I don't think—"

72

"He also happens to be the biggest shit in the town. Did you know that too?" His voice was echoing from something; it had a kind of ring to it. "Did you?"

Kistner had moved away. He was standing over there by the desk. His hands weren't in his pockets any more. He was writing something on a pad.

"The biggest shit in the whole of this goddam town and it's for *him* to tell us what *he's* going to do about *my* sister! You know that?"

Something was trickling on his face and he wiped it with his fingers and looked at them and was surprised to see it wasn't blood, though it occurred to him it shouldn't be blood, he hadn't hit anything, it was just the hospital and that pump in there and the tube in her throat and all those people in white and everything, making him think of blood.

"What?"

The other man had just said something.

"The desk in the recovery ward. It's just along there at the end of the corridor."

Kistner was standing with him in the doorway, a hand on his arm. David was holding the piece of paper. It had some writing on it: *Valium 5 mg. #10, one T.I.D. for tension. NJK.*

"They'll look after you, Mr. Pryor. A perfectly normal reaction, so you don't have to worry." A telephone was ringing again. "I'll be in touch with you, of course."

Dr. Matheson to Pathology, please.

Late sunshine was in the windows, throwing rectangles of warmth across the floor of the Intensive Care Unit, orange-tinted in contrast with the new full-spectrum lighting. There weren't many people here at this hour and none of them was moving around: Tracy was checking the crash cart for its correct complement of drugs (it had been used twice during the day, once successfully) and Denise was on the

73

stool at the nurses' station watching the monitor screens. Miss Dean was standing in the doorway of Room 1, her short figure erect and her slightly large head poised as if listening, her hands in her white linen coat. The visitor in Room 6 stood equally still, looking down at the patient. They were like figures in a tableau, the sunlight stealing on them as the day grew quiet.

Dr. Matheson, please.

Three of the MA1's were running, the sound of their pulsing sometimes coming into unison, then separating again. Miss Dean heard them but did not listen to them; she was only subliminally aware of the change in the sound background since this morning, when there had been a fourth ventilator running. She liked the evening hour at Garden Grove more than any other; by this hour the day had grown wise, and many unknown things had become known; the frenetic rush of the morning had abated, as happens with a fever, and things were more comfortable.

She would be here for another two hundred forty-one evenings; she had counted them on a calendar. That didn't seem many, compared with all those thousands.

Someone had just come in and she turned and saw Dr. Rand heading for Room 6. The patient in there intrigued him: Mrs. Terman's physical trauma didn't account for her continuing coma, and he thought he was missing something. Perhaps he was.

Scott looked at the young man.

"Are you a relative?"

It was a moment before he answered, lifting his head and focusing but not really seeing Scott.

"No."

"He's Mr. Newby." Miss Dean was in the doorway. "I allowed him a few minutes. This is Dr. Rand, the attending physician."

Newby still didn't seem to be taking anything in, though

74

he kept his quiet brown eyes on Scott. He looked like a young professional of some kind; not an executive—his sports clothes were too casual—but maybe a scientist on his way up somewhere.

"Are you a friend of hers?"

Another couple of seconds went by.

"I guess."

Miss Dean stood attentively in the doorway, her stethoscope hanging from her neck, a strand of white hair falling away from her head: during the day she had tucked it tidy a score of times, perhaps more; it varied from day to day, from year to year. Someone was calling to her from the nurses' station and she turned away.

"You wouldn't know," Scott asked the visitor, "how this happened, I suppose?"

"How what happened?"

"The accident. You know there was an—"

"Oh. No, I don't know why." He was staring down at Claudia Terman again. "How bad is she, Doc?"

"We're not sure. Did you know her well?"

Newby looked up quickly. *Did* I?"

"Do you."

"Oh. Not really." He went over to the second bed and sat on the edge with his hands on his knees, looking at Claudia. "Not really."

"How did you work on Miss Dean?"

He looked up. "I beg pardon?"

"How did you persuade Miss Dean to let you in here?"

"Oh. I wouldn't go away."

Scott looked at the chart, not hurrying. He was heading for home in a few minutes but at this hour it didn't take much to make him stay for a while; the evening was the time when you weren't chasing your tail any more, and you could catch things you tended to miss during the day's pressure, sometimes important things.

"Did she use drugs, do you know?" As the silence lengthened he added: "You don't have to answer, and if you answer it's in strict confidence."

In a moment: "No. She didn't."

"Can you be sure, since you don't know her well?"

"Yes. She doesn't even eat meat."

"Is she highly strung? Would you say?"

"No. She puts it all into tennis, and things like that."

Scott hooked the chart back and glanced up at the monitor screens. The readings were steady. "This marriage of hers—do you know about that?"

"It didn't work."

"Was it very upsetting for her?"

"It was."

"Over what period of time?"

"Not long. They broke it up seven weeks ago."

"Exactly seven?"

Newby got off the empty bed, looking at Scott with a slight twist to his mouth. "Exactly seven. And for someone who doesn't know her very well, I know her very well, right? That's just the way it is."

"What I'm looking for, Mr. Newby—what's your first name?"

"Brian."

"What I'm looking for, Brian, is some kind of a mental or emotional stress in Claudia that could be aggravating the physical trauma caused by the accident."

"Well, I guess seven weeks of a broken marriage could qualify."

Brian looked down at the quiet face with its closed eyes and the electrodes trailing across the pillow. "Do you have the strange feeling there's nobody here with us? I mean we're talking about her as if—" He broke off and took a breath, moving past Scott to the doorway. "My God, all that beautiful vitality . . . where did it go?"

Scott Rand reached his home in Seal Beach soon after seven o'clock that evening, unusually early. Eve didn't remark on it but took it as a sign that he meant to relax his schedules, according to her suggestion. She whipped up a particularly attractive *Pâtes au beurre* and opened some Riesling to celebrate.

Twelve miles along the coast at Newport Beach the small dinner party at the Yacht Club lasted until almost eleven. Christina Kistner had a flair for entertaining those people who not only enjoyed each other's company but lent substance to Neil's image as a successful man. This evening there were two rising young film actors, a prominent banker, an Arabian horse breeder and three Japanese industrialists. The medical world was represented by Arnold Blatsky, the eminent surgeon, and Joshua Smythe, once personal physician to the Attorney General and recently out of a professorial chair at Stanford. Both wielded influence at the boards at Garden Grove Hospital. On the distaff side there were four wives and three mistresses present.

Neil Kistner admired, as usual, his young wife's unerring management of the evening, during which the two young actors agreed to swap mistresses, the announcement being made amid general and well-mannered laughter from which only the three Japanese industrialists abstained, their wives being present. Further cachet was lent to the evening by the appearance of the showroom-polished custom-built Stutz at the entrance of the Club, driven there by one of the valet-parking boys precisely on cue as the guests were leaving—another instance of Christina's flair for effective stage management, evoking the delight of the young actor-proprietor at the reception of his new toy by those in his party.

"One of these baubles," announced Christina, "I must possess."

It got a polite laugh but Neil Kistner knew she was serious, by her glance to him as she said it. His wife was not so impractical as to demand tokens of homage from Saks and Cartier at frequent intervals, but when something really took her fancy she made it known. Beautiful, charming and intelligent, she graced and appointed her husband's life style, enjoying her role and playing it with an understated brilliance to their mutual advantage. Tonight's calculated throwaway line would reach the gossip columns of a dozen selected magazines, nationwide, before the weekend; and it would be followed shortly by photographs of the proud owner taking delivery. The message was terribly simple: anyone able to afford this kind of car must be first-class at his job.

There was another aspect to the little charade. Tonight, as the Kistners and their guests waited under the columned porch for their cars, Christina was throwing her mate a challenge to which his masculine pride would respond: for the "bauble" that stood dazzling them all in the lamplight came in, with its Italian body and gold-plated accessories, at more than forty thousand dollars.

Her birthday was, by chance, in six weeks' time.

Not long after the dinner party at the Yacht Club had broken up, a young man was arrested in a downtown bar in Buena Park for breach of the peace. He wasn't very drunk but he was very noisy, and admitted having harangued the bartender and several customers on the subject of modern medicine, sundry references having been made to "the fucking incompetence of those fucking doctors" who "ran you around in circles while their patients were dying."

The police were satisfied, after questioning, that the party under charge was suffering considerable stress due to the fact that his sister was in critical condition following a traffic accident, and he was released with a warning to go straight home.

78

At Garden Grove Hospital the early part of the night passed without major incident.

Soon after the late staff came on duty in Cardio-Pulmonary one of the patients in the CCU—Mr. Mario Mancini—was moved to Room 9 of the observation complex on the instructions of Dr. Thayer, the attending physician. In consultation with Dr. Rand it had been agreed that the patient's CPK and SGOT enzyme levels had returned to normal, that the HBD had remained within satisfactory limits and that there had been no recurrence of the chest pains. The feeling was that the attack had been one of angina pectoris and that the crisis had passed. Dr. Thayer had proposed a four-day sojourn in a private room under close observation, with ambulation permitted on the second day, under telemetric monitoring.

Mancini made no objection to being moved, though he took care not to exert himself or talk overmuch. In his new room he was given a light meal and allowed to sit up in bed for an hour, his dark glasses on and his head turned to watch the lights of the freeway from the window.

His night nurse, Frieda Hoff, suggested leaving only a bedside lamp burning so that he wouldn't need his dark glasses, but he said he preferred to wear them, as he felt "lost" without them. She left the door wide open and told him to ring his bell if he needed anything, however small, because they wanted him to make as little physical effort as possible during the first twelve hours of the observation period. He said he understood.

Mario Mancini knew quite a lot about medicine, though he hadn't mentioned this to any of the staff, perhaps because his knowledge had been derived solely during his three years at medical school a long time ago and they wouldn't be very interested. He had intended becoming a physician in those days, and his studies had absorbed him; he had passed all his interim exams with consistent A's, which was typical of the efficient way he tackled everything he did.

Probably he would have made an excellent doctor, but for the fact that as an orphan he had always lacked security and was therefore avaricious. There was a good living in medicine, but at medical school he had learned it would take time to earn it. An observant young man, he had noticed where the real money was in this field: it was in drugs. Much of a doctor's work was in prescribing them, and for patients who were eager for them to the point of mania. Any physician who failed to prescribe at least two drugs for a new patient would soon lose him.

But it wasn't the doctor who reaped the benefit: it was the pharmacist, and beyond him the man who actually manufactured the drugs. So ten years ago Mario Mancini had left medical school and joined a pharmaceutical firm, a modest back-room enterprise in Chicago that had since become one of the largest manufacturers of antibiotics in the country, thanks partly to Mr. Mancini's dedicated work and talents as a chemist and partly to the ruthlessly competitive policy of the company and its talent for cultivating useful contacts in the business field.

Its name was Fiorenzo Pharmaceutical of Chicago, Inc., and today, at the age of forty-one, Mario Mancini was third vice-president and in charge of the Los Angeles branch.

As he sat propped against the pillows in Room 9 of the observation complex, his head angled to watch the lights of the freeway traffic a half mile distant while his thoughts absorbed him, the beat of his heart was displayed on the EKG screen at the CU station and also on a slave monitor in the Intensive Care Unit at the other end of the corridor. The rate was steady at 77 beats per minute, only five above normal.

At 11:35 P.M. Julie Sears, on night duty in the ICU,

began making routine printouts of the EKG readings for the six patients in her charge, and of the EEG reading for Claudia Terman. At this time she noticed an acceleration of the brain rhythm to 8 cycles per second in the alpha region and an increase in the heart rate to 101 beats per minute, the greatest change since approximately the same time last night, at 11:19.

Julie went into Room 6 to make a physical check, but found the patient in a quiescent state with a temperature of 98.7 and no signs of perspiration or restlessness. A series of pain-stimulus tests—ordered by Dr. Rand in the event of the patient's condition moving toward consciousness—had no effect on the monitor screen readings.

As last night, the nurse decided there was no need to call Dr. Rand at his home, but noted the change in her report so that he would see it in the morning.

Shortly before midnight Arlene Wyatt was on duty in the recovery ward, seeing to a patient just in from the operating room following a pneumonectomy. At present there were no complications either evidenced or expected, and it was necessary only to carry out routine postoperative procedures, checking the pulse and blood pressure at frequent intervals and keeping the airway clear.

A few minutes later, when Arlene was going back to the nurses' station with a tray of instruments, she felt an attack of migraine coming on, as had occurred twice on the previous night. This time she was conscious of sudden urgency, a feeling that she must do something immediately, though she had no idea what it was. Within a few seconds the migraine grew intense and the tray began shaking in her hands, so violently that she had to run the last few yards to the nurses' station and put it down.

Her heart pounding, she believed she called out to someone—perhaps to Kathy, who was on duty with her—before

81

she was snatching up a pencil with great force, snapping it in half and at once seizing another to begin writing feverishly on the scratch pad near the telephone, without knowing why, knowing only that she could not stop herself.

Chapter 6

Dr. Glezen, please. Dr. Glezen.

Most of the night staff heard the call and their reaction was much the same. This was the only exception to the rule that the paging system should be restricted to code alerts during the dark hours, so that the patients wouldn't be unnecessarily disturbed. Don Glezen concerned himself a great deal with terminal cases, for whom there was no difference between night and day, and a call for him at this hour—a few minutes after midnight—would mean that someone, somewhere in the great rectilinear labyrinth of Garden Grove, was near death and in need of comfort.

Dr. Glezen. Dr. Glezen, please.

There was no location given. "Carcinoma Ward" was never referred to over the speaker system by name, and there was no code number for it. Cancer was not an emergency.

At ten minutes after midnight Don Glezen called the switchboard and was told he was needed in Recovery. He was only a little surprised: in Recovery there were no terminal cases, and if a patient died there it would be during an intensive battle by the medical staff to keep him alive; there would be no place for a psychologist. On the other hand, the staff sometimes had a problem with someone in such pain—usually in a bone—that narcotics failed to deal with it; and his training in clinical hypnotism could often help.

When he reached the recovery ward he found Arlene

Wyatt at the nurses' station and Kathy checking an IV drip halfway down the room.

He looked along the rows of beds.

"Who is it?" he asked Arlene.

"It's me."

He now saw that she was pale and shaken-looking.

"What happened?"

She didn't know what to say, how exactly to put it. It would be like admitting to something embarrassing, a drinking problem or a loss of reason; she didn't want to hear the words said, making her fright a reality.

"I guess I shouldn't have called you, Don."

On duty she normally used his title, but during her sessions with him after Roger's death it had been necessary to establish an informal relationship so that he could work on her problem, and at this moment she needed his help again.

"Sure you should."

He was looking around him for a clue but didn't see anything; the place was in perfect order, except for a broken pencil lying on the floor.

"Thank you for coming," she said, and knew she was just putting it off.

"Feeling a bit depressed, Arlene?"

His voice was low and resonant, its tone easing her. Those months ago, she'd asked him to put her into hypnosis and suggest it was perfectly okay for people to die, and you didn't have to grieve. He'd refused, telling her that grief was the real way out and she had to take it, or later she'd come to know she'd cheated, and wouldn't forgive herself.

"No. I'm not depressed. All that's okay now." Her voice stopped again, and she felt angry at herself for not having any guts. "It's this, Don. Look."

As she put the three pieces of paper in a row on the desk he could feel the fear coming out of her; in his daily work he was familiar with it.

She watched his quiet and attentive face as he read the scribbled messages by the light of the desk lamp.

For God's sake help me.

He tried — kill — and he'll — again.

Won't anyone help me? He's — to — now. Oh God I'm so scared.

Don read them three times, then took them right under the lamp and tried to make out the illegible words. In the third message, one of them looked like *close,* to read: *He's close to — now.* Was it: *to me now?*

"Did you write these?"

"Yes."

"What do they mean?"

"I don't know."

He hitched one leg across a stool, watching her with his large contemplative eyes, letting the hint of a smile come to reassure her. But he was thinking of a child, a twelve-year-old girl at a school for the mentally retarded in Santa Barbara, six years ago, almost seven.

"Did you write them at intervals?"

She told him about them. The last note was written ten minutes ago. Kathy had been at the other end of the ward and hadn't seen anything this time.

"You felt a compulsion? Felt you *had* to write *something?*"

"Anything. Write *anything.*" She took a deep breath and let it out slowly, shutting her eyes for a moment. It was okay now that Don was here. She wasn't going crazy or anything. If she was, he could fix it.

"You just had to *write,*" he said. "You didn't know what you would put down."

"I only knew when I saw it there."

"It was like taking dictation?"

She almost laughed. "Absolutely." He was right on the button.

"Any migraine?"

"What?"

"Did you feel any migraine?"

"How did you *know?*"

He laughed gently, tempting her to laugh with him, letting the tension out. She felt suddenly it was some kind of game they were playing.

"The migraine went," he said, "as soon as you'd finished writing." He made his tone a statement this time, wanting to show her that he knew these things, so she'd have faith in him, in his apparent omniscience.

He looked at the messages again, leaving her quiet, letting her absorb the relief of his knowing.

After a moment she said: "This must happen to other people. Or you wouldn't know these things."

"Sure. To a whole lot of people. I hear they've started a club."

She laughed now for a different reason, almost for joy. He was making jokes, so she couldn't be going crazy after all. Then she was leaning her head against him without knowing she was going to do it, and saying, "Oh God, I was so scared, Don."

"You didn't have to be." He held her shoulders until she straightened up and stood away from him, embarrassed that she'd needed his comfort so badly.

He didn't think she was reiterating the last part of that particular message in her mind—*Oh God I'm so scared*. It was a natural thing to say, a natural way to put it. She *must* have been scared, doing a thing like this, losing control. Like the twelve-year-old girl in Santa Barbara.

"You feeling better now?"

He was looking around the desk, for the list.

"I'm feeling great." Arlene was laughing at herself a little, wondering how it had all happened, going across to the mirror on the wall over the blood unit, getting her blond

86

hair in shape again and wondering how it had gotten to look like this anyway, when nothing *physical* had happened to her; maybe she'd put her head in her hands or something, while she was waiting for Don. She didn't care any more; nothing mattered, because she wasn't going crazy.

"But you began feeling great," Don said, as if half to himself, "before I came along." He was going through the list of patients currently in the ward. "Or rather, just *after* you finished writing the message."

In a moment Arlene said simply: "Yes." She watched him steadily. He knew so much about this; it was kind of spooky. "Just after."

"You felt—well, delivered?" He went on looking at the list, sometimes glancing along the ward.

"Yes," Arlene said low. "Like I'd kind of got through a whole day's work, just in a minute. Was that the tension coming off?"

Don smiled faintly. "You know almost as much about this as I do."

He put the list on the desk where it belonged. He hadn't found what he was looking for.

"Don."

"Yes?"

"Is it going to happen again?" She went on watching him.

Kathy was coming back to the station and he picked up the three slips of paper and put them in his pocket, strolling to the doors as he talked, so Arlene would follow. "Well, that depends on a lot of things, which I suppose is the one universal answer you can use for any question under the sun." When they were a little way along the corridor and out of earshot he said: "Yes, it may happen again. But don't let that worry you."

"That's easy to say." She couldn't forget the way the tray had started shaking in her hands, making her put it down.

"If you can just tell me what's going on, maybe—" She shrugged helplessly.

"I'm not sure, but I have an idea." He kept his voice low, watching her small strained face under the lights as he made up his mind how much he could tell her, and where he must stop. "This looks like a paranormal manifestation, of the kind I've run across once or twice in my researches. It's nothing new, and certainly nothing we need feel any alarm over. The paranormal is only a name for a place we don't want to recognize—the real world outside the very narrow view we allow ourselves of the universe. And the universe happens to be the most normal thing there is, with every one of the atoms in it following its laws: including the atoms in our own bodies. Out there, the most incredible things can happen, but they're only incredible—and therefore frightening—because we don't know anything about them: and we don't want to know. We cling to ignorance as our defense, for fear we'd find out something we'd rather not accept."

In the ward, one of the patients had woken up, and they heard Kathy going along to see to him. Arlene stood listening, in case she was needed. Don said nothing till she looked up at him again.

"Am I making any sense?" he asked her.

"I guess you're trying to reassure me. But I don't know why I wrote those wild things. It—"

"You didn't."

In a moment she said: "But it was my—I mean—"

"All right, the mechanics were yours: the pencil and paper and the requisite muscular contractions—okay. But you didn't think up the words. The important thing you have to understand, Arlene, is that there's nothing wrong with *you*. Somebody's using you as a contact, that's all, hoping you'll help them."

88

The dark green TR-2 stood on the ramp in the end garage of the Los Angeles Police Department repair and maintenance section, the windshield half hanging off and the snow from the safety glass scattered between the bucket seats. There'd been a leak from the gas tank and the mechanics had siphoned it dry; battery acid had pooled under the hood from a split in the casing and they'd mopped it up so it wouldn't cause any corrosion. Then they'd gone over the whole car for the second time and come up with a blank, except for the dent.

The dent was approximately four inches in diameter and a half inch deep at the center and carried a film of smoke-gray paint around the edges, which had been checked under a blowup lens and found to be smoke gray, which didn't surprise anybody. The lens also showed, though, that the dent had been made by a glancing impact while the car had been stationary, or by a glancing impact while the car had been moving at a speed of 5 or 10 mph faster or slower than the other vehicle that must have made it.

There had to be another vehicle because there wasn't anything smoke gray around at the crash site; unless the dent had been made at some other time. To find out, they told a patrol to pick up Joe MacArthur at the Hitchin' Post service station, where, according to Claudia Terman's friend at her apartment block, she used to get her gas. Joe MacArthur refused to be picked up because he said it was bad for business for him to be seen around in some crummy patrol car, but he went along to the LAPD in his own beat-up 1957 Dodge truck and took a look at the dent in the left front fender of the TR-2.

"It wasn't there Saturday."

"Last Saturday?"

"Sure, last Saturday, that's what I'm tellin' you, ain't I?"

Joe bit through the end of his cigar butt and threw it in the corner under the NO SMOKING sign. He didn't have too much time for these boys: they got their gas at the Arco across the street from him.

"You're certain about that, Joe?"

He began walking out, just as an indication of his feelings. "Holy cow, you ask me if there was a dent the last time I set eyes on the car, an' I say no, there wasn't a dent, not on Saturday, an' I didn't say I didn't *think* there was a dent, y' get the difference? Let's try it again, shall we? No dent. No, not, negative." He got out a new Carlos y Garcia and split the end with his thumbnail and lit up and threw the match in the corner under the NO SMOKING sign and waited till nobody said anything; then he let them drag him back and ask him a lot of questions about the condition the car was in Saturday, the last time he saw it, and whether Mrs. Terman had been complaining about anything, like the brakes or the steering, or had got him to fix anything for her, anything that could have sent the car rolling over and over on the Garden Grove Freeway at 2:31 on the morning of Sunday the fifth.

He said no, negative, nix, and they believed him. Joe had a good reputation among the local boys—"a pain in the ass but real hot on mechanics," as one of them put it. He said he hoped he'd been of help to them because it had cost him almost a full hour's working time, though he realized he was doing a public service. He added that you could get Carlos y Garcia in packs of ten, full size, and they said they'd have to put in a voucher for the cost and it might take a week or two but they'd deliver. As soon as he'd driven away in his beat-up 1957 Dodge truck they picked up the match and the cigar butt from the corner beneath the NO SMOKING notice before the chief came around and saw them there.

Despite everything, Joe had been a real help. The dark green sports car may have suffered a minor collision at any time between the hour when Joe had last seen it—at 5:20 P.M. on Saturday the fourth—and the hour when it crashed

90

—at 2:31 A.M. on Sunday. But one theory on the cause of that crash was now valid: that on Sunday morning the TR-2 had collided with another vehicle, color smoke gray, at a low relative speed but at a much higher road speed at which the resulting damage had been considerable.

Soon after Joe's leaving the LAPD repair and maintenance garage the police began looking for a smoke-gray car with minor damage to the bodywork and possible traces of dark green paint. At this point they had no reason to suspect the collision had been caused deliberately.

Scott Rand was at Garden Grove before 9 A.M. and was checking the patient in Room 6 some twenty minutes later. He read the report left by Julie Sears twice and compared it with her report of the night before.

At 11:19 on the fifth there had been a change in Claudia Terman's condition, with an increased heart rate to 103 bpm and an accelerated brain rhythm into the alpha region between 7 and 8 cps. At about the same hour—11:35—on the evening of the sixth her condition had changed again, the EKG showing 98 and the EEG showing 7 cps, both readings being comparable to those of the night before.

The addenda to both notes were also similar: *Quiescent state, no undue perspiration, temperature 98.7. Pain-stimulus tests negative.*

"Dr. Rand?"

He didn't answer. The door was open and they could come in if they wanted to. He hoped they wouldn't. This was the first time a consistent pattern was emerging from the dozens of printouts and reports on the Terman case, and even though it concerned no more than a single repetition phase it caught his attention, because these were vital signs and they had twice indicated a return toward consciousness and at approximately the same hour of the day.

A candystriper was in the doorway: he noted her uniform at the periphery of his vision. She didn't say his name again. He checked the patient physically, noting the dry skin, the small pupils, the light pulse, the inability to assist the ventilator when he moved the valve control. Her condition was the same as it had been since she had been brought in here on Sunday morning, varying only on those two occasions for approximately fifteen minutes each time. Tonight he would stay on for a few hours and watch for a repeat phase. If Claudia Terman's brain approached the conscious field he wanted to be there and try to help her.

Going out of the room he almost bumped into the candystriper.

"Dr. Glezen is in your office, Dr. Rand." A short plump girl with high color and anxious eyes. "He said he didn't want to disturb you."

"So why are you disturbing me?"

She started to say something, realized she didn't have any answer and just stood there swallowing. He didn't remember having seen her before.

"How long have you been here?"

"Two days."

"All right, then you have forty more years to go, so slow down a little. Don't do anything until you've watched trained people do it first, and don't talk too much. When you're talking you can't listen, and if you listen for forty years you still won't know it all, any more than I will, so you can see there's absolutely no hurry. Thinking is also a help: if an experienced doctor doesn't want to disturb me, there could be a message in it for you. It's not a bad rule never to disturb a senior staff physician when he's on his rounds, unless the place is on fire. Is the place on fire?"

"No, Dr. Rand."

"All right. When it is, come and see me again and we'll put it out between us."

92

About eleven o'clock he took a break and called Don Glezen.

"What can I do for you?"

"I just wanted a little talk. How long do you have?"

"I'm all right for time."

"Can I come up right away?"

"Do that. We'll have some coffee."

Don found him in his office ten minutes later, and dropped into the visitor's chair, waiting until Scott got off the phone. He'd known him several years, ever since Scott had taken up his residency, and knew him to be a good physician, rather on the conservative side and therefore hard on himself in terms of working hours and his attitude toward patients. He was sometimes a nuisance to the board of control, kicking at new regulations designed to provide shortcuts to compensate for the lack of trained staff, and had once had a showdown with Charles Jordan, the Administrator, over a question of whether candystripers should be allowed in the Intensive and Cardiac Care units. Jordan had prevailed, arguing that even if these young trainee nurses occasionally got in the way and made minor mistakes they took a lot of trivial but necessary work off the shoulders of the RNs, and at the same time learned at first hand the special procedures followed in units where crises were the norm and the life of a helpless patient depended on how hard the staff could fight for it.

Don watched the lean quiet figure behind the desk, trying to place the difference between this man and the hundreds of other men he'd seen sitting with a telephone. It took a moment or two because it couldn't be seen in what Scott Rand was doing, but in what he was *not* doing: he didn't have his feet on the desk or his eyes on the ceiling; he wasn't doodling or toying with a pencil or swinging his foot; he was sitting perfectly straight and perfectly still and listening with all his attention to what was being told him on the

93

phone. It was, Don thought, a restful and instructive sight, and he would refer to it in his next article for *Persona*.

"Then we'll run another test," Scott said. "We'll run as many tests as we have to. Tell Dr. Fineman, will you?"

In a moment he hung up and went on gazing straight in front of him for a while, then made a note on his pad, talking before he looked up at Don Glezen. "The more we discover about the human body, the less we know."

"It figures," Don said. "We're all busy trying to cure people from the outside, instead of letting their own bodies do it from the inside, where the action is." This conviction was his reason for choosing clinical psychology.

"They need help," Scott said, and tore the top sheet off his pad, filing it.

"They need it less than they think they do. How's Eve today?"

"What? Fine." He looked up at last. "At least I think she is. I haven't seen her today." It occurred to him he sounded disinterested. "She's always fine. What can I do for you, Don?"

"I'm not sure, really." He didn't look at Scott, but at a cloud in the window, a bubble of cumulus floating above the smog. "Do you know anything about psychometry?"

"Yes. It's an allergy. Try vitamin E." He was ready to listen to Don Glezen on medicine or psychology, but this paranormal business wasn't in his line, though Don had tried to get his interest now and then. "What about that coffee?"

"I'll pass." He decided on a direct approach. "I've been looking all over the hospital for a brain-damage case, and I thought you might have one." He looked down from the cloud into Scott's clear and attentive eyes. "A case with what we might call puzzling complications."

Scott was getting up and Don noted that; he believed he'd touched on something.

"Head injuries are always a bit puzzling, as you know." He picked up his stethoscope from the desk and put it on top of the filing cabinet, where he kept it for most of the time.

Don watched him from the chair.

"I've worked out a model for this one," he said evenly. "I'm looking for someone in a state of coma 4, who has theta waves across the screen." He waited. Scott said nothing. "Someone who could be suffering from psychic shock. Emotional shock, if you like."

He went on watching Scott Rand.

Scott stood quite still, his hands behind his back, not looking down at Don, not looking anywhere. His fingers were moving a little, though it was barely noticeable.

"Someone," Don said, "who's terrified of something."

Scott looked down at him now.

"Have you seen my lists?"

"No."

"You said you've been looking all over the place."

"I have."

"You could have called the desk," Scott said. He was feeling irritated and he didn't know why. "They would have told you."

"I know." Don got out of the chair and stood facing him, excited and not wanting to show it, because Scott Rand wasn't receptive to anything outside the known laws of science and he'd be difficult to handle. "But I wanted to talk to you first."

"Why?"

"Because I think you've got a case like the one I've described, and I wanted to tell you about it—before I could have known."

Chapter 7

Fifteen minutes ago a Code 1 alert had gone out over the paging system, but since then the telephones in the Intensive and Cardiac Care units had remained quiet. Whoever it was the ambulance had brought in, they didn't need the specialized survival equipment and techniques offered by Cardio-Pulmonary.

It was now 10:35 P.M. and the quiet that came with the dark hours had settled over Garden Grove. At this time the ICU was staffed by Julie Sears, Fran Engel and an aide. Also at the nurses' station tonight were Don Glezen and Scott Rand, both still in their white coats and unofficially on duty.

"He's too young to retire."

"It's what he has to do, Scott."

Their voices were low. They leaned against the station counter, their arms folded. The nearest telephone was within reach of Don's right hand.

"Is it that bad?" Scott Rand asked quietly.

"Yes. It's that bad."

They were talking about Dan Taylor. Today a third suit had been filed against him for malpractice, this one linked with his drinking problem.

"It's getting bad," Scott said with a shrug, "for all of us."

He looked again at the two monitor screens, checking the sixth band down. Don looked again at the digital wall clock as the figures flicked to 10:43.

"That doesn't make it any better for Danny," he said.

"All right, I'm just extrapolating this thing. People have begun suing us for not taking enough trouble in diagnosis, so now we take twice as many X rays and bring in twice as many consultants, and we get sued for performing unnecessary medicine."

Scott had fought this issue with the board of control and nothing had yet been resolved as concerned policy. More than half the time it wasn't the physician's fault when a death occurred, and there just wasn't the time to pin it down to the real culprit: improperly functioning temperature controls in the lab refrigerators, slack Emergency Room personnel with unwashed hands, undetected Rh problems in the obstetrics ward because the blood hadn't been typed, faulty EEG and EKG monitors and alarm circuits in the Intensive Care Unit.

This was why he'd asked Phil Byers, the respiratory therapist, to check out the MA1 in Room 6 at two-hourly intervals, and why he'd asked the EEG and EKG technicians to check out the monitors twice a day: because the Claudia Terman case had what Don Glezen described as "puzzling complications" and the cause might not be in her body, but in one of the machines that were linked with it as her means of survival. But Scott didn't think so.

He thought the cause was in her body, in her brain.

During the time that had passed since Don had come into his office this morning he hadn't discussed the case further. Don hadn't wanted that. "I'm going to have to convince you about something," he'd told Scott, "and I have to do it my way."

His way was that they should meet here in the ICU at 10:30 P.M. and watch the Terman monitors. Scott had intended to do that in any case, to see if this patient's condition would show a change for the third time at approximately this hour.

97

The sound of voices came again, and Don moved, going over to the open doorway of Room 3, where one of the nurses was talking to the patient.

"Is it still uncomfortable?"

"Not really. It's just that I can't sleep."

It was Mrs. Graham, who had been transferred from Recovery last night. Don went quietly to stand beside the nurse.

"Hello, Doris. Have we been keeping you awake?"

"No. I like to hear people around." Her voice was stronger than this morning; the monitor was registering a fluctuating beat in the low eighties, again an improvement.

"I know you, Doris. You're the partygoing sort."

She was able to smile; that too was new. Last evening Don had been called to the recovery ward to help her with her pain, which had been mostly fear.

"I'll bet you miss Arlene, don't you?" He held her fragile hand for a moment.

"She was wonderful to me."

"We'll have her up here for a minute, to say hello."

"I wouldn't want to trouble her. It's—"

"She misses you too."

Her eyes were closing, and he didn't say anything more. Sometimes his voice alone made them drowsy, when they were under sedation.

He went back to the nurses' station and looked at the Room 6 band of the EEG, to refamiliarize himself with its pattern.

"Is she all right?" Scott asked him.

"She's fine." He glanced at the clock again, reading 10:49.

Scott still hadn't probed him on this thing and he was appreciative. He could have talked to Scott for hours in an attempt to convince him his theory was valid, but it would have been in abstract terms. Scott would want proof and he'd want it in figures. Don wasn't sure he could show him any; this was a long shot and he knew it.

"The problem with defensive medicine," Scott said quietly, "is that we're—"

The green phone began ringing.

"Excuse me," Don said, and picked it up. "ICU, Dr. Glezen."

The digital clock flicked to 10:50.

"Arlene Wyatt has just come in, Doctor."

He began watching the EEG monitor, Band 6.

"Thank you." He pushed down the contacts and dialed Recovery. "Dr. Glezen. When Arlene gets in, would you have her call me at the ICU? Thanks." He hung up and said to Scott: "The problem with defensive medicine—?"

"Is that we're no longer thinking of the patient's welfare. We're thinking of the doctor's."

Mrs. Engel came across from Room 3 with the chart, newly annotated. The temperature was down again and the fluid balance showed an intake deficit.

"You'll have to take care of that, Fran."

"I'm trying to keep pace with the diuretic, Doctor." There was a veiled rebuke there.

"Then phase it down."

Fran Engel always had something she couldn't keep pace with: the diuretic, the airway clearance, the edemas. And life, Scott thought, itself.

Don was answering the phone again. "Arlene, would it bother you to come up here for a couple of minutes? Doris Graham wants to say hello."

He watched the EEG screen. The rhythm on Band 6 was unchanged.

"How is she?"

"She's fine."

"I'll ask Betty to hang on for me."

"Do that."

99

Don put the phone down and went on watching the monitor.

Scott had gone across to Room 3, maybe to supervise the correction to the fluid balance.

The clock moved to 10:57.

Four minutes later Don heard the doors of the elevator along the corridor thumping open, and turned his head to see who came out. It was Arlene. He looked back to the monitor screen and listened to her footsteps, quick and light on the vinyl-tiled floor.

"Good evening, Dr. Glezen."

"Hello, Arlene." He didn't look away from the screen. "She's in Room 3."

"I'll go see her."

He nodded.

The pulsing green line kept up its steady rhythm at 5 cycles per second. He heard Arlene's rather husky voice as she talked to Doris Graham. There was still no change on the screen.

So it wasn't going to work.

A long shot was a long shot. Period.

In a few minutes Arlene came across to the nurses' station with Scott Rand.

"She's doing great!"

Don looked away from the monitor at last.

"You've cheered her up." He noticed Arlene was looking at ease and rested from her day's sleep. Last night he had sacked out in his office instead of going home, in case she had another experience; there hadn't been one. Maybe there wouldn't ever be one again. "While you're here," he said as an afterthought, "would you look in at Room 6 for me?"

"Sure. Who is it?" She went across to the open doorway.

"Somebody new," Don said, and began looking at the monitor again. Then he said sharply: "Scott."

They both watched the screen. On the sixth band the

100

rhythm was accelerating from the theta into the alpha region through 9 . . . 10 . . . 11 . . .

Don didn't turn his head.

"Scott. Are you watching?"

"Yes." He looked briefly at the wall clock and back again. It was 11:07. The EEG reading had steadied around 11 cycles per second and on the EKG the heart rate had risen to 109. This had happened last night, and the night before. He didn't know why it had happened.

Don had known why.

Arlene stood in Room 6, about halfway from the door to the nearer bed. She saw the woman in the bed. She saw the light coming through the doorway and through the slats of the window blind. She felt the air very still, very clear. She breathed it. She heard the machine pumping near her. Nothing in the room moved. She stood quiet, seeing a long way, listening a long way through the still clear air. She floated through it, through the cool echoing air.

"Arlene."

Floating through the air, going away into it, beginning to spin, while the face on the pillow turned slowly, spinning with her.

"Arlene."

Someone's hand. Spinning and turning through the tunnel of the air, giddying. Their hand squeezing her arm.

"Arlene."

Yes. Turning.

"Yes," she said, and walked with them, walked away, seeing the panels of light above her everywhere, and the telephones, and Dr. Rand.

"Are you all right?"

"Why shouldn't I be?"

She felt someone taking their hand away from her arm. It was so warm in here: everybody complained about it, all

101

over the hospital; they kept the air conditioning set at too high a temperature.

She could see Doris Graham through the other doorway; she looked like she was asleep now. It made Arlene feel reassured, because sleep was a healer. She'd just seen someone else asleep, but couldn't remember where.

"She's a wonderful patient," she said.

"Who is?"

"Mrs. Graham. No wonder she's pulling through—she's so positive. But there's a fluid imbalance—did you see the chart?"

"Yes. We're working on that."

Dr. Rand and Dr. Glezen were watching the monitor screens, and she watched them too, for a moment. The EKG and EEG readings for Room 6 were both slowing progressively.

"I'll get back to the ward," she said.

"I'm going down there myself," Don Glezen told her, and they went to the doors together. Then the migraine began and she had to turn around and go back to the nurses' station, where Dr. Rand stood watching her as she broke into a little run and hit the desk because she couldn't stop, hurting her arm but in a strange way not feeling it as she snatched the pencil near the telephone and began writing, jabbing at the pad.

Don't leave me . . . Please . . . now . . . God's sake don't leave me now.

The meeting took place before noon on the following day in Scott Rand's office. He first took Don Glezen and Ernst Stein to look at the patient in Room 6, then led them to the narrow pastel-green room at the end of the corridor, where Don dropped into the vinyl chair and Ernst elected to lean with his back to the wall near the window, the sunlight sparkling on his gold-rimmed glasses as he watched the other two men.

"Tell me again," he said in his soft tones. He'd forgotten nothing of what Don had told him over the telephone, but wanted simply to listen for any changes to the story that might be made. Sometimes that could be revealing, in terms of what the teller was trying to make himself believe.

Ernst Stein was a psychiatrist whose services were available to Garden Grove in cases where a problem came up regarding a difficult patient. He had his office in the next block, opposite the Memorial Grove, and kept certain hours of the day clear of appointments, when he was able, so that the hospital could count on his help. A prewar refugee from Berlin with American citizenship, he had established an impressive record for his researches into dementia praecox and paranoia; he was also gifted with children, who saw him as someone out of a storybook, with his short plump body and round face, and his soft confiding voice with its lingering trace of an accent.

Scott Rand disliked him for various reasons but had agreed to get him in here when Don had suggested it; Stein had a brilliant brain under his tan bald head, and they could use it. He listened to Don's recapitulation and put in a couple of his own questions before Stein could say anything.

"Doris Graham wasn't involved in these reactions?"

"Oh no. I just wanted to get Arlene up here, and Doris gave us an excuse. We'd have used a different one if we'd had to."

"Were you expecting a reaction," Scott asked him, "when Arlene came into the hospital?"

Ernst said: "Reaction?"

"From Claudia Terman."

"Ah yes."

"Not really *expecting*," Don said. "It was—"

"Hoping for?" Ernst asked softly.

103

"Well, sure. The paranormal excites me, so I'm always on the lookout for new evidence. But my hopes can't affect an electroencephalograph that isn't hooked up to my head, can they?"

Ernst said nothing, but stood with his arms folded across his expensively tailored chest, gazing mildly at the picture of Scott Rand's daughter on the wall. He thought that perhaps an electroencephalograph *could* be affected by paranormal means, but it would hardly advance the inquiry; he had never seen evidence of the paranormal and had no reason to place his belief in it, though that was no proof that it didn't exist.

"The thing is," Scott said, "or *one* of the things is that similar changes were recorded on the two previous nights, when Arlene Wyatt did *not* go into Room 6. I've questioned the night staff on that."

"I certainly wouldn't say," Don told him, "that there mightn't be another source of excitation somewhere affecting Claudia. There could be several. All I'm suggesting is that Arlene is seemingly one of them."

Scott was lining up the five small sheets of paper along the edge of his desk; the scratch pads at the nurses' stations were uniform throughout the hospital, drawn from Central Supply. The fifth message had been written early this morning, an hour before Arlene went off duty.

Don't let him find me . . . Where did you go?

In a moment he said with a hint of emphasis: "Arlene Wyatt was badly upset by the death of her husband, I believe." He didn't look at either of them.

Don left it for Ernst, who carried more authority than he did: the little man by the window was more experienced in this field.

Ernst said in a moment: "She is quite stable." There was a pause. "In my opinion."

Scott's question came rather fast and he was aware of it but didn't care. "Have you examined her recently?"

Ernst Stein wrinkled his forehead. "There is no need."

Scott realized he could put the obvious question—why not? Or he could say nothing. He said nothing, because he didn't care to put an obvious question to a man like Stein, who would be more than ready for it. In the silence he was aware of himself again, aware of his attitude and his thinking; Stein had got his back up, as he usually did, because of his faint smile and his soft voice and his air of looking through your eyes at the back of your head, of listening to your every word as if in private disbelief, and his trick of leaving a silence for you to jump into—a little too fast.

But then Stein was a trained observer of human behavior. How else would he act? It wasn't really Stein that worried him: it was the idea that Claudia Terman was in some way "unusual"—to the extent of influencing one of the nurses and even blocking her own recovery. This kind of thing was right out of his field and he didn't understand it, and was therefore instinctively against it. Even afraid of it. Because Claudia's life at present depended on the machine that was breathing for her and he didn't want to bring these outlandish considerations into it. She was in coma 4, the state described on the patient chart as *fully unconscious, no reactions to stimuli;* and with her mind quiescent her body had a chance to regain its vital forces and return her to normal.

They could keep her body alive indefinitely, but there was nothing they could do about her mind.

Don was talking, in his low resonant tones. "Ernst, can I have your thoughts?"

Stein smiled. "Certainly. Which ones?"

"Do you believe this is a case of the paranormal?"

"No."

Don tilted his head. "But on the phone you said you

105

thought it was possible that Claudia Terman was influencing Arlene Wyatt by thought transference—didn't you?"

"Ah yes. But I don't think it has anything to do with the 'paranormal'—as I understand the term."

Scott looked up. "What do you think it has to do with?"

"Telepathy."

"Is that all?"

Ernst spread out his pink plump hands. "'All' is so relative, isn't it?"

Don Glezen got out of his chair and stood by the bookshelves, wanting to look down at Ernst, not up. Ernst wasn't easy to talk to: his mind was intricate and one felt inferior; they'd talked about it more than once, and Ernst had laughed it off, though he'd seemed rather pleased.

"Spell it out for me, would you, Ernst? What do you think is happening?"

It was like getting blood, Scott thought, out of a stone. Then he checked himself again: a psychiatrist was a listener, an observer. He wasn't primarily a talker. And it wasn't any use feeling hostile about him because Stein was a professional and could help them and they needed his help because along there at the other end of the corridor a young woman was lying as near death as the touch of a switch and there might not be much time.

Ernst pushed his hands into his pockets, looking along the rows of palm trees that bordered the boulevard, the reflected sunlight flashing on the gold earpiece of his glasses. "Very well. In the first place I believe that Arlene Wyatt is not responsible for the *content* of these messages. She suffered a traumatizing experience in the loss of her youthful husband almost a year ago, and Don and I were able to help her back to what one terms 'normal.' This took several months and of course we came to know her rather well. That is why I suggest there is no need for an examination."

He turned from the window and began looking at them with sharp periodic swings of his head. "A consultant might well think otherwise, but I see no evidence of paranoia in this young lady. If there were such a state of mind present, it would have begun slowly and our good friend Don Glezen would have noted signs of depression, a growing mistrust of her colleagues and so forth. They would have come to you as a routine procedure, surely, to report such a thing?"

"Yes," Don said, "they would." Personnel relations was one of his official concerns at Garden Grove.

"Very well. We have no evidence, either, of any physical brain damage in Arlene Wyatt, nor of any recent emotional experience that might unbalance her mentally. We are left with the possibility that some person has threatened her life during the past few days, in which case a normal individual would go to the police or seek help from her family or close friends. She would not begin to scribble random messages to nobody in particular." On a thought he added: "Your anesthesiologist here, Mr. Brickman, is a very close friend. It was he who enabled us to bring Arlene through her bereavement so satisfactorily, and I would expect her to reveal any fears to him, rather than leave notes around the place."

"She was talking to him this morning," Don told him, "in the recovery ward. She called me the moment she'd written this last message—I'd asked her to. Bill Brickman was there."

Scott looked up at him. "Was she scared?"

He couldn't forget the look on Arlene's face last night when she'd snatched up the pencil.

"Yes," Don said, "she was scared. She—"

"But not because of the *content*," put in Stein quickly.

"No." Don lifted a hand and dropped it. "At least I don't think so. I think it was the compulsion that scared her. She's

107

a very capable person, and she didn't like—well—something else taking over."

"How long," Ernst Stein asked him softly, "does she take to recover from these experiences?"

"Only a few minutes. There's a definite process at work—a compensating process. First the migraine and the compulsion and the writing; then a quick recession of the migraine and a sense of relief—of deliverance."

"No ill effects?"

"No."

The telephone rang and Scott answered it and said he didn't want to be disturbed unless there was an emergency. Putting the phone down, he said: "You think Arlene Wyatt is stable, and not paranoiac. You believe Claudia Terman is forcing her to write these messages. How stable, then, is Claudia Terman? Or how paranoiac?"

"We would need her history," Ernst said at once.

"How far back?"

"All of it, ideally. But the last few months, essentially."

Ernst was interested to note that Scott Rand was prepared to accept his theories on this case, though not at face value: he'd ask for proof of some kind. But he might not be the ultraconservative practitioner he'd always seemed, and that would be helpful.

Don slipped a question in. "Can paranoia be induced by a head injury?" He was looking at Scott.

Scott hedged. "We could ask Kistner."

"Paranoia," Ernst Stein said, "is psychic. It involves the psyche, not the brain." He gazed out of the window.

Scott found himself resenting the man's certitude, but had no means of challenging it. He would still ask Kistner, though.

Stein was going on suddenly, swinging his short body away from the window. "I think this is a case of shock, but it would interest me tremendously to know what *kind* of shock this patient suffered. It has to be partly psychic, of course, and somewhere there is an extra dimension we seem to be missing. What kind of accident was it?"

"A car crash," Don said.

"Very well." Ernst was speaking much faster than usual, and less softly. "In many crashes there is intense fear at the time of the event and immediately preceding it, as you know. In a head-on collision when the driver sees he cannot avoid it he realizes he may be severely injured or even killed. But in most highway crashes the other driver is a complete stranger, who wishes no slightest harm—in fact he will make every effort to avoid the collision. But suppose—for example—the other driver happens to hate you so much that he is prepared to lose his life in taking yours?" He spread his plump hands out. "We all like to be loved, even those who won't admit it. And we are all dismayed by another's hate: it strikes at our ego with almost demonic force."

His head began swinging again from one to the other. "In the light of these messages we might propose—as an example—that Mrs. Terman believed not only that she was about to die in that accident, but also that it was someone's intention that she should do so. That is what I mean by the 'extra dimension' to her psychic shock."

He waited impatiently for their reaction.

Don spoke first. "You mean it could have induced paranoia?"

"On the contrary. Paranoia is the fear of *imagined* persecution. Of course, she could have *imagined* another driver was trying to kill her, I agree."

Scott Rand felt his scalp tighten, and when he spoke he heard something odd in his voice. "The police don't know how the accident happened. They're very puzzled."

The silence went on until Ernst began jingling the coins in his pocket. "Of course, I was simply offering an *example*

109

of how psychic shock can be reinforced." Then he looked directly at Scott. "Was there another vehicle involved?"

"They don't know."

Don said quietly: "Claudia knows."

There was another silence. Possibly the same thought was in all their minds: on the face of it this could be a case of a psychiatrist's revealing the existence of a crime by his assessment of the victim's psychic state.

Ernst said in a moment, rather slowly, "We might certainly watch for any signs of an enemy, in Mrs. Terman's background, either imagined or real." He gave a sudden short laugh, whose falseness left the other two just as uneasy. "But I'm sure we are letting our imagination run too far!"

Scott let a few seconds go by. "Ernst, did you know we can't find any *physical* reason for her continuing state of coma?"

Ernst Stein blinked. "No." He tried to laugh again but didn't manage it. "Now that is *very* interesting. Of course, there could be a dozen reasons. The inside of the human head is complicated."

"Would you feel that this patient's psychic condition is preventing her recovery?"

"That's too broad," Stein said immediately. "*If* the fears expressed in those messages are Mrs. Terman's, and *if* there are indeed no physical problems, then yes, I would say that her state of mind is causing an inhibitory block, the mechanism being similar to that found in psychosomatic disease."

Scott got up and came from behind his desk, his uneasiness growing. "There could be no significant brain damage present, but the psyche could be manifesting the symptoms?"

"Conceivably."

"Don?"

"I agree. I mean, I agree there's the possibility."

"You mean she could be"—Scott threw out a hand help-

110

lessly—"trapped down there in the theta region and trying to call out to us?"

"Yes," Don said in a moment.

"Couldn't it be just a nightmare?"

"No. She's not in the deep delta region where sleep occurs. She's in the region where mystical experience takes place. Including telepathy."

Scott stopped pacing. "So what do we do?"

"We could try proving our theory," Ernst said blandly.

"How?"

Ernst looked at Don. It was he who had proposed this idea, before they came to see Scott.

Don said hesitantly: "There's only one way I think we could do that." He didn't feel ready to put this idea on the line, because there were certain risks. On the other hand, time was running short, for Claudia. "We could send Arlene down there with her, into the theta region. If she agreed to go."

Chapter 8

At this hour the shadows of the taller palms along the boulevard began to rise against the windows on the west side of the hospital, casting surrealistic images on the walls of the corridors inside. It was the season when the sun, sinking enormously behind the trees, set the hills and the whole city ablaze for the last few minutes of the day.

Dr. Matheson to Lab 3, please. Dr. Matheson.

Cars were turning out of the parking lots, forming a chain of colored links, and along the freeway the traffic was slowing as it made room for the influx from the ramps. The Goodyear airship floated low across the coast, with the sun leaving a streak of crimson across its envelope that changed it to a vast tropical fish.

Candystriper to the Pharmacy, please.

The day had gone well for some, in Garden Grove, and for others badly.

Triplets had been born in Maternity 1 and they were doing fine, though one of them, a girl, had a slight mark on her cheek.

Doris Graham had been transferred to an observation room and had eaten a poached egg for the first time, with a little spinach. She said it was like Christmas.

A patient under surgery at 4:30 in the afternoon had suffered a cardiac arrest, and Dr. Gomez had gone into the chest within thirty seconds, cutting through the fourth intercostal and using both hands to massage the heart while his team opened the IV route and administered drugs. It wasn't successful. Defibrillation was started and twice got a response but that was all. Gomez went in again for twenty minutes and there were repeated shocks given, together with epinephrine. It wasn't successful.

The shadows of the palm leaves grew hazy against the walls, and for a few moments the evening took fire from every tree and hill and building; then it was dusk, and the pallid glow of the headlights began threading through the streets like a procession of fireflies.

Dr. Brickman to ICU, please. Dr. Brickman.

Scott Rand was already there at the nurses' station, talking to Miss Dean. An hour ago Don Glezen had called him, saying that Arlene had agreed to the experiment. (That was the word he'd used, because that was what it was, and nobody tried to make out it was anything else.)

She was due here at seven o'clock.

Scott had spent more time in his office today than with the staff and patients, which always disturbed him. However watchful you were, paper work demanded more and more of your time as the day wore on. There had been several interviews, one of them with David Pryor, another with Patrick Terman. David was changing almost daily, Scott noticed, becoming quick-tempered and progressively losing weight. Patrick was much the same as before except that his frustration was increasing and he again asked what the chances were of an operation succeeding. Scott had said he was against the idea and told him to see Dr. Kistner if he wanted a second opinion.

He'd asked both men about Claudia's background and personality, and had later seen the young man Brian somebody and questioned him too, compiling a history from the sum of their information.

At ten minutes to seven Ernst Stein arrived in the ICU and introduced the man with him as Dr. Wallengroom, a psychiatrist at General, whom Stein had invited here as an observer. Scott remembered his name from an article in a medical journal but had never met him; he was a brooding individual with an immense brow and shadowed eyes that contemplated rather than regarded what they saw; there was contemplation even in his hand as it held on to Scott's for longer than usual while the dark eyes brooded.

Baines was different. Dr. Redford B. Baines came through the open doors at a minute to seven at something just short of a trot, jerking his head around as if looking for an ambush somewhere, then seeing Wallengroom and pumping his hand with an air of relief to find an ally. Neither Scott nor Ernst Stein knew him, so they introduced themselves while Wallengroom contemplated them all from a little way back. Apparently Don had sent him along.

"He was very mysterious," Baines said, and waited for someone to answer. No one did.

Don Glezen arrived with Arlene at ten after seven. She didn't look at anyone after a first glance in greeting, and the tight little smile died quickly as Don began talking to her alone in the doorway of Room 2, which was empty.

At 7:14 a couple of technicians came into the unit with an electroencephalograph and began setting it up. At this point Ernst Stein and Don Glezen took the visiting psychiatrists aside and briefed them, answering questions and elaborating on their theory. Scott went across to Arlene and told her they appreciated her cooperation and would keep her for as short a time as they could.

"I'm in no hurry, Dr. Rand."

He didn't know if she was always as nervy as she seemed now, or if she were keyed up about what they were going to do. She was small and fine-boned and a little doll-like to look at, quick in her movements and constantly turning to glance around her at the others as if she wished she weren't missing what they were saying. Her blue eyes were of the kind that in most people had a light in them, but it wasn't there; one would have had to know her, Scott thought, in the time before her husband had died, to know if the light had ever been there at all.

"Dr. Brickman isn't here yet," he said.

She looked up quickly.

"Is he coming?"

"He asked if he could, and it's fine with me; but he's still in surgery." Dr. Lessiter had been in there for the last five hours with a spinal laminectomy that had developed complications.

"When do we begin?" She said it rather brightly.

Scott took her arm. "How much sleep did you have?"

"Five or six hours."

"How much do you normally have, during the day?"

"About that. I don't need much."

"When you feel good and ready," he said, "we'll make a start." He went with her past the central desk, his hand still on her arm. "It's all pretty flexible, Arlene; we can break off whenever we like, and call it a day. I'm sorry we got you along here, for something so unimportant."

He began looking at the monitor screens as they passed the nurses' station. Tracy was there with Miss Dean, watching them too, as instructed. So far the sixth band was stable at 5 cycles per second. They'd started running a printout.

Everyone had been talking in low voices and now they stopped as Scott and Arlene reached the open door of Room 6. Don was smiling to her, and Dr. Wallengroom stood aside, looking down from his somber height as she went inside the room.

Scott's eyes flicked upward to the EEG monitor on the wall and saw the reading accelerate from 5 cps through 7. They were all watching it now: Don, Ernst, Baines, Wallengroom. It had been a feature of the briefing the visitors had been given a few minutes ago: if there was a reaction from

115

the patient as Arlene came into the room, the overall theory had a basis, and demonstrably. It was at this moment that Scott realized how confident Don Glezen must have been, to get them all here in the almost certain knowledge that a reaction would show up. There wasn't time to think about it now.

He looked down at Claudia.

Claudia Marianne Terman, Caucasian, twenty-seven years of age, married, no children. "A will of her own, maybe a bit obstinate, but she knows where she's going"— David Pryor. "A bit inexperienced, that's all. I mean, most married guys go after a girl now and then, without meaning anything. But she doesn't seem to know that"—Patrick Terman. "If you have to ask, she has a kind of perfection. I'm not sure how to express it. Have you ever watched a sea gull, I mean for minutes on end, wheeling and diving and feeling out the wind? That's a kind of perfection, and that's what I mean"—Brian Newby.

Hell of a temper. She slammed into me, you better believe it.

The only time she did anything stupid was when she married that bastard. That's why we'd been quarreling—over him.

She plays tremendous tennis, without kind of trying, or even caring. It's just a way of using her body, a perfect way. Is that what you want to know? What else can I say?

She just wanted all of me, see? Totally. It had to be the biggest goddam love affair the world had ever seen—or else. So we had to get married, though of course I didn't want to.

We've always been buddies. I mean, she was the original kid sister and it was my job to look after her. But she mostly looked after me—that's just like Claudia.

It's the most wonderful thing I've ever seen. She just goes curving in, and the water closes over her, without any

116

splash or anything. She does it like she does everything—perfectly.

Enemies? No, I would've known.

Oh no, people liked her, I guess. Even I did, for a while.

A girl like her? You could only love her, the way she was.

Claudia Marianne Terman, all those things and none of them any more, lying here in silence with part of her life a machine. A dark head on a pillow, the raven-black hair tangled a little by now and the hollows of the cheekbones deeper in shadow, the result of a steady weight loss of twelve pounds in less than four days, it said on the chart.

Someone had closed the door and Scott looked up.

Miss Dean was in here, and Tracy, the senior nurse in the unit. There might be physical reactions, he'd warned them, and the blood pressure would need controlling. Tracy was looking rather tense, he thought.

"Is she going to sit up, Dr. Rand?"

"No. She'll lie on the other bed."

Don was there, arranging the two pillows, crossing them.

"We'll need another blanket."

Someone went quietly to the closet by the window.

The technicians worked for twenty minutes before they were satisfied with the readings. There was nothing for the others to do except watch the Terman screens and check her visually, sometimes drying her face; in the last few minutes she had begun sweating a little, though the EEG reading had gone back to the theta region at 5 cps. It had thrown Ernst Stein for a moment, but Don suggested it was simply because the interaction was initially electric, expressed as a nerve impulse, and there was a natural discharge of its potential—"the way a battery runs down."

At 7:44 the technicians said they were satisfied with the hookup. The monitor screen was on the side table near the

117

second bed, where Arlene was lying. Don had put a new scratch pad and two sharpened pencils within reach of her hand and told her repeatedly they were there.

"Scott, can we have those three phones out there switched down to low?"

"All right."

He asked Tracy to see to it.

"And I'd like the lights in here turned off."

Miss Dean went to the switch and there was now only the diffused light coming through the slats of the screen from outside.

No one talked any more. The rough hiss of the ventilator was now the only sound. They began listening to it consciously, needing a focus for their attention.

Scott stood against the wall opposite Arlene's bed, with a direct view of the two electroencephalographs. Claudia's was now reading 6 cycles per second, a fraction higher than the norm for her condition. Arlene's was producing 27 cps, near the extreme high range for the beta region of full consciousness.

Miss Dean and Tracy were on each side of the bed, the charge nurse sitting with her back to the MA1 ventilator and in a position where she could watch both Arlene and Claudia and the monitor screens.

Ernst Stein stood by the curtained window, next to Dr. Wallengroom, the tall psychiatrist dwarfing him. Dr. Baines was a little cut off from the others, perched on a stool near the fresh-linen closet. The two technicians were by the doors, both of them watching the new EEG screen.

Don sat on the edge of Arlene's bed and took her hand.

"You look a heap better than most of our other patients, I'll say that."

But her hand felt cold. She didn't smile. Or try.

"All there is to do," he said in his low tones, "is to relax."

118

He waited, but she said nothing. "As soon as you feel ready, just let me know."

They all listened to the machine breathing for Claudia.

In a moment Arlene said almost inaudibly: "I'm ready."

"You're sure?"

Three, four seconds. Five.

"Yes."

She looked up at him.

He looked taller than before. That was because she was lying down in the still air. They were all watching her. She thought she had said something but didn't know what. The thing was not to feel—

And we can break off whenever we like. All we do is relax, and let things take care of themselves. Just let your-self go limp, let everything drift away. Think of a big round "O"—it's a zero—it's nothing—you're thinking of nothing.

Sometimes they looked up at the wall. They were all here because she—then she didn't know why they were here. She was thinking of nothing, but nothing was a lot of things to think, it all wouldn't stop. The thing was not to feel—

Until your mind is a blank. Like a big white wall with nothing on it, just white, wherever you look, just blank. The big black "O" is fading away now, into the white wall, becoming invisible, becoming nothing. Sleep now. Sleep.

She couldn't see them any more. She was alone in the still air, with his voice echoing, spiraling into the silence. It was taking her with it. The thing was not to feel—

Sleeping now—

Not to feel scared.

Sleeping now, just drifting away, deeper and deeper, down and down. You are thinking of nothing. Your mind is a blank. You have no thoughts. You are just you, and noth-ing else.

Alpha, a voice said.

119

A voice said: *Shhh.*

There is just you here, and of course there is Claudia. We all know Claudia, and we are here to help her. You want very much to help Claudia. Think about that. You want to help Claudia.

The white wall going darker, except for the round light globe floating on it. All alone now in the wind, the still air gone away and the wind rising and everything streaming by in the dark and *it's scary* like this all alone in the rushing of the wind *I'm scared* but it won't stop and won't stop and won't stop.

You want to help Claudia. We all want to help her. You can do it better than we can. If you want to write anything, here is a pencil.

The roaring of the wind through the dark with the round light globe out there in front, sometimes moving, sometimes not moving, everything else rushing by and I'm not scared any more but I don't know why.

Sleeping deeply, down and down, with nothing to worry you, down and down, thinking of Claudia, thinking of helping Claudia. If Claudia tells you anything you can just write it down. Here is a pencil.

Voice. *Theta.*

The wind rushing and the big light swinging ahead, the moonlight in my eyes, my hair blowing in the wind. The road like a path to the moon, and a red light below, very small, tiny, the warning light on the gas gauge, remember, remember in the morning, we're low on gas. Brilliant light in the mirror and all around me, sudden and white and blinding, a car behind me and very close and coming closer, it scares me, *who is it, who are you?* I'm scared. The heavy rushing of the tires alongside and the shine of metal and glass *and now I can see his face* but he's no one I know, a man just looking at me, staring at me, watching me, watching . . . and I know what he's come for—I know what he

120

wants to do and I'm so frightened of him *and there's no one to help me . . .*

A bump and the roaring so close and a bump again and the wheel tugging and the smell of rubber and heat and the feel of the whole world lurching, the lights blinding and the sky swinging over and over *he's going to kill me* and over with the glass smashing and splinters of it flying ice-bright into the dark, *kill me,* the big moon rolling down and down, *kill me,* down and down, *kill . . .* down into the dark and the killing, the dying, the dying away . . . away . . .

"Don!"

"All right, I'll—"

"Dr. Rand? She's—"

"Yes. *Get her back.*"

"Ernst, do you think we—"

"Let them handle this."

"Tracy, look after Mrs. Terman."

"Don, you'll have to—"

"Easy, Arlene, easy. You're less drowsy now, you're beginning to wake up, but take your time, easy, easy now."

The monitor screen was still producing theta waves of 5 cps but Arlene was writhing, her legs twisting and her slight body shaking, one of her hands reaching out and trying to claw at something—

"Ernst, can you—"

"Yes. It's all right."

Their faces were set and they glanced at one another and away, staring at the monitor screens and the tortured figure on the bed, startled as she screamed suddenly—

"He wants to kill me, don't you understand? He tried to kill me and he'll try again!"

"Arlene, he's not here and you're perfectly all right, we're all with you and we'll take care of you—you're waking slowly, slowly and easily, taking your time. You're coming back now, Arlene, and we're waiting for you."

Don's eyes flicked to the screen again and saw 10 cps . . . 11 . . . as the brain rhythm passed into the alpha range of light meditation.

Over the seconds the Claudia reading followed, but less steadily, fluctuating, racing ahead and then falling behind as Scott Rand watched it, glancing across to the EKG, where the heart rate was still pulsing at more than 110 bpm and now rising a little, falling a little. He looked at Amy Dean.

"What do you have?"

"One hundred seven, Dr. Rand." She held the antique hunter watch at an angle, to catch what light there was, her other hand at Arlene's wrist.

Scott looked down at Claudia's face again. It was perfectly composed, the lips together and the eyelids still. The anguish in Arlene's mind was in her own—it *was* her own—but nothing in her face or hands or body showed that it was there.

"Easy now, easy, you're waking up, Arlene, waking up and opening your eyes, slowly opening your eyes." Don glanced toward the door. "Can we have the lights on, someone?"

As the light flooded the room they saw the perspiration shining on Arlene's face, and Tracy used tissues to wipe it away. Ernst Stein kept his hold on the thin trembling wrist as Don went on talking her back to the conscious level.

The EEG beside the bed showed the brain rhythm rising into beta through 17 . . . 19 . . . 21 cycles per second. The Terman EEG readings had fallen away after following for those few moments: Claudia's brain was now functioning deep in the theta region again, below 6 cps. She had not moved during the whole of the experiment.

The door opened quietly and Scott glanced up, seeing Bill Brickman. They nodded briefly, then Scott brought his attention back to Arlene. She was still restless, and beginning to cry silently now, as a child does, her face wrinkling. Soon tears were coming.

"You're almost awake now, almost awake . . . You can open your eyes when you feel you want to . . . open your eyes. We are all here with you, and it's all over now."

Dr. Wallengroom, statuesque against the window, was watching the man who had just come in, noting his concern for the subject on the bed. Dr. Baines had left the seclusion of his corner to come closer and stare down at Arlene Wyatt. He had been listening—they'd all been listening—to the spate of subliminal material that had come from her during the hypnotic induction, and he had been trying to piece together the brief passages that had been intelligible— the reference to the accident with the car particularly, which had been brought out in a series of half-sobbing phrases.

Baines knew nothing of Claudia Terman's history, or what had brought her to the Intensive Care Unit at Garden Grove; and he was reluctant to put the one question that occupied his mind, because the answer could radically change some of his strongest convictions, and he was conservative of his ideas and hated to have them altered.

"You are awake now, Arlene, you are fully awake. It is all over and we are very happy with what happened." Don glanced across at the monitor screen and saw a reading of 25 cps in the region of full consciousness. She should be waking now, but she still lay crying quietly, and he didn't insist; the aftermath of the psychic trauma was still an influence. He wouldn't have suggested this experiment had he known how violently her mind would be affected; but since it had been carried through he could only hope that Scott Rand was now convinced that the source of those messages was Claudia Terman, that she was existing in a constant state of terror and that until her terror could be removed she might never physically recover.

He waited, giving Arlene time to surface. Beside him he heard Baines, the uneasy-looking psychiatrist, talking to Ernst Stein in a low voice.

"I was only partially briefed, as you know. Can you tell me why this patient was brought here? I mean Mrs. Terman?"

"The symptoms are of brain damage." Ernst was stroking Arlene's hand and wrist, rhythmically, following Don Glezen's example.

"I mean, what caused the damage?" Baines asked him quietly.

"She was in a car crash." He jerked a look at Baines and saw he'd got the point.

"Good God."

"There are more things, Redford, in heaven and earth . . ."

Baines went thoughtfully back to his stool in the corner near the fresh-linen closet. Before he accepted the idea of subliminal telepathy he tried the only loophole he could think of for the moment: Arlene Wyatt, as a member of the nursing staff, would know the cause of Mrs. Terman's injury, and might simply have been affected by her proximity at the theta level, to the point of experiencing a form of nightmare the theme of which was a car crash. (If one, for example, were to spend the night in a cell next to a condemned man, one might expect to have bad dreams about being shot at dawn.) But there were two objections to this idea: Arlene Wyatt's reactions had been far too intense, and the outpourings of her subconscious had been far too consistent. Despite the presence of unintelligible passages in her recounting of the accident, she had given a clear and logical picture of it, in orderly sequence.

In his daily work Redford Baines listened to countless reports of nightmare, and over the years had learned a great deal about its mechanism and characteristics. At this moment he was prepared to dismiss the only loophole in the argument for subliminal telepathy.

He looked once at the brooding Wallengroom, wanting to talk to him but knowing it was too soon. Dr. Glezen was now bringing the subject to full consciousness, and as the EEG began producing waves of 28 cycles Arlene Wyatt opened her eyes and looked uncertainly around her.

Bill Brickman bent over her.

"You feel okay?" She looked at him but didn't answer. "Arlene?"

"Hello, Bill." It was a whisper.

He stood back, wanting to ask someone what had been going on in here. She'd told him earlier that she was to take part in an "experiment" but hadn't said more than that. She looked traumatized and he'd talk to Scott Rand as soon as this was over. The experiment may not have been Scott's idea but he was in charge of it and he'd let it go on to the point where she'd broken into tears, and Bill Brickman was going to see it didn't happen again.

Ernst Stein took his plump hand away from Arlene's wrist as Don sat back on the edge of the bed, giving her his most reassuring smile.

"You were great," he said quietly. "Really great." She shut her eyes for a moment, then opened them again, sitting up as they helped her, reaching for the box of tissues and blowing her nose.

Scott asked for someone to get some coffee for her. Bill Brickman was trying to speak to him but he shook his head and moved away, trying to absorb the implications of what had happened. Finding little Ernst Stein in front of him, he said abstractedly: "Is it one-way?"

"Is it what?" Ernst gazed up at him with his soft imaginative eyes. "Ah yes—you mean the thought transference. It doesn't have to be, of course. But from the history of the patient—I mean since she came in here—I can't see any evi-

125

dence that her mind has been reached from the environment." He thought for a moment. "Has anyone tried?"

"No. Unless Don has."

They both looked at Don but he was busy helping Arlene reorientate.

"If it's only one-way," Scott said in something like despair, "I don't see how we can help her." He looked down at the peaceful face of Claudia Terman, the truth confronting him with the force of a shock: *she was always like this*. Lying here with a machine breathing for her and her body attended by devoted slaves, she went on living at the mercy of her own mind and its unceasing state of terror, *every minute of the day, every minute of the night*. Her face at peace and her body motionless, she was living through the turmoil they had just seen in Arlene a few minutes ago, and though she was capable of sending out her distress signals to the environment—through Arlene—she seemed to have no idea that anyone was receiving them: hence her pleas of *why won't someone help me?* and *don't you understand?*

It was as if she were buried alive in a glass coffin and hammering to be let out. They could see her and they could hear her, but there was nothing they could do to smash it open.

When Arlene had been led out of Room 6 and was sitting at the nurses' station with Bill Brickman, drinking coffee as if her thirst would never stop, Scott spoke for a few moments to Don Glezen.

"All right," he told him, "I'm convinced."

"So now we can do something," Don said.

"Yes. But I don't know what."

The two technicians were leaving the unit, carrying the boxed electroencephalograph and their instruments. Amy Dean had said good night a few minutes ago and left for home: she was due in surgery at 5:30 tomorrow morning.

"There are two ways we can go," Don said in his low

126

unhurried voice. "We can try opening up some kind of two-way communication, reaching Claudia's mind and reassuring her that we're all protecting her and that nothing can happen—nobody can get at her. Or we can work outside, in the environment, and try to locate the exact object of her fear, and eliminate it."

Dr. Thayer, please—Code 1.

Thayer was on call tonight.

"But this is something new," Scott said, and felt himself instinctively resisting ideas beyond his field. It occurred to him that it might be a good thing all around if he resisted less and accepted more, or at least kept an open mind. The experiment had shaken him and he wasn't ready for another ride on this metaphysical roller coaster that Don had going, and he'd have to make an effort to keep up. For Claudia's sake.

"It's new to you, Scott. Not to me."

"All right. I'm prepared to believe Claudia is contacting Arlene telepathically from the theta level. You've just given us a demonstration. But all you've demonstrated is that she's in that room over there reliving the crash and her conviction that someone was trying to kill her. But now you're talking about the 'object of her fear.' Couldn't that be only in her imagination?"

"It could," Don told him. "I don't think it is."

"This 'object' then: you think it's a person—the man who apparently tried to kill her? And you think she's right when she says he'll try again?"

"Yes, to both questions."

Don waited, not wanting to present a detailed argument. Scott had been impressed by the experiment and might be more receptive now than later, when the emotional component would be absent.

"You don't have anything to support this theory, Don?"

127

"Not really. Not enough to convince a diehard like you."

"Look, Don, I'm a clinician."

"So am I. We're just using different tools. But I'll tell you one thing: I think the police ought to be told what's happening here."

"The police . . ."

"They don't know why Claudia crashed. She thinks she does. And they ought to be told." Scott said nothing, so he went on: "It's one of the ways we can go, right? An attempt to find the 'object' we're talking about. Maybe the police can find him quicker than we can."

"You'd have to ask Jordan."

Charles Jordan was the Administrator of Garden Grove.

"Right. I'm going to do that." Don backtracked for a moment, deciding to give Scott Rand the only practical support he had for his theory. "While the police are working from their end, we can work from ours. And we might start with the fact that Arlene isn't the only source of excitation to Claudia's subconscious. Remember that on the two earlier evenings when the report showed that her brain rhythm and heart rate had both changed substantially around eleven o'clock, Arlene wasn't anywhere near the ICU." He waited three seconds. "So who was?"

Scott was getting into his car at a few minutes after nine the same evening when the desk clerk came running out of the building.

"You're on page, Dr. Rand!"

He slammed the door of the car behind him and went up the steps. She said he was wanted in the Intensive Care Unit, and he took an elevator. In Room 6 of the ICU he found Denise Ross and an aide, with one of the interns up from the floor below.

128

"There's increasing arrhythmia, Doctor," Denise told him.

He was already watching the electrocardiograph and saw the heart rate moving through 129 beats per minute. It had risen earlier, during the experiment with Arlene, but had subsided before he'd left the unit. Now it was hitting a new high.

"We'll give it a little time," he said.

Denise continued checking for edemas and the young intern went back to the labs. Scott took a gulp of water from the fountain and went across to his office, trying not to worry about the arrhythmia, and worrying. It could be psychogenic: Don would probably think so.

By 9:30 the heart rhythm was hitting 140 bpm and the blood pressure was lowering. At this state he entered *ventricular tachycardia* on the chart and ordered a direct counter-shock by electronic cardioinversion. It wasn't effective.

"Is Arlene Wyatt still in the building?" he asked Denise.

She was puzzled because it seemed irrelevant; Arlene wasn't on the staff in the ICU and there was no shortage at present. But she went out to the central station and asked for a page call.

A few minutes later there was a call from the reception desk in the main lobby, reporting that Arlene Wyatt had left the building soon after eight o'clock.

Denise gave Scott Rand this information and he thanked her absently. If the tachycardia was psychogenic it wasn't being induced by Arlene's presence anywhere nearby. But then Don had suggested she wasn't the only source of influence. Was there another, nearby? It was impossible to know, and Scott settled down to concentrate on the physical condition, trying another cardioinversion and failing again.

"Denise."

She came across from the station.

129

"Yes, Doctor?"

"We'll try Pronestyl, intravenous." He worked out a low initial dosage and saw it administered and sat for a few minutes watching the screen of the EKG. The heart rate was pushing 190 and the blood pressure was falling progressively and he started worrying about a kidney shutdown. "I'll be in my office," he told the nurse. "Call me if the rate hits 200."

At 11:25 the arrhythmia in the patient in Room 6 reached 203 beats per minute and Scott Rand ordered a third dosage of Pronestyl of four times the strength. On the printout the rate had declined to 195 over a period of fifteen minutes, indicating that the drug was now exercising a minimal effect but not enough to control the condition.

The rapid beep of the monitor was distressing to Denise and the other nurse; their trained imagination was picturing the feverish pulsing of the small ventricle inside Claudia's body, and they spent most of their time in or near Room 6.

Before midnight Scott abandoned the current treatment and ordered an initial dosage of quinidine in 5 percent glucose and water intravenously; and now he remained in the room while the nurses went back to their rounds. The heart rate was at this time a grueling 240 beats per minute and the blood pressure was reacting in slow swings to the specific treatment. Watching the monitor screen, Scott found it impossible to believe the condition could be psychogenic: if the rate increased to 300 bpm and beyond, the patient would go into adrenal failure. There would be another way of saying it was psychogenic: that Claudia was deciding, in the hidden regions of the theta rhythm, to kill herself.

Ten minutes after the first dose of quinidine the rate began falling. A second dose was administered and the decrease continued. At midnight the heart was beating at a

130

lowering 130 per minute and Scott came out of Room 6 wiping his face, his eyes still narrowed from strain.

"That was awful," Denise said shakily. She should have gone off duty at eleven o'clock but had stayed on.

"It was," Scott told her. "But it looks like we've got it under control. It's time you went home."

Dr. Thayer, please. Code 1.

A red light began winking at the nurses' station in the Intensive Care Unit and Julie Sears noted it. The time was nine minutes after midnight and this was a standby call: an ambulance was coming in and the patient might or might not be a case for transference to the ICU from the Emergency Room. All that was known by Communications was that he was already on artificial respiration and in grave condition.

ER personnel, please—Code 1.

Statistically the patient had seven chances in ten of reaching the hospital alive and five chances in ten of making the ICU.

At 12:16 Fran Engel found an edema developing on her patient in Room 7 and began the Lasix therapy.

At 12:21 the green telephone rang at the nurses' station and Julie answered it, to be told that the ICU facilities wouldn't be needed for the patient now in Emergency. There were no reasons given and she didn't ask any questions. The caller was an intern and she took the opportunity of telling him that the patient in Room 1 who had been brought in from Emergency two hours ago was now responding to the drugs and starting to assist the ventilator. Julie asked him to pass this information on to Dr. Thayer.

As she hung up she heard Fran asking for help, and went over to Room 7. The edema was difficult to get at and Fran wanted the patient turned. He was a heavy man and it was a

131

few minutes before they managed to move him over and settle his limbs comfortably. Fran continued the treatment.

On her way back to the nurses' station Julie found one of the cardiac patients, Mr. Mancini, standing halfway between the desk and Room 6, peering around him through his dark glasses.

"And where are you off to?" she asked him cheerfully. They all liked Mr. Mancini; he was considerate and never gave any trouble.

"It's my first time out on my own," he said ruefully. "I was trying to find the bathroom."

He stood there looking helpless. He was a short man but strong, with a thick hairy neck and arms that hung out from his sides, like a wrestler's. Julie thought he looked like an amiable bear.

"It's the other way, Mr. Mancini, at the end of the corridor, to your left."

"Thank you."

"Do you need help?"

"No. No, thank you."

He turned away.

Chapter 9

Soon after nine o'clock the next morning Dr. Kistner called Scott Rand in his office and said he had received authority to operate on Claudia Terman.

"Whose authority?" Scott asked him at once.

"Her husband's."

"You can't accept it." He was holding his breath.

There was a slight pause.

"I beg your pardon?"

"When did he see you?"

Another pause. It was one of Kistner's little tactics: he gave these pauses to suggest either that he hadn't quite heard you correctly, or that you didn't understand what you were saying, or (as in this case) that you shouldn't be asking such a question in the first place.

"I received him in my office late last night, at his request." Kistner's tone was overprecise, admonitory. Even the word "received" was heavily formal.

Scott stared unseeingly at the Western Pharmaceutics calendar on the wall. "Did he sign anything?"

"He signed the required form, and asked me to proceed as soon as possible if I considered the matter urgent. I do."

The coiled white telephone cable, lying across Scott's arm, quivered slightly to his heartbeat. On the other side of the door he heard someone saying his name to someone else; he didn't know who and he didn't care.

"Where are you now?" he asked the surgeon.

"I am just out of the operating room."

Despite the man's studied tone Scott detected fatigue. He'd been in surgery for three and a half hours and would be taking a break.

"I'd like to see you, Neil." He tried a conciliatory approach but found it difficult. "I could come right away."

A pause, to suggest surprise at the request.

"If you wish."

"Thank you. In your office?"

"Yes."

Scott hung up and went along to the ICU and told the charge nurse where he was going and took the elevator to the ground floor.

Neil Kistner looked tired, but only those who knew him well would see it; he was a man of great energy, and even nearing the age of sixty he could outlast far younger men at the operating table, or for that matter on the tennis court. On the few occasions when he showed fatigue it was because he'd been driving himself.

"I'm sorry you've decided to take this attitude," he told Scott. Neil always attacked first, if in doubt. "Won't you sit down?"

He moved heavily behind the big carved desk and took off his thick-framed glasses, folding them and putting them down, looking at Scott with steady gray eyes. Usually he paced the royal-blue carpet of his spacious office when he was interviewing people, but this morning he was content to sit.

"I'm not taking any 'attitude,' Neil. You know me. I'm only concerned with clinical facts. We don't need to go into the details again—you can see the latest reports if you like. As the attending physician I must tell you that the patient has a condition of ventricular tachycardia and that we're having difficulty controlling it. Surgery is out of the question."

"Oh, really? Why?"

The question seemed naive, and wasn't. Scott decided on the obvious answer. "I told you. This is a case of severe arrhythmia."

"But you said you're controlling it."

"With difficulty."

Kistner paused, his large head on one side. "How? May I ask?"

He had no right to ask, and knew it. He was a surgeon and this was the physician's field—unless an operation was agreed on.

"We tried cardioinversion and failed. We tried Pronestyn and failed. The patient is now on large dosages of quinidine."

"What is the heart rate at present?"

"About 80."

"That sounds quite satisfactory." With studied innocence the surgeon spread his hands. "I have been asked to operate, you see. And so far you've shown no acceptable objection. You've succeeded in bringing a condition of 'severe' arrhythmia—I think you said 'severe'?—down to a normal sinus rhythm. If you can do that now, you can do it in the operating room."

Scott knew this argument could develop out of all usefulness. He chose another tack, and hit hard.

"Did Terman take a lot of persuading?"

The two men looked at each other in a moment's silence. "Persuading?"

"To sign the required form."

In a moment: "Would you care to be more precise?"

"Yes." Scott got out of his chair. "Like some of your colleagues you've performed more than one totally unnecessary operation and you've performed it for the sake of the fees." He could hear the anger in his tone and didn't bother to control it. "Maybe you've done it a dozen times—or a hundred times. I don't know. I realize it must be tempting, particularly if you live high on the hog, as you do. A working physician doesn't have the same kind of temptation—he's got to cure the patient or fail, one way or the other, without any dramatics. *And without any avoidable risks.*"

Neil Kistner watched him, his eyes turned slightly upwards.

"In this patient," Scott told him, "the risk is very high. And it's avoidable. If you try to go ahead I'll fight you all the way."

Kistner didn't move. He sat with his elbows on the desk and his thick talented hands clasped in front of him as he looked up.

"Would you care to make these accusations before a tribunal?"

"It's come close to that, hasn't it, in the past?"

"There have certainly been others like yourself, yes, ready to denigrate their more successful colleagues. It's usually from jealousy, don't you agree?"

"Sure, that happens." Scott turned away, not wanting to look at him any longer. It wasn't so much what the man had done that angered him; it was the hypocritical stand he was taking, of the outraged innocent. Scott would have felt less contempt for him if he'd simply said: "You're calling me a crook. All right, prove it. And meanwhile get out of here."

Kistner rose from his chair slowly, putting his large hands into his pockets, one of them jingling some change. "Is there something . . . special," he asked blandly, "about the Terman case?"

"In what sense?"

"In the sense," the surgeon said slowly, "that you don't want anything revealed in the operating room, when I go into the brain." He became offhand. "The best of us make mistakes, however hard we—"

"That's a little unsubtle, for you. I've nothing to cover

136

up. There's no incentive for a physician to break the first injunction of the oath and harm the patient—as there is for a surgeon." He faced Kistner across the enormous desk. "Do you intend trying to take this case into the operating room?"

Kistner came from the window, looking everywhere except at Scott, as he did when he was lecturing at the college. "I think perhaps I should explain the situation to you. It's very simple. Your patient's closest relative has asked me to operate on her, and has signed the required form. He has placed his trust in me to proceed as I think it's best for the patient. In my professional opinion I think we should take her into surgery as soon as we possibly can, in the hope of saving her life—which she may lose if we delay any further." He looked at Scott now, coldly. "I would be obliged, Doctor, if you'd see that Mrs. Terman is prepared for operation with all speed."

Scott called Patrick Terman and asked him if he could come to the hospital.

"There isn't any point, Dr. Rand."

"We should talk about your wife. She's in my care and it's customary to consult the attending physician before asking for major surgery. If we—"

"I talked to you yesterday, didn't I? For about an hour. Is that all we're going to do? Talk? Or are you getting the message, Dr. Rand? I want some action."

Scott heard some kind of background noise on the line, but couldn't identify it. "Did Dr. Kistner tell you there's a distinct risk if he operates?"

"Sure. There has to be, I understand that. But there's a risk of her dying if we *don't* do something—right? Listen, my wife and me broke it up, okay? But that doesn't mean I don't care any more what happens to her. She's a nice kid, what the hell, and I feel kind of responsible for her, don't you understand?"

Scott identified the background noise now. It was a ball game.

"If you really feel responsible, Mr. Terman, you'll come along here and talk to me and a few of my colleagues before you take the risk you seem set on taking, in your wife's name. I would see that you received no bills for the consultations."

"Jesus, you're talking about bills while the life of that kid's running out? That's exactly how Dr. Kistner put it, so you think I don't realize?"

Probably for the first time in his life Scott wanted to smash someone. Kistner.

"What other dramatic and persuasive arguments did he have for you, Mr. Terman?"

"I don't get what you—"

"Her life isn't running out, as my colleague put it. She's in trained and dedicated hands and—"

"For Christ's sake, Doc, I've listened to you and I've listened to him and I like what he said and I liked the way he said it, I think he carries a lot of weight. So I did what I've got a right to do, and made a decision—okay? I signed the form—okay?"

Scott held back for an instant because he'd said far more to Kistner than he'd intended, and he'd used stronger terms. Maybe he regretted some of it but it was too late now. But it wasn't too late to say exactly what he intended to Patrick Terman. He kept his tone impersonal.

"Did you ask Dr. Kistner what his fee would be?"

"His what?"

Scott had the impression Terman wasn't listening. It was probably the ball game.

"His fee. How much it would cost you."

"Uh—no. How much?"

"It's not for me to say."

"You could give me an idea, couldn't you?"

138

"Yes. It won't be less than four thousand dollars."

There was silence on the line, except for the faint cheering of the crowd.

"Four thousand?"

"Yes. Minimum."

"So what? Listen, my contract gets me top dollar, so it's only money—okay?"

"Then there's no problem," Scott said tightly, and hung up.

David Pryor was waiting for him in the ICU when Scott came back from a scratch lunch in the coffee shop: there hadn't been time for Eve to make him a sandwich this morning, so it had to be junk food or nothing and he needed the protein.

"You're losing weight," he told David.

"Surprise."

"Did you get my call?"

"Yes."

"Sit down." Scott closed the door. "Would you like some coffee?"

"For God's sake," David said in a kind of moan, "will you just tell me what's *happened?*"

Scott looked at him quickly. "Nothing. Nothing bad."

The young man let out a breath and dragged his fingers through his hair. "Now I'd like some coffee."

Scott went into the corridor and brought back two styrofoam cups and gave David one and dropped the sweetener and the non-dairy creamer onto the corner of the desk where he could reach it.

"Have you seen your sister?"

"Yes."

"There's no change. But Terman's asked for an operation. Did he tell you?"

David sat perfectly still with his hands on his knees. "What sort of operation?"

"Exploratory."

"What does that mean?"

"What it says. They want to open up the suboccipital area and part of the skull and go in and look at the brain stem in case there's anything to see."

"In case? Just *in case?*"

"Correct."

David began massaging his knees, very slowly, back and forth, looking all the time at Scott Rand with his dark head tilted, as if he could listen better that way. "You're against that."

"Yes."

"Can't you stop them?"

"I don't think so."

"Are you going to try?"

"Yes. I wanted to know how you feel about it, David."

"How *I* feel?"

"You're her brother."

David got up and spilled some coffee and didn't notice and said as if he were holding himself back, as if he'd like to say more, "I can only feel what you people tell me to feel, don't you realize that? Am I any judge of what we should do for Claudia? That wouldn't be so bad—I could leave it for the experts to decide—it's their job. It's when the experts can't agree among themselves what we should do that I get worried."

Patiently Scott said: "You've listened to me, and you've listened to Dr. Kistner. There's—"

"Who's he?"

"The neurosurgeon."

"Oh, right, Kistner, right." He shut his eyes for a moment, squeezing them. Looking at him from behind his desk, Scott realized he was looking at a man he couldn't

140

heal. David was losing weight and producing adrenaline he wasn't getting rid of and losing sleep and there wasn't anything he could do for him except put him on Librium or Valium until his sister recovered or died and he could start thinking about something else. He wondered how much of David's anguish was due to the "fight" he'd been having with Claudia before the accident, and the fact that they hadn't made it up before it was too late.

"The only way you can decide," he told him gently, "is to decide whether you think I'm right, or Dr. Kistner is right. And you can't rely on the technical data we've both given you, because you're a layman. I'm about as experienced as he is, and we're both good at our jobs. If I said any more it'd be unethical."

Which was pretty funny considering some of the things he'd said to that baseball player on the phone this morning. (*What other dramatic and persuasive arguments did he have for you, Mr. Terman?*)

David Pryor looked down at him, his eyes narrowed against the light from the window and baggy from lack of sleep. He used to think you went to doctors when you were sick, or when your sister was sick, and they'd know what to do. But they didn't. And he hadn't found that out by reading it in the newspapers or talking to people; he'd found it out because Claudia had smashed herself up and might be dying.

"Unethical," he said very softly, and the word went quietly down and down in the silence, like a stone in a pond. "So how do I decide? Do I have to be a judge of character? But suppose one of you is a good guy and the other's a shit, does that mean—" He broke off, squeezing his eyes shut again. "I'm sorry, I—"

"That's all right, don't worry."

"It doesn't mean the good guy's *right*, does it? Oh Jesus, I didn't know it could be like this."

141

"Why don't we let it go, David? Look, I'm going to contest the proposal of surgery in front of a medical board, and I don't have too long. You'd be welcome to the hearing, unless someone raises an objection. I'll let you know when we're going to convene."

David's body sagged a little as the tension came off, and he looked around for the chair. "Okay. I want to be there."

Scott waited for half a minute to see if he wanted to say anything else, anything off his own bat. He didn't. That wasn't necessarily because he couldn't think of anything, but because he was thinking of too many things and he couldn't get them straight in his mind.

"There's another aspect to this case," Scott told him, "and I think you should see two of my colleagues. One is a psychologist and the other a psychiatrist."

David's face slowly went blank.

"You think I'm going off my head?"

"No, it's—"

"Well, *I* think I'm going off my head."

"You're under stress, that's all. These two men have studied Claudia's state of mind, and—"

"Claudia's state of mind? But she's in coma."

"We'll tell you about it, David. For the moment I want to ask you something I asked you already: do you think she might have had any enemies?"

He had to wait a little before David said slowly:

"I don't see how she could have. Not Claudia. I mean, she—you know, she had a mind of her own, but—"

"I mean a real enemy. Someone who really hated her. Or was frightened of her. Or who wanted her out of the way. Any of those things."

"There's Terman."

Scott felt a jolt and had to start thinking. "Terman. He wants to marry someone else, doesn't he? Wants a divorce?"

"Yes. He keeps—he kept on at her about that. The di-

142

vorce. That's why we had our fight, see. I said why didn't she let the bastard go, and she said it wasn't any of my business." He lowered his head, looking at the carpet. "I guess it wasn't. But I don't think he'd do anything to her, I mean—"

"Never mind. The thing is, David, that my colleagues and I believe she's frightened of someone." The dark head came up. "Very frightened. Terrified. And we believe she's staying in coma because it's a kind of shelter; and all the time she's there she can't breathe, or get well again. That's why I don't think surgery should even be contemplated— apart from the physical high-risk factors already present. And that's why I'm going to put the case before a medical board. It's the only chance we have."

Mr. Mancini had been permitted a poached egg for lunch today, and had enjoyed it. There had been some white grapes for dessert; the sweet seedless kind they grew here in California. His day nurse, a thin red-headed girl called Patsy who always liked talking to him, said the grapes had been brought for one of the patients by a visitor, but were "going to waste." She didn't explain why the recipient couldn't eat them.

His wristwatch showed him 1:14 in the afternoon. He had been looking at it occasionally today, getting used to the need to know the time again. He knew quite a lot about the routine of the Cardiac and Intensive Care units by now, through asking the nurses; they said how nice it was for a patient to take such an interest in their work, when most people were so wrapped up in their own problems they didn't think about anyone else.

He knew the names of nearly all the patients in the Intensive Care Unit at the far end of the corridor, and what most of them were there for. He did very little reading, though they brought him old copies of *Newsweek* and *Reader's Digest* and *Christian World;* he liked to sit upright against the pillows and look out of the window and "do his thinking," as Patsy smilingly called it.

He always thought about business, and matters closely connected with it. The assets of Fiorenzo Pharmaceutical were currently in the region of fifty million dollars and the company was expanding at a steady pace, thanks mainly to its aggressive policy in marketing and advertising and to the flair of several of its directors for establishing useful and powerful contacts, some of them in Washington. Much of the firm's success, on a more technical level, was due to the synthesis and development of three broad-spectrum drugs, Phenoxitin, Lipinol-100 and Vitalium. A fourth, Adrenon, had already proved its worth against a broad range of tropozite and cyst states in the laboratory and was just now undergoing its final clearance tests required by the FDA; based on adrenyl-phenox derivatives, it provided an efficient and powerful antidote against the basic organic toxins in the Western Hemisphere group, and three weeks ago the final testing project was started at West Coast Research Laboratories in Los Angeles.

If the trials were successful, Fiorenzo Pharmaceutical would profit substantially in launching the drug on a market eager to reward its potential for the benefit of mankind. Enthusiasm was very high within the company, and a massive promotion campaign was ready to hit the media.

It would be unthinkable, everyone at Fiorenzo was agreed, that this new weapon in the crusade against disease should fail in its trials at West Coast Research.

Mario Mancini stared out of the window, the heads of the palm trees reflected in his dark glasses. Though he was a patient man, he was beginning to miss the active routine of his work as third vice-president of Fiorenzo and head of the Los Angeles branch; and he intended to leave the hospital in a few days. Dr. Thayer and his staff had already commented with surprise on his rapid recovery from the attack

144

and the pathological condition engendered by it, so that he must stay a little longer and let them claim due credit for his rehabilitation.

His three years as a medical student had given him an understanding of the diligence, hard work and dedication required of hospital staffs, and he was full of praise for the treatment he had received at Garden Grove.

Don Glezen was already waiting in the staff room when Scott reached there soon after four o'clock the same afternoon, bringing David Pryor with him since Kistner had raised no objection. Ernst Stein arrived a few minutes later and the three of them explained their views to David, going over for him the phenomena of the messages and the experiment involving Arlene Wyatt last evening.

David listened with his head on one side and his hands on his knees, looking mostly at Don Glezen, whose low resonant voice held his attention. David had an open mind on the subject of telepathy, but found it hard to picture Claudia involved in what amounted to extrasensory perception; though she was athletic and held a degree in the sciences she wasn't totally an extrovert: she had gone into TM and biofeedback a year ago and was still interested. But the idea of her being terrified of someone subconsciously while deep in coma, and of her sending out a form of signal asking for help, left him bewildered.

By the time Don Glezen had gone over the case for him, and the psychiatrist Stein had added his opinions, David was more ready to accept their theories; but he said very little at this stage, and put only a few random questions.

"If she's so scared of this man, why doesn't she just tell us who he is?"

"She could," Don said, "very easily. But she doesn't think it's necessary."

"But that's—I don't understand."

145

"She is functioning in the theta region," Ernst Stein told him, "far below consciousness. She cannot reason: she can only emote. What we are listening to, in these messages, is a continuing scream of fright. It's like being in a nightmare, Mr. Pryor: we shout for someone to save us—but we don't say from what. The monster is so real, and so close, that we are sure everyone else can see it too."

David said in a moment: "Christ. She's that bad?"

"She is that frightened," Don told him carefully. "It's her fear we should be working on, instead of opening up her brain with a knife." He chose the brutal words deliberately: it would strengthen David's convictions and help him fight the opposition at the medical board.

Scott was silent. There was no point in adding to the boy's anguish by telling him how big a risk his sister would be running, in physical terms, if the operation was allowed to go ahead. He'd hear it revealed anyway, when they convened.

The summons came at twenty minutes past four, and they joined the group of specialists in one of the smaller conference rooms. Charles Jordan, the hospital Administrator, was in the chair, and the members included three surgeons, three physicians and a neurologist. One of the surgeons was Blatsky, a resident, and one of the physicians was Smythe, recently from Stanford. Both were socialite friends of Neil Kistner.

The hearing lasted almost an hour. Careful consideration was given to Scott's point that the condition of drug-controlled ventricular tachycardia offered a grave risk to the patient's life during the stress of an operation; as the physician he said he could not guarantee maintaining control—by whatever means—of the tachycardia, and would accept no responsibility in the event of Claudia Terman's death.

Kistner's answer was also considered carefully. He claimed that had he been allowed to go into the brain at the time when the patient had arrived in the hospital, the present condition of tachycardia might well have been avoided. He felt that if further delay were permitted, further complications might well set in, taking this woman ever closer to a terminal condition. He was not impressed by Dr. Rand's "washing his hands of all responsibility," since misfortune in the operating room might be met with *as a result* of the "delaying tactics" employed by Rand from the moment when he—Kistner—had suggested surgery.

The other members of the board spoke in their turn.

David sat silent for the most part. He could not be invited to give medical opinion; he was here "to speak for the patient," as Charles Jordan had put it, since he knew his sister well and could perhaps help them decide what she herself would have wished.

Someone asked if Patrick Terman had been invited here this afternoon.

"There was no need, gentlemen," Kistner told them briefly. "He has considered the opinions of experts and feels we should operate as soon as possible, in the hope of saving life."

Scott remained silent. Any reference to the husband's motives would be out of order and unacceptable.

In the final vote taken, both Smythe and Blatsky opted for surgery "without hesitation and without any reservations." This had been expected by most of those present.

Jordan summarized at some length. The nub of his statement was that there appeared to be a choice between risks, and both would seem rather high. This much had been freely admitted, and Dr. Kistner had not pretended otherwise: he had said he would do everything in his power to minimize the risk to life during his work on the patient, but admitted it would remain high. On the other hand it seemed a time for "extreme measures" since "routine medical methods" had signally failed.

At 5:15 the meeting was brought to a close, on the decision to operate on Claudia Terman as soon as possible.

Talking for a moment to Dr. Lessiter as they came out of the conference room, Scott asked him a question. He knew there was no real answer; it was just that his mind had become numbed by the realization that all his experience and capability had been set aside, and that any power he might have had to fight for his patient had been taken away. His regard for Lessiter was very great, and Scott was perhaps groping for a morsel of consolation at a time when everything seemed lost.

"What are her chances?" he asked the physician.

Lessiter turned to him in faint surprise.

"What chances?"

Chapter 10

"So you just signed the form."

This place smelled of leather and gym shoes and sweat. Two men were sparring in a far corner and another one was punching the bag with steam-hammer blows. A few were just standing around, talking and laughing, towels around their necks.

"I mean, you just signed the goddam form." David threw out his hands, to mean he didn't understand how it could have happened. "Without even calling me or leaving a message for me saying what you were going to do. Don't you see?"

Patrick Terman watched him. There was a towel around his neck too, and sweat on his face. His bright blue eyes were wide open, excited-looking as he watched his brother-in-law. This boy Dave had been at him before, getting on his back about "what he'd done" to his sister. What had he done anyway, for Christ's sake? She'd gone off sex and he'd met Terry and that was it, bingo, they were just made for each other. So what? He had to have sex, didn't he?

"Look," David said more quietly, "I'm her brother, remember?" He waited this time, so Terman would have to say something. In some part of his mind he listened to the hammering of the gloves against the punching bag.

"How could I forget?" Patrick said. Then he shut up again, because he didn't have to take anything from this little jerk. Pryor was an inch shorter and fifty pounds lighter

149

and didn't look like he'd ever been inside a gymnasium before in his life.

"You were a total stranger when you met Claudia, remember? You were just a—a baseball player. You—"

"What do you mean I was *just* a—"

"I mean exactly that. It's all we knew about you when—"

"It's all *we* knew? I married your sister, not the both of you." He waited a couple of seconds. "Did you miss her too much?"

David felt his body tense and a kind of hammering start inside his head, like the punching bag, but softer. He had to look away from the bright wet face in front of him, with its hair dark with sweat and sticking to the forehead in ringlets. He had to keep his temper, because he'd come here to ask this bastard to change his mind and call the hospital and tell them it was all off, they had to leave her alone.

Because he'd begun seeing things very clearly during that meeting this afternoon. It had been like his mind had been a kind of searchlight suddenly, with its beam playing on the minds of the people there, Dr. Rand and Dr. Kistner and the rest of them, so he'd been able to see inside. He'd felt very alert suddenly, very much on his toes, like he'd been smoking—which he hadn't. The medical details had been way above his head, and he hadn't really heard them; he'd been too busy looking at those people and getting their vibes. And there hadn't, finally, been any question about it.

Rand and Glezen wanted to help Claudia. The little baldheaded guy with the accent—he forgot his name but he was a shrink—had been so high on the technicalities of this "case"—they meant Claudia—that you couldn't tell if he wanted to help her or not. A couple of other guys were on Scott Rand's side, but the rest were with Kistner. And he hadn't dug that man's vibes at all. He'd been so damn sure of himself that he hadn't even talked much, and when he talked at all he made it sound like he'd just stepped down

150

from Olympus to tell this bunch of morons the score. "It is my opinion, gentlemen, that I can be instrumental in saving a life here. Should you agree, I'd be anxious to offer my services while there is time."

But it hadn't been what he'd *said,* or what any of them had *said,* that had made up his mind. It was the vibes he'd got. In this strange way he'd looked inside of their heads and seen very clearly what was there. And there didn't have to be any operation. Not for Claudia. Because it would kill her.

So this bastard had to tell them he'd changed his mind. He just had to keep his temper with him, and talk the whole thing out, and go tear up that form.

"Look, Terman, you weren't at that meeting." He hadn't called him Patrick since the time she'd said it was all off, after only eight months. "Maybe you—well maybe you had something more important to do. That's okay, but—"

"You bet your sweet life I had something more important to do, buster. I'm a baseball player, you know that? I'm on the Wildcats and this is the middle of the goddam season! Doesn't that mean anything to you?"

Yes, David thought bitterly, it meant you couldn't stop playing with a ball just because your wife was dying.

"The thing is," he told Terman, "that if you'd had time to be at the meeting I think you'd have been convinced they shouldn't operate on Claudia."

Patrick stood watching him, bouncing slightly on the balls of his feet.

"What did they decide?" he asked with elaborate patience.

"It doesn't matter what *they* decided. It's what *we*—"

"Oh for Christ's sake, Pryor, who are you trying to kid? Do *we* know better than those medics? What are they for?"

Some of the athletes standing around stopped talking and watched the two of them, wondering who the young guy

151

was in the crumpled sports clothes and the dusty shoes. He looked pretty teed off about something.

"Hey, Pat!" someone called.

"Coming!" Terman called back.

"You know Dr. Rand?" David asked him. He had a long way to go, and by Terman's attitude he didn't think he was going to get there.

"Sure I know Dr. Rand."

"He's her physician. And he's dead against surgery. And two of those other people were in agreement with him. I'm just telling you, it was only *some* of them who—"

"Hey, Pat!" the man called again.

"Okay!" Patrick turned back to David, punching one fist against the flat of his other hand impatiently. "Look, friend, I talked to Dr. Rand and I talked to Dr. Kistner and I listened to both of them good and hard, see? And I made up my mind. And I signed the fucking form, and if you don't like it you better just get used to the idea. I'm not going to wait around any longer while she's in that place with all those people running around after her and a machine breathing for her like it could go on for months, you know what I mean? I'm—"

"*You're* not waiting around? What's the hurry, Terman?" He knew what the hurry was.

"Life has to go on, doesn't it?"

"What's the hurry?" He wanted the bastard to admit it.

"Look, buster, they're waiting for me over there. Come in again sometime when I'm less busy, okay? She'll be in good hands with that guy Kistner, you know that? So you don't have to worry. If we—"

"You want to get married again, don't you? Isn't that why you're in a hurry to—"

"That's none of your goddam business."

"My sister's my goddam business!" David tried to get the edge off his tone, to stop his hands bunching like they were.

152

But all he could see was this pug face with its curly hair and its bright blue eyes, the face of the man whose sweaty sexy masculinity had found such a response in Claudia's unawakened libido that she'd gone the whole way with him, even into a marriage that had left her scarred from her own self-discovery. "I didn't know I was like that," she'd told David after the breakup. "I didn't know I was looking for a—for just an *animal*." She'd talked to him about it, because she'd had to talk to someone and he was closest; and he'd tried to say the right things, like all girls go through that phase, and some of them can't even pull out, things like that. Then there'd been the fight, when she kept on delaying the divorce and he'd said she was secretly hoping Terman would forget the other girl and take her back. She'd flared up at that, and there'd been a door slammed; and the next thing he knew was that the highway police were telling him to get to the hospital.

He said as quietly as he could to the man in front of him: "I want you to change your mind. She doesn't need surgery. It's going to kill her."

Terman half turned away from him, catching a pair of gloves from someone. "I made the decision and there's no reason to change it. Why don't—"

"*You want to kill her! You—*"

"Oh Jesus Christ, I—"

"That'd be cheaper than a divorce. Quicker."

"You know how much that operation's going to cost me? Four grand! Four thousand goddam—"

"*I want you to tear up that form.*"

It was all he could think about: a signature on a bit of paper that was going to let them—what had Glezen said?—"*take a knife to her brain.*"

He couldn't see Terman very clearly now, but he saw Claudia somewhere near, the way she'd been, laughing her clean white laugh when they'd talked, hitting a fast ball

153

back to him with that sudden fire she had. He could hear her voice, though far away, too far away for him to hear what she was saying.

"You're nuts," Terman told him. "You—"

"*I want you to tear up—*"

"You're obsessed with that goddam little—"

Flash.

It happened in a kind of *flash* and David saw a whole kaleidoscope of images in slow motion as his fist surged away from him and the knuckles met the skin of the face in front of him and puckered it deeper and deeper till it rocked the head back and back as the bright eyes slowly squeezed shut and the blood began coming from the ripped skin and Terman's arms opened, sticking out at right angles as he went down and away, down and away.

Someone said: "Jeees-us *Christ.*"

The slowness was over now and David saw Terman hit the resined boards of the floor and slide toward the wall, his legs doubled and one of the boxing gloves skittering ahead of him. Then he was still, and didn't move again.

David went out to the street and walked fast, trying to shake away the thought that he hadn't done any good, or anything he'd intended.

Scott Rand was on the ground floor of the North Block when the doors of the emergency entrance banged open and two paramedics came in at a run with a stretcher. The patient was thrashing about and giving a lot of trouble, so he went along to help. This was just before nine o'clock in the evening and the Code 1 calls had been sounding for five or six minutes.

By the time Scott reached the Emergency Room there was a whole bunch of people there because the calls had asked for "all available personnel," which at this time of the evening meant as many as could get there, wherever they

154

were and whatever they were doing. This was because the radio messages coming in from the ambulance had repeated the phrase "wildly delirious."

It took seven of them to hold the man down. His temperature was 106 degrees and they took a white blood cell count of 40,000—four times the highest norm. His name was Sonny Cohen.

A few more people came in but left again because the situation was now under clinical control, though four orderlies were still having to hold the patient still. He was incoherent and in acute shock, with blood pressure at 70/30 and a central venous pressure of close to zero. Scott ordered rapid cooling with an ice blanket and fans to reduce the fever, and a regimen of salt water and plasma.

Arterial blood gases showed the patient to be grossly acidotic, and Scott asked for an IV of sodium bicarbonate. Gomez came in and he asked him to take over the case, beginning with bacteriological analysis of blood, urine, stool, sputum (if they could get it) and spinal fluid. An antibiotic cocktail was pumped in just before Scott left the Emergency Room, and morphine was given.

"Someone call his wife, or whoever. Get the history. You need any of my staff, Ramon?"

"I can manage."

By 9:50 Scott was back in the Intensive Care Unit, where Arlene Wyatt had taken over from Tracy, the senior nurse on the 3 P.M. to 11 P.M. shift.

The arrangement had been made with the cooperation of Miss Dean and the charge nurse in Recovery, a few hours before the medical board had sanctioned Dr. Kistner's proposal to operate on the patient in Room 6. It had been Don Glezen who had suggested that if Arlene were to work in the Intensive Care Unit her presence near Claudia might reassure her and speed her recovery. Arlene had suffered no lingering trauma from the theta-induction experience, but still remembered a little of the fear she'd felt at the time—"like deep pain you can still feel back there behind the anesthetic," as she'd said to Don. For this reason she'd hesitated before agreeing to change her duties, but had made up her mind immediately when she heard that Claudia was going into surgery.

Coming on duty late this evening to work through the remainder of Tracy's shift, she had gone into Room 6 with Dr. Glezen and Dr. Rand, feeling a little scared as they'd watched the heart-rate and brain-wave readings accelerate across the monitor screens, then slow again after three or four minutes. If the woman in the bed could have opened her eyes or smiled or said her name before sleeping again it would have seemed almost normal that she'd been communicating by telepathy, even while unconscious; but she was only a face, a mask, and showed nothing of the mind that had been reaching out to Arlene's in such desperation, in such terror.

But she wasn't any kind of monster, Arlene thought as she looked down at her: she was a young person much like herself, and helpless—a thousand times more helpless. There'd been no way, really, she could have refused to come here and stay close to her as she was prepared for surgery. Dr. Kistner had revised his schedules, passed two cases over to Dr. Lessiter and arranged to take Mrs. Terman into surgery at 11:30 tonight, on the premise he'd expressed frequently: that if they were going to operate they should do it in time.

Scott Rand looked at the monitor screens the moment he came into Room 6, reading an elevated 90 beats per minute and an accelerated 9 cycles per second, both of which indicated a state of excitation. In Arlene's absence the quinidine treatment was keeping the heart rate below 80.

"Has that change become typical?" he asked her.

"Yes, Doctor."

156

She was looking tense, and her voice was overquick, overbright. It didn't surprise him.

"When you leave the room, are there fluctuations?"

"No. She's pretty well leveled out at these readings."

Don Glezen had asked her to check the monitor screens at the nurses' station every time she left Room 6 and Claudia's immediate proximity.

"Do we have all the reports in yet?" Scott wanted to know.

"Yes, Dr. Rand. I filed them at the station."

He went to check them over. Most of Claudia's medical history was precisely known, and this final series of tests was meant simply to update it: a chemical screening battery covering calcium, inorganic phosphorus, glucose, uric acid, cholesterol, total protein, albumin, total bilirubin, alkaline phosphatase, LDH and SGOT. These were routine studies and part of the established preoperative work-up, to cover the chance of infection and metabolic imbalance. Coagulation studies had been made because of the risk of hemorrhage, and Scott had ordered blood typing and cross-matching in case the need for transfusion arose during the postoperative phase.

Pre-anesthetic medication had been started already and Arlene had been assigned to the task of its continuance. While he was at the nurses' station Scott noted that the last two-hourly printouts from the EKG and EEG monitors showed a progressive state of excitation in the patient; but he had no means of telling whether this was due to Arlene's presence in the room or to some subliminal awareness by Claudia that her life had been placed at risk.

At 10:12 P.M. Bill Brickman, as the physician-anesthesiologist, visited the patient and confirmed his own premedication orders.

"How are you feeling?" he asked Arlene.

"Fine."

157

"What kind of fine?"

"Okay fine." She gave him a quick smile.

Bill had called her during the day, at an hour when he knew she wouldn't be sleeping. He'd heard something of the theta-induction experiment and seen earlier this evening that she'd been subtly affected by it: she normally lived on fine-tuned nerves and her movements were quick and positive, but these characteristics seemed now exaggerated, as if she had to prove that nothing had changed, nothing was wrong.

"Are you going to let them do it again?" he asked her quietly as he finished writing the form.

"Do what again, Bill?"

"Use you as a guinea pig."

She snapped the end off an ampule, deftly and precisely. "Is that what I look like tonight? I don't feel like one." Another bright smile.

He said nothing more. He had no authority over Scott Rand or Don Glezen, and no right to dictate to Arlene what she should let herself get into. But it wasn't easy for him to stand by while she took the risk of being hurt.

"Bill," she said as he turned to the door.

"Yes?"

"I'll be okay."

He said in a moment: "Sure. But if you need me any time . . ."

"I know."

At 10:35 Scott called his wife for the second time this evening and said he'd be home late or might stay at the Grove in one of the treatment rooms.

"Alarms and excursions, darling?" Eve asked him absently.

"Did I wake you up?"

"No. I was meditating."

"I'm sorry, I'll—"

"I could have left the phone off the hook if I'd wanted to. Which alarms, and which excursions?"

He realized she probably didn't care.

"Claudia Terman."

"Oh. Are they still going to operate?"

"She's due on the table," he said tonelessly, "in an hour."

"But you said there's a risk. A big one."

"Yes."

"Then why are they—" she said and broke off. In a moment she spoke again. "Is it Kistner for this one?"

"Yes."

She knew Kistner's reputation.

"He's too bloody ambitious," she said, "isn't he?" Scott didn't answer. "How did he swing the decision, this time?"

"Like he always swings it. He's a power figure, and people think they'll get some of it for themselves, if they—" He stopped and left it at that. He suddenly felt he didn't know the answers to things any more.

"I hope it goes all right, darling. I really do. Will you call me, when it's over? Whichever way it goes?"

"I'll try," he said, and they hung up, because there wasn't any more to say.

When he went back into Room 6 he found that Denise, one of the ICU nurses on this shift, had helped Arlene turn the patient and shave the light hairs that had started to grow again in the suboccipital area surrounding the sutured closure; shaving now extended to a periphery of six centimeters across the base of the skull. An operating-room nurse had looked in to see how the premedication was going, and had left again.

A call came through soon afterward to say that Dr. Kistner had returned to the hospital after a short break at home. He had asked about Mrs. Terman's status and been told it was appropriate.

A few minutes before eleven o'clock Arlene primed a

syringe with cephalothin, one of the premedication antibiotics, and pressed the plunger to squirt out a few drops and clear any air that might be present. The room was quiet except for the rasping of the MA1 ventilator, and she was alone.

The drops came squirting from the tip of the needle and flashed in the light as they fell. She didn't see where they went. The needle caught the light too, shining along its whole length as she squeezed the area of flesh on each side of the median cubital vein. The air was very still in the room and she could feel it against her face, cool and still, like silence. She positioned the tip of the needle against the blue vein's swelling, feeling a lightness, a spiraling away through the air, the shine of the long steel needle beginning to spin and break up into many needles, spinning slowly like the spokes of a wheel. She pressed the glass cylinder forward and pressed again, but the tip didn't go in. But it didn't matter, there'd be no harm done, it was important that no harm was done, spinning in shining silence, terribly important to do no harm in the stillness and the coolness of the air, do you have a problem? No. No problem.

Let me do it.

"I think," she said from somewhere else, and stopped.

"All right."

"I think it's sticking," she said, and tried again; but Dr. Rand took it from her and she stepped back to make room. The air was less cool now, less still, and she heard the hiss of the ventilator's spirometer and Denise's voice on the telephone outside.

Scott took the syringe and pressed one or two drops from the needle in case Arlene had pulled on the plunger inadvertently, letting air in. The median cubital stood out from the flesh between the thumb and finger of his left hand and he drove the needle in, pressing the plunger and finding a slight resistance before the zigzag crack appeared suddenly

160

along the transparent cylinder. He pulled out the needle at once.

"I need another syringe."

"Yes, Doctor."

He took the broken one under a light and checked it, but saw nothing that could have made the plunger stick or the plastic break in this way. But once in a thousand times a syringe was faulty, so this was a thousandth time. He dropped it into the trash bin and took the new syringe from Arlene and filled it and drove the needle into the vein, injecting the contents. Arlene noted it on the chart.

"Was that the final antibiotic?" Scott asked her.

"Yes. The cephalothin."

He nodded, looking at Claudia's face and noting its color, seeing no change. Her skin had been pale and sometimes waxen, because of the sweat sheen that sometimes gathered, ever since her admission to the ICU; her eyelids had never lost their stillness, nor had her mouth ever moved of its own accord. Her face was now an indelible image in his memory, and the thought of her brought it to mind at once, the pale skin and the shadowed cheekbones, the blueblack contrast of the eyebrows and the hair, the firm mouth and the long-healed scars of the adolescent acne, the small white lobes of the ears.

Sometimes he looked at the three photographs of her that he kept in his office, trying to believe that the mobile smiling face of the earlier Claudia Terman was the same as the painted sculpturing in Room 6. He'd never managed it. The woman in there was different, a changeling, driven in her mind by terror and reaching out for whoever would help her.

This evening he'd been through the expected eleventh-hour phase of searching desperately for a way of stopping the operation—ethically or unethically, reasonably or violently. Now he was out on the other side, knowing he had to

161

go with it and see it through. The medical board had convened and all aspects had been taken into consideration and a decision had been reached. And there was nothing he could do about it now.

"Dr. Rand?"

He turned away from Claudia's bed and went out of the room.

"We have a Mr. Cohen being transferred, Dr. Rand, from the E.R. Will you be supervising?"

He looked at the digital clock. "No, I'll be in surgery at a quarter after eleven. But I'll see him in here and we'll get out a call to Dr. Thayer."

Denise began talking on the phone again to Emergency.

In Room 6 Arlene topped up the IV for the patient and felt her skin, noting the onset of dryness due to the premedication. There were no more injections to give until Claudia was put onto the trolley and taken down to surgery. Everything was in order and it was now a question of waiting and making minor routine checks.

For a few moments Arlene perched on the stool by the door to rest her feet, watching the pale face of Claudia Terman and telling herself that everything was going to be all right. From the moment she had come on duty tonight for the first time in the Intensive Care Unit she'd been expecting that sudden attack of migraine and the frightening urge to write and go on writing, with her hand shaking and her stomach knotted up and her breath half blocked in a kind of scream that she couldn't get out; but it hadn't happened. Nothing at all had happened, nothing to show that Claudia wasn't deep in a peaceful sleep, and safe in her dreams. For this she was grateful.

Dr. Kistner to Operating Room 1. Dr. Kistner, please.
The wall clock in the ICU showed 11:10.

"Denise, will you check Mrs. Graham for me?"

162

"Sure."

Nurse Fowler, please. Nurse Fowler to Operating Room 1.

Miss Dean had arrived, as she often did, after going home to her one-room apartment and putting her feet up on the sofa and sleeping for an hour before boiling an egg and eating it with anchovies. Her home was in Garden Grove; the apartment was a gesture to her independence, and sometimes a refuge.

Dr. Brickman to Operating Room 1, please. Dr. Brickman.

These were routine calls, part of the fail-safe system that guarded against errors and accidents and confusion in the surgical field at Garden Grove. The staff now being called to surgery should know they were due there at this time; some, in fact, were there already, and others on their way. But a reminder was in order, in case someone was sleeping in a treatment room after a grueling emergency, or engrossed in the reading room with X-ray pictures covering the frosted screens, or dealing with a terminal case where pain was dominant and had to be overcome.

Or simply in case someone had forgotten. It happened.

Dr. Westlake, please. Dr. Westlake to Operating Room 1.

Westlake was to bring a student into surgery.

Just before 11:15 Mr. Cohen was brought up from the Emergency Room and Scott saw him into Room 2 and gave him a brief check preliminary to Vern Thayer's taking over. The patient was still under morphine and his temperature had shot up again to well above the hundred mark, and Scott ordered further cooling procedures.

Dr. Thayer, please. Dr. Thayer to ICU.

Scott went across to Room 6 and found Arlene readying the IV hookup for transportation and removing the catheter.

163

"Are we set?"

"Yes, Dr. Rand." She pulled away the adhesive tapes from the EEG contacts on Claudia's forehead and smoothed back the dark hair.

"Did you call—"

The beaker of instruments on the shelf by the door spun twice through the air and smashed against the wall, the glass fragments flashing in the light as they scattered below the bed. Neither Scott nor Arlene saw it directly: it was the sound of the shattering that made them turn their heads. Suddenly the room was quiet.

"Are you all right?" Scott asked Arlene.

"Yes," on a breath. Her face was white.

He looked down at the mess of glass and metal again. Neither of them had been near the door or the shelf, and no one had come in.

"Dr. Rand?" It was a voice from outside. He didn't answer.

They were both looking at Claudia now, at the pale serene face against the pillows. There was no movement, no expression. Scott looked up and saw the heart rate had increased to the eighties on the electrocardiograph; the EEG had just been disconnected and he couldn't tell what the brain rhythm was.

He looked at Arlene. "Someone left it too near the edge of the shelf. We'll have to watch that in the future."

She nodded, swallowing.

Denise was in the doorway. "Dr. Rand, I have Surgery on the line. Are we ready to move Mrs. Terman?"

He turned slowly.

"Yes. We're ready. And get a broom in here, will you? There's some broken glass."

164

Chapter 11

At 11:37 P.M. a nurse took a piece of chalk and wrote on the blackboard: *Operating Room 1. Pvt. Service. Exploratory neuro. Kistner.*

The only constant sound in the room was that of the portable MA1 ventilator as its spirometer hissed regularly. The doors had been closed a few minutes ago and the red light was on in the corridor outside.

Neil Kistner was scrubbing at the row of basins, with a nurse helping him. Scott was talking quietly to Don Glezen, gowned and masked. Nearer the operating table, Dr. Westlake, a physician-teacher, was pointing out details of the initial procedures to his student, a young man from back East. Dr. Brickman and his anesthetist were controlling the induction of a minimal dose of intramuscular analgesic: after talks with Scott Rand, Bill Brickman had decided to assume that the patient's coma could conceivably lighten or even give way to consciousness, creating the need of a painkiller during the operation.

Arlene was standing a little apart from the others, watching an operating-room nurse washing the surgical site with safety soap and alcohol and then painting it with 1 percent Hibitane in spirit solution. A moment ago Bill Brickman had said a word to Arlene, asking if she were "okay fine." She had said that she was; but her smile looked shaky.

Because the beaker *may* have been left too near the edge of the shelf to be safe if anyone brushed it in passing and dislodged it—but no one had done that. No one had been near. She could have believed it had been left so close to the edge that a background vibration had set it moving, and that her own nerves had made something scary out of it; but Dr. Rand had gone very quiet too, and had made a point of "explaining" how it had happened.

She was trying not to think about it now, but it wasn't any good: the explosion of glass and the jangling of the metal instruments were still echoing in her mind as she watched Claudia.

The scrub nurse had moved to the operating table, bringing her trolley; she was now helping to arrange the towels around the suboccipital area. The pillow had been pulled forward to the end of the table and two others inserted so that Claudia's brow and chin were supported in her facedown position, with enough room for the tracheal tube to remain clear and without risk of compression.

One of the "clean" nurses, already scrubbed, gowned and masked, had chanced to touch her mask when she was adjusting the gown, and was back at the row of basins to scrub again.

Scott remained near Don Glezen. They were no longer talking. He'd decided not to tell Don what had happened in Room 6 just now: it was unnerving and irrelevant at a time when Claudia's life was so finely in the balance. Their concern at the moment was that the quinidine should manage to keep the ventricular tachycardia under control at this crucial time, and that Claudia's subliminal terror should remain at theta level and not become conscious, in the field where intense physical pain would overwhelm her.

Scott was now watching the monitor screens exclusively.

An hour ago David Pryor and Brian Newby had arrived at Garden Grove and were now sitting outside the operating room. David had asked if he could be present at the operation, and been told that strict regulations didn't permit that.

He had been promised a chance of seeing his sister as soon as she was transferred to the recovery ward.

"Smoke?"

"No."

David lit up and began pacing again between the rows of turquoise-colored padded chairs of the waiting room.

Brian Newby watched him for a while, sitting sideways on a chair with his arm hooked over the back and his legs out straight, his jacket open because a button had come off and he'd looked for it and couldn't find it. He thought David looked very like Claudia, both dark and intense and with very clean-cut faces, like a male and female model. But that was only their looks. If David was anything like his sister he had a lot of personality, a lot of style.

"D'you know her well?" David was asking him, suddenly coming to a halt.

"Not really. We work in the same place."

"West Coast Research?"

"Right."

"So—" David began and left it and took up his pacing again.

"So what am I doing here at midnight?"

"I didn't ask you anything," David said from quite a way off, six or seven chairs away. He couldn't remember Claudia's ever having talked about a Brian Newby.

Brian watched him and didn't say anything more. He was trying to see Claudia's face in the face of her brother, and Claudia's movements in her brother's movements, in the way he was walking, his feet slow but his head glancing up, glancing around every few seconds in a kind of impatience for something to happen, someone to communicate with: *that* was Claudia.

"What do you do?" he asked David.

"Solar heating. What do you do?"

167

"I told you."

"Oh yes." He dropped his cigarette into the big sand-filled can that stood at the bottom of the pillar. "I can't stand those damned things."

"That's because you go at them like a forest fire."

David stopped and looked down at him, blowing out the last of the smoke. "You're pretty observant."

"It's my job."

They both looked at the big wall clock again, chancing to do it at precisely the same time. It was 11:47.

"Did she have any enemies?" Brian asked.

"No. I told everyone."

"So did I."

David came and sat down on the chair next to Brian, just with the tips of his buttocks, leaning forward near the edge, getting out the cigarettes and lighting another one. "Jesus Christ, I didn't want them to do this."

"Do what?"

"Operate."

He'd had only one scotch tonight. One double. Normally he never drank, and then he'd hit it that night and got arrested. Now he was leveling out. He hated scotch as much as he hated these damned things.

"But they advised it," Brian said.

"What?"

"These doctors advised doing an—"

"No. *No.* It was that *bastard.*"

"Which bastard?" Brian leaned away from the back of the chair now, interested.

"Her husband. Don't you know her husband?"

"No." Brian remembered seeing a man in the lobby at West Coast once; he'd come in and was asking for Claudia. A lot of muscle and hair in a tee shirt and track shorts, walked on his toes. "Does he look like a beach bum?"

David swung his head. "You could say that."

168

Brian sat still for a while; he'd been swinging one foot and now stopped, to sit still. So that was her husband, the man with—but it was ludicrous. And of course sickening. He knew she was married for a time and had sometimes glimpsed a face behind the reflections in a windshield in the West Coast parking lot, a figure in white in the distance at the tennis club talking to her. He'd assumed it was her husband, but had never thought about it, like you never go on scratching once it bleeds; now he knew what he looked like. A beach bum. What had gotten into her? Claudia: Mrs. Beach Bum.

He went on sitting still, so nothing would hurt.

"He signed the form," David said.

"Did he?"

"After that, there wasn't anything I could do." David got up again, pacing with short and slightly toed-in steps to the end of the row of turquoise-colored padded chairs and back, grinding the cigarette out in the sand, looking up and around to see if anyone had come in. During the day this place was crowded when he came through; now it was deserted, in a kind of way disjointed, as if they'd come here at the wrong time. As indeed, Jesus Christ, they had.

He saw Brian's eye on the clock again, and looked at it himself. A minute had gone by since the last time he'd looked, not seventeen years or anything. A whole minute.

His knuckles felt sore again. They were beginning to heal, then he shoved his hand in his pocket or through a sleeve without remembering, and the healing skin broke again.

"As a matter of fact," he said, "the last time I saw him he was on the floor."

"Is that right?"

Brian's voice sounded a long way off; but then he was almost at the other end of the row of chairs.

"Yes," David said.

169

"Is that how your knuckles got that way?"

The voice sounded disbelieving.

"Yes."

"Good heavens."

An odd expression, rather Old Worldly. He didn't know who Brian Newby was, except that he was the guy sitting at the other end of the row of chairs. He was smaller now, looking along the perspective of the waiting room at David and perhaps saying something that was too quiet to be heard.

"Yes," David said again, though no one had asked him anything.

He looked at his knuckles, with his hand spread out and the patches of blood making a line against the white of his hand, scaring the hell out of him as the faces came and went, peering down close at him and then drawing back, their mouths hidden in whiteness.

One of them had a knife.

Don't, David told him, and stood shivering in the middle of them all, looking around for a way of escape. There wasn't any. So it'd have to be the other thing. Like with Terman in the gymnasium. *Don't you dare.*

Shivering.

Only their eyes showing above the whiteness, and the shine of their knives, the shine of their knives in the cold. He could hear his own breath panting as if he'd run a long way; but he was only shivering, because of the cold.

Leave me alone, he said, but they still held on. He tried to move but they wouldn't let him. One of them was peering into his face, saying don't worry, everything's okay.

Of course, he said.

"Come and sit down."

He began moving now. The hand on his arm was moving him, and he sat down in one of the padded chairs and Brian sat down in the one next to him.

"Shall I get you some coffee? There's a place open."

"What? No. No, thank you."

"You're okay now," Brian said, and stopped peering at him.

"Of course."

"I don't have a sister," Brian told him, "but if I had one, and she were in there having an operation, you know how I'd feel?"

"No."

"Like you do."

He looked at the clock again. It said 11:49.

The anesthesiologist and his anesthetist stood at the head of the operating table, monitoring the patient's reactions, looking for restlessness, seeing none as yet.

The circulation nurse was standing by farther down the table, so that she would be on the surgeon's right when he came to take up his position.

Dr. Westlake and the student sat on stools at the other side of the table. They were "dirty"—that is to say, they were masked and gowned but not scrubbed. They would be moving no nearer the table than this.

Arlene was now standing in a group with Dr. Rand and Dr. Glezen, near enough to the table to follow the procedure but far enough back to be out of the way.

The scrub nurse was now moving to the table to take up her position with the trolley, immediately on the left of the surgeon's position. Dr. Kistner was left-handed.

The digital clock read 11:47.

The ventilator pulsed softly, breathing for the patient.

Claudia Terman lay face down on the three pillows, with the tracheal tube leading away from her to the ventilator, and the IV container hanging above her on its chrome stand, the tube leading down to the vein of her left arm.

The main lamps were now fully on, and in a moment Dr.

171

Kistner came across from the basins, his hands powdered and the gloves comfortably in place. The scrub nurse moved slightly to make room for him: she had been standing too close.

He looked down for the first time at the prepared site of operation at the base of the patient's skull. His eyes were a slate-blue color, not cold-looking but deep, contemplative. For a few moments they were quite unblinking as he noted the disposition of the towels surrounding the suboccipital area and the shaved skin.

The wound was beginning to heal without too much inflammation, and he noted that the sutures were meticulously placed, as only Scott Rand would do it. Scott was all right, and knew his stuff; but he was so fussy.

"How is everything, Dr. Brickman?"

Outside surgery he called him Bill; in here he preferred a certain degree of formality: it reduced tensions and purveyed reassurance.

"Everything's go, Neil."

Dr. Kistner looked down again at the exposed area. There wouldn't be any complication about going in: he'd be working less than an inch and a half below the surface of the neck; nor would there be any complications in opening up the critical field for exploration; but at that stage some problems could arise: it depended on what precise form the damage had assumed.

He cut the sutures.

Handing the snips back to the nurse, he felt a slight pocket of air at the tip of a finger, inside the glove, and squeezed back the rubber to disperse it before he took the scalpel and placed its point at the end of the healing wound, since there was no argument for cutting a new opening.

Watching him, Scott Rand noticed particularly the bright flash of the blade as it spun away in an arc, just before Kistner's knees began jackknifing and he went down, lurching in an effort to save himself, but failing, hitting the floor with his left hand still clutched at his chest.

The meeting convened at a few minutes after ten o'clock the next morning in the Administrator's office was brief but effective, since major decisions were made.

Charles Jordan was a thin, cautious and self-effacing man with some kind of tragedy in his background that no one seemed to be sure about, though some believed it concerned one of his children who had not survived. To balance his retiring disposition he was gifted with a stone-wall obstinacy that had resisted quite a few attempts to make Garden Grove a really "progressive" institution, designed to attract the kind of physician and surgeon who thrive on what Jordan himself called "exotic showmanship" both on the ward and in surgery.

This degree of conservatism was difficult for the others at the meeting to break down. Those present were Scott, Don and Ernst Stein, and it was an indication of the hospital Administrator's respect for their combined reputations that he put up only a token resistance. His resistance was low this morning in any case: it was a bad day for Garden Grove, and he was no less shaken by the sudden death of Dr. Kistner than any other member of the hospital staff.

Scott was quiet, leaving most of the talking to Don and Ernst. Ironically he had been the person most active in the attempt to save Neil Kistner's life, since he was on the spot and had the necessary equipment and assistance on hand. They had gone to work as a team, first trying closed massage and artificial ventilation, with injections to stabilize metabolic imbalance. This failed to bring about contractions of the heart muscle, so they went into electroshock therapy, again with no result. At the three-minute stage when brain damage would have been setting in they injected adrenaline and calcium directly into the left ventricle and gave further defibrillation. There had been no response, and ten minutes later they stopped work, there being little point in bringing back to life a man whose brain would by now be heavily and irreversibly damaged.

Neil Kistner had been fifty-eight years old.

Scott sat listening to Ernst Stein as he explained their theories to the Administrator.

"As you realize, Charles, we are talking about the hypnagogic consciousness that precedes full delta-wave sleep. I agree with Dr. Glezen that the linear, free-flow transcendent nature of the theta level of consciousness—or hypnagogic sleep, if you will—is ideal ground for the onset of psychic experience. It is in this state that Mrs. Terman has existed since her admission to the Intensive Care Unit—or at least since the electroencephalograph was hooked up."

Don spoke shortly afterwards, leaving Charles Jordan time to make his shorthand notes, for which he was renowned. There had, Don said in answer to a question, been another case of psychometry in his experience: a twelve-year-old girl in Santa Barbara had written desperate messages under compulsion, though only for a short time.

"I was called in by the principal of her school," he told them. "The girl was mentally retarded, and had never studied parapsychology or even shown any interest in ghost stories. Her urge to write was intense during the whole of one hour—it was soon after dark on a winter evening. At first the messages pleaded for help, then tailed off after a time to give simple directions, saying something like 'You can find me on the beach, where the tall trees are, and the boats.'"

Don paused, looking at Ernst and Scott in turn. "I persuaded the police to make a search of the area south of the jetty, where there were groups of tall palm trees. They found a girl of ten buried under stones, and the medical evidence suggested she'd been there since last evening, and had been viciously assaulted."

174

Jordan's pencil made a soft scratching sound. "'Last evening' was when the other girl wrote the messages for help?"

"Yes."

"Did the police question the girl?"

"Very closely. But she'd almost forgotten the incident." As an afterthought he said: "I didn't think of taking her down to the theta level, as I did with Nurse Wyatt."

Jordon had been told about Arlene's induction, and the five messages were on the desk in front of him. Scott had described how the beaker had crashed down last evening, saying simply that he was prepared to believe Don's suggestion that it had been a case of telekinesis, similar to the "faulty" syringe that had cracked in his hand.

Don was speaking again, and Jordan watched him for a moment over his half-moon spectacles, his narrow head turned a little to the left, the side on which he was slightly deaf.

"Try to accept the idea just for a moment, Charles, and view what I'm going to say from that standpoint." In a moment he went on with quiet emphasis: "She didn't have to do very much. She didn't have to throw him out of a window or send his car into a wall or anything." He leaned forward. "She only had to effect the electrochemical system of a small organic pump."

Jordan glanced at some notes on the desk. "This was the third heart attack Neil had experienced in the past four years."

Don hung in there. "And it was the final one. And it was the easiest to induce, because the heart was weak."

Scott sat half listening to the argument. In his own mind he was now convinced that Claudia had extended her capabilities from telepathy to telekinesis, the ability to affect organic or inorganic objects at a distance by the power of her mind at the theta level. A few days ago he would have gone to Ernst Stein for a checkup if this kind of idea had entered his head. Today he accepted what Don had accepted long ago: that "reality" was a narrow band in the conscious spectrum and limited by man's reluctance to credit anything that couldn't be proved on the test bench, since he was a technologist and not a philosopher.

Scott was therefore conscious of Claudia Terman's true condition: a state of terror that was driving her to acts of desperate protestation. He was going to leave it to Don to make what rescue attempts he could, through parapsychological means and possibly with Arlene's help in getting to Claudia's mind and reassuring her. He himself would try the other and more practical way: through somehow locating the man who was the subject of Claudia's terror, the man who had "tried to kill" her and would "try again."

Don't let him find me, her last message had implored.

"I think," he told Jordan when there was a chance, "we ought to call in the police."

The Administrator put his lean head forward an inch.

"The police?"

"Claudia Terman is dead scared of someone who apparently tried to kill her. The police don't know how she came to crash. If we're to believe her messages—as I do—we have to believe some kind of assailant is 'close' to her. It could mean he's somewhere in the building. She—"

"There's a great deal of conjecture in this, Scott, and—"

"Sure, there aren't any facts. Except she's dying and I want to save her if I can. We all do." He waited for two seconds. "Don't we?"

Don and Ernst were listening hard; it was the first time anyone had thought of getting the police in. Don didn't take to the idea: he'd prefer to call in a parapsychologist with an international reputation, like Dr. Lawrence LeShan of Chicago or Dr. Tiller of Stanford University. Ernst felt privately that the police would probably throw out the very

176

ideas they were trying to put across to Jordan, and increase his skepticism.

"I would expect," the Administrator told Scott, "a certain degree of ridicule, if we proposed these theories to a hard-working Los Angeles policeman."

Scott brought out the ace.

"I've talked to the LAPD on the phone this morning, quite unofficially and without mentioning names or anything. I asked them two questions. One was about the night of the car crash on the freeway: would there have been a full moon dead ahead of any driver going in the direction Claudia Terman had been going at that hour? They had to ask around the office, while I tried to remember where the moon had been last night and work back from there. They got it first: yes, the moon would have been right in Claudia Terman's eyes that night—which ties in with what Nurse Wyatt told us when she was under thetagenic induction in Room 6. A lot of her words were unintelligible or indistinct, but we all agreed she'd mentioned the full moon."

Jordan said nothing for a moment, and Scott had the feeling he was annoyed at his having called the police without saying he meant to do so. But with a man like Jordan you had to take things into your own hands if you thought he'd stonewall you at the outset.

The Administrator said at last: "And the second question you put to the police?"

"I asked them if they thought anyone else was involved in the accident, either by chance or as an agent. They said they now believe a second car was involved."

After a moment Jordan said carefully: "That may mean nothing, of course."

"Or everything."

Scott decided at this stage that he wasn't going to let the

man stall him. If Jordan wouldn't call in the police he'd go and see them himself.

"I'm afraid I don't see any reason for bringing the *police* into this, Scott. Not right now." The emphasis on *police* made it sound extreme, Scott thought, even outrageous.

"Then I'll spell it out for you, Charles." He kept his tone neutral but it was an effort. "I think there are two good reasons—even vital reasons. As the attending physician it's my responsibility to do everything I possibly can to bring this patient out of coma and start her breathing for herself again. I now believe she is psychosomatically inhibited from recovery by latent fear, and by fear of a specific person. If we can find that person and take away his power to harm her, I think she could make a spontaneous recovery and breathe again for herself." He glanced across to Don and Ernst, who understood the workings of the human mind better than Jordan. "It's surprising how the most common-place phrases we utter are a true guide to our deepest feelings; and one of them is appropriate now. After a period of anxiety or fear, we often say: 'Now I feel I can breathe again.' In the case of Claudia Terman, I think this is literally true."

Don inclined his head and said quietly: "I'll give you ten for that." It was one of the most significant aspects of the psyche and its expression, and almost a complete explanation of autosuggestion in a nutshell: as we think, so we are.

"It may be," Scott said, turning back to Jordan, "that the police can find this man, and deal with him. My second reason for calling them in is a corollary to the first: if they can find him they might do it in time, before he can make another attempt on Claudia Terman's life."

He sat watching Charles Jordan. It was a while before he spoke. "I'm afraid I still don't—"

"Let's stop being afraid, shall we?" Scott got out of his

chair and began moving because he couldn't sit still any longer. He knew this was not much more than formal resistance on Jordan's part but he was impatient with it and it was time to let the man know. "Let's do something instead of hedging around the subject just because it's a little bit mind-blowing, Charles. *I* was like that only a few days ago, and Don had to spell this whole thing out for me like I was in first grade. Now I'm convinced and if I can't communicate my convictions to you then I have to go the other way and see the police myself—because Claudia Terman is *my* patient and I'm responsible for her welfare and her safety and I think she's in danger." He looked at his watch. "I have a busy morning, like you do. You'll want to think about this for a while." On his way to the door he said: "I won't do anything for the next hour—say, eleven-thirty."

He was viewing the Sonny Cohen X rays in the reading room at five minutes after eleven when the paging system called him to a phone, asking him to ring the Administrator's office. Charles Jordan told him he had already notified the police and they were sending a man from the detective branch right away.

Chapter 12

Detective Frank J. Cody reached the hospital within twenty minutes of Jordan's call to the Los Angeles Police Department and saw Scott Rand in the Administrator's office on the sixth floor. Jordan himself arrived soon afterwards, back from a meeting of the trustees.

Cody listened to Scott's detailed scenario of the situation for twelve minutes without a single interruption. He didn't want to sit down and he didn't want any coffee and he didn't want to listen to the random interjections that Charles Jordan kept slipping in while Scott was talking, and he showed his impatience by standing with his back half turned to the Administrator, watching Scott most of the time with steady expressionless eyes the color of black olives.

He was a man who revealed himself more than most others by the way he stood and the way he walked: he stood with his shoulders slightly forward and his square crew-cut head an inch down as if he'd just seen the objective and was about to take off before it saw him and ran. The way he walked was an extension of this characteristic: he took short quick steps that had in them the potential for a sudden burst of speed if it became necessary. He was, and looked, a forward-facing, forward-thinking organism with a tightly controlled brain and enough energy to take him through the nearest wall if the door were shut against him; and his associates knew many people who had shut doors against Frank

Cody during his nine years at the LAPD, most of them now using a federal box number as their address.

He also had a very lovely wife, an ex-Miss America who on her way down through unsuccessful auditions and small-time Las Vegas nightclubs had met Frank Cody one day in Saks Fifth Avenue, where she was on the point of putting a gold-plated elephant with emerald eyes into her handbag while the assistant was telephoning. That was twelve years ago when Frank had been a store detective, and now there were three kids with the faces of angels and a nice little place out there in the hills and on the mantel a small gold-plated elephant with emerald eyes, which Frank had paid for in cash. Marie-Ann hadn't liked it when she'd seen it there on the shelf but he'd talked her into accepting it: "Don't get the message wrong, honey. It doesn't say don't ever do it again, it says thank God you did it that time when I was there, or I wouldn't have found you."

His real reason was that he had learned the wisdom of blotting out a traumatic memory by changing its meaning.

He had learned many other things since then, most of them from the Los Angeles detective-inspector who had had the imagination to call in Peter Hurkos, the psychic, to help him locate the killers of Sharon Tate. Frank had been suitably impressed by the result, and had opened his mind to the possibilities offered by parapsychology in criminal investigation. He had therefore been detailed to check on the Claudia Terman case when the Administrator of Garden Grove had said on the phone that there "appeared to be certain extraordinary aspects to the affair, possibly involving the paranormal."

When Cody had listened to Dr. Rand he turned to Jordan and said: "These messages. Can I make copies?"

"We'll see to it for you." Jordan folded his thin hands in front of him, a well-known gesture that meant he was settling down to a fairly prolonged dissertation. "Now you've

181

heard Dr. Rand's theories, Mr. Cody, you'll probably feel inclined to—"

"I'd like Mr. Cody's reactions," Scott cut in quickly, "just as they come." He knew Jordan's propensity for what in court would be called leading the witness.

"I don't have any reactions," Frank Cody said with a look of bland innocence. "Not yet."

"I didn't want you to feel," Jordan tried again, "that people of our—shall we say—*responsibility* allow ourselves to accept *any* unusual interpretations of—"

"Can I see the patient, sir?"

"Er—yes, I—"

"I'm on my way there," Scott said, and moved for the door. He was glad Jordan made no further attempt to cloud the issue, because he would have had to put him down in front of Cody. Jordan was responsible for the running of Garden Grove and it was an immense task and he did it pretty well; but Scott was responsible for this one patient and he didn't want anybody getting in his way. That phrase of Ernst Stein's had got stuck in his mind and it drove him through most of the day: *What we are listening to is a continuing scream of fright.*

He had to stop the screaming.

"Just like old times," Cody said.

"You've been inside an Intensive Care Unit before?"

"You bet. Half drowned. A kid got into a canal."

Scott took him past the nurses' station without introducing him to Miss Dean or anyone else. The staff in the ICU were jittery this morning as it was, because Garden Grove was a close-packed society and news got around fast. It was said there was something odd about Dr. Kistner's sudden death and that it was something to do with the patient in Room 6. Some of the ICU staff had been on duty during Arlene's induction yesterday and had formed their own varying conclusions. In addition, news got around fast in Garden Grove because most of it got around on the telephone, and during the last few minutes an exchange of calls on quite other subjects had carried the incidental information that the visitor in the Intensive Care Unit at this present time was a police detective—who had asked at the desk in the lobby to see Charles Jordan, with whom he had an appointment. Frank Cody's presence was giving a lot of substance to established rumor.

"She doesn't," he said, "look terrified."

He and Scott were alone in the room.

"The whole of our theories," Scott told him, "rests on the idea that she is. You'll be seeing Dr. Glezen and Dr. Stein before you leave here: they've been paged."

"Which is which, Dr. Rand? I mean, one's a—"

"Glezen is a clinical psychologist; Ernst Stein is a psychiatrist."

"Thank you." He looked up at the two monitors. "This is where she's been showing her reactions?"

"For the most part. She also has temperature changes and blood-pressure fluctuations."

"She hasn't breathed since she came in here?"

"She hasn't breathed since she was found on the freeway near the wreck of her car."

Cody was wandering around looking at things as he talked. "So if you flipped that switch, or pulled out that plug, that'd be it, would it?"

"Yes."

"I'm not thinking criminologically. I mean, I realize that no one could just come in here and—"

"Sure, we—"

"I just think it's amazing, a whole live human being plugged into the wall, like a hundred-watt bulb."

"Like a computer, perhaps."

183

Cody gave a sudden white smile. "I only got it half right, Doc, didn't I?"

"Do you need to see anything more in here?"

"No. I could have germs, right?"

Outside the room Scott said: "You'll be meeting Dr. Glezen and Dr. Stein in the Administrator's office, where we just came from. I have to be on my rounds now. When you leave here, what sort of action will you be taking?"

"Routine." Cody looked steadily into Scott's eyes, wondering if they were always jumpy like this, narrowed in what looked like anxiety. Medicos normally looked pretty stable. "I'll talk to her husband, her brother and the people where she worked—"

"Looking for some kind of enemy—"

"Right. Someone, anyway, who might own a car with smoke-gray paint."

"You believe there was actually a collision?"

"We're pretty sure."

Scott thought of Patrick Terman again, then dismissed the idea. That kind of thinking was for Cody, and he didn't look as if he'd miss anything.

"Also, I'll ask you and your staff here to keep an eye open for anything unusual—any strangers in the corridors, anyone unauthorized in the vicinity of her room, any calls you receive from people who don't give their name, asking for news of her progress. And obviously I'd want to know myself about her progress. If she could say just a few words to us . . ."

"I'll pass on your request. We hoped we could keep quiet about the police being involved, but that's not possible."

"Or even advisable." Cody looked at him quickly. "It's really surprising the things people get to see and hear which they'd normally miss." A brief smile. "We're a nuisance, but also a stimulus."

Dr. Rand, please. Dr. Rand to Cardio. Lab. 1.

184

They were all still working hard on Mr. Cohen.

"You have to go, Doc."

"Yes."

Cody watched him steadily for a couple of seconds. "I guess this thing has got you a little nervous, hasn't it?"

"Nervous?"

Scott could sense his own reaction: too quick, too defensive.

"It'd certainly hit me that way," Cody said.

Scott said low and with a lot of emphasis: "If we're right, that girl in there is in constant terror; in fact it's all we can do to counteract the adrenaline she's pouring into the bloodstream. I don't know how long her body can stand it, psychosomatically, but I hope it's long enough to give *you* time to do something."

Bill Brickman hadn't touched his coffee.

"You need a week's leave," he said.

"Who doesn't?"

"I don't," Bill said. "Because they're not using me as a guinea pig."

Arlene had her hands on the edge of the counter, near her empty plate. She'd been getting the impression her hands had begun shaking, ever so slightly, in the last few hours; and already she'd got into the habit of hiding them or supporting them so it didn't show. Especially when Bill was with her.

"What am I for, Bill?"

"Nursing the sick. Not for Don and Scott to use for their exotic experiments." He wanted her to look up at him but she wouldn't, because she knew he was right.

"Would you like anything else?" the waitress asked, and took their plates away.

"That's it, Maggie." Bill got out his wallet but didn't look away from Arlene, wishing to God he could think of the

185

right way to convince her she was going into this Claudia thing too deep. He'd never seen her look this way before—anxious, jumpy, withdrawn. And that awful bright smile—not awful, she was pretty as hell, but the falseness of it, the lies it told: *everything's okay, I know what I'm doing*.

"I'd like to talk to Scott," he said quietly.

She looked up now. "What about?"

"You. I want to ask him to put you back in the recovery ward and—"

"People don't *put* me places, Bill. I—"

"Okay, but—"

"I could have refused, when they asked me to change duties, and I could have refused to let them hook me up to—" But she heard her voice getting shrill and she stopped, looking away from him, wanting to go. "It's my life, Bill."

He put his hand over hers. "I know. But sometimes we're our own worst enemies. We let ourselves get into things we —well, we can't handle."

She slid her hands from under his and got off the stool, looking in the mirror and looking away quickly, hardly recognizing herself and knowing Bill was right and wanting to tell him; but she couldn't, and she didn't know why. There were the yesterdays, when she'd been a nurse at the hospital doing what she had to do and doing it the best she could, handling herself efficiently and knowing, somewhere in the back of her mind, where she was going. Now there were the todays, a group of experiences that had sunlight and darkness and clocks and sleep and waking all in a row but not making any divisions, making only one continuing and deepening experience—the time of Claudia—that had begun when she'd grabbed that pencil and scribbled with it while her left hand had supported her head because of the migraine, the time that was still going on and taking her deeper, deeper every minute and every hour, in a kind of

186

spiraling downwards into something that frightened her so badly she couldn't even scream.

And she ought to pull out before it was too late, but she couldn't. Three times she'd been on the point of saying yes to Bill, yes she'd go back to the recovery ward or take a few days off, away from Garden Grove, away from Claudia; and each time she'd almost prayed he'd insist and take this thing into his own strong hands and *make* her pull out; but each time she'd put him off, deceiving herself and deceiving him by relying on the one quality she loved in him above so many others: his willingness to respect her sense of privacy that had made a refuge for her since Roger died.

So if she knew all this, what was stopping her from getting out while there was time?

Claudia.

"Are you going back there now?"

He meant the Grove.

"Yes. Are you due in surgery?"

"At three." He looked at his watch. Arlene wasn't due back until three either, now that she was working the afternoon shift. It was a quarter after two right now. "We could go around by the park," he said, "if you like."

For more talking. For more persuasion.

"There are some things I have to do in the ICU."

But try harder, Bill.

"Just let me talk about it on the way there, Arlene." He left a five on the counter and held her arm as they made their way out. "Give me a chance to get through to you."

"You're getting through all right, but it's no good, that's all. I *have* to see this thing finished."

Go on talking, Bill. *Tell* me. *Make* me pull out.

His car was in the lot and he opened the door for her. "You mean finished, one way or the other? Okay, she goes on living or she dies, and that'd be a shame but at least she'd let *you* go free, you know that? And that's all I'm thinking about. She's just another patient and you're—you."

She clipped the seat belt on. It was five minutes but the statistics said you were most likely to have an accident within five miles of your home.

"Bill, will you please talk about something else?"

Something that'll shake me up, get me out of this trap I'm in. Something, *anything*.

"Okay. Okay." He made a left and saw the upper stories of Garden Grove topping the skyline. "Let's talk about the fact that it's your life and you have to do what you want with it. I'll go along with that. God knows how I will, but I will."

Candystriper to Central Supply, please.

"Miss Dean."

"Yes, Dr. Rand?"

"Did you just get in?"

"Yes."

"Denise says there's a dry IV in Room 1. Find out how it happened, and if it was negligence I want the person responsible to come and see me in my office."

"Very well."

Amy hadn't heard him speak like that before; normally he would just have said: "There's a dry IV. Find out how it happened, will you?" She was quite capable of having a nurse fired without notice and he knew it.

Scott was on his way to his office when he saw someone in Room 6 and went in there. It was David Pryor, and he was standing looking down at his sister on the bed. Her head was a little on one side and he could see part of the shaved area at the back.

"Good morning, David."

He hadn't called to say he'd be here and Scott wished he had. Nobody in the Intensive Care Unit liked people wan-

188

dering in and out on the spur of the moment; they were handling life and death in here and sometimes the borderline was narrow.

"You know something?" David looked around at him. "This morning I felt great because she'd just escaped being butchered in the operating room. All I could think about was that she'd been given a reprieve." His voice was very tense, very precise, and Scott noted the articulation of deep anger. "*Given* a reprieve!" He looked down again at the quiet figure in the bed. "Nobody *gives* this kid anything, not a goddam thing. I've had time to think this whole thing over, Dr. Rand, and I want to know if that bastard is going to call in another surgeon, and I want to know how much longer you people are going to push my sister around when all she wants to do is live." His dark head jerked up again to look at Scott.

In a moment Scott said: "Did you see anyone at the nurses' station before you came in here?"

"The where?"

"That central desk out there."

"No."

Scott saw that his face was expressionless now, because it's difficult to be angry when there's something you don't understand—the cerebration gets in the way of the emotion.

"Did you see anyone at all before you came in here?"

"Yes. One of those girls."

"She gave you permission to come in here?"

David's eyes came wide open. "Oh, *that's* what you're getting at!" He took a step toward Scott. "You want to know if *I* got permission to come and see my own sister! Jesus Christ, do you know what you're saying? She—"

"Forget it," Scott said. "I'm satisfied."

David stared at him. "*You're* satisfied. Well, I'm damned if I am! Is this all that medical science can do these days—

189

ship this poor kid from one place to another while you're trying to make up your mind what to do with her?"

It was the shaven head, Scott thought, and the reaction from the news that the operation wasn't going to take place. And the realization that his sister's destiny lay in everyone's hands but his own: in the hands of Patrick Terman, whom he despised, and those of a bunch of medical men who couldn't agree on how to save her life.

"Medical science," he told David, "has so far got her from a wreck on the highway to this bed without letting her die."

"How do you know she would've died?"

The boy seemed far gone.

"People who stop breathing normally do."

"So you kept her alive. What for? For this?"

"How much sleep did you get," Scott asked him, "after you left here at one o'clock this morning?"

"How much would you think?"

"I have one thing you might like to hear, David. I don't know if Terman's going to call in another surgeon, but there's no question of an operation now. Claudia's blood pressure has gone up several points since last night, and there's a consistent increase in the heart rate."

David tilted his head. "That's *good* news?"

"These changes aren't dangerous, but they'd make surgery too high a risk."

David looked down at his sister again and for a while didn't say anything more. Scott took a call from the nurses' station and came back after a few minutes.

"It's having to see her like this," David said very quietly without looking up, "and not being able to do anything. Not being able to take any kind of responsibility, while everyone else seems—" He left it.

"I understand," Scott said.

"You know something?" he looked up now. "She's my

190

kid sister. I mean, she always has been. That makes a difference, did you know? Do you have a kid sister?"

"No."

"Well, you have to look after them. Our dad went when she was nine years old, okay? I was twelve, then. And when Mother took off a year later—because she couldn't live without Dad, it was like that between them and it wouldn't have mattered if there'd been a dozen of us kids, she'd have had to go—well, when she took off, there was just the two of us, and an aunt we didn't really know, and who didn't know how to handle us. All she could think of was how to keep our hands out of the cookie jar, and how to stop us reading in bed under the sheets with a flashlight."

Miss Wilson to Pathology, please. Miss Wilson.

It sounded as if they had the biopsy ready on Mr. Cohen. He was the star patient today, with the fever still on the rampage.

"So it's really a question," David said slowly, "of responsibility. I should have it all, and I don't have any."

"I see that," Scott said.

"But you don't *know*." David wheeled around, dragging his hair back with splayed fingers as if he could get his head straight if only he could get his hair straight. " 'I understand that'—'I see that'—okay, but you can't *feel* it." More quietly he said: "How long is she going to be like this?"

"I can't tell you."

"If she ever recovers, will there be any brain damage?"

"I can't tell you."

"I mean, will she be a—a kind of *thing*, one of those—oh God, will she talk okay and play tennis and—will she be *Claudia?*"

His eyes were very bright and Scott wondered if he was using ups or one of the amphetamines. "We have to wait, David," he said. "We have to be patient."

David went on looking at him, and Scott couldn't tell

191

whether he was hoping he'd say something more, something reassuring, or whether he hadn't even heard what had just been said to him, but was away on his own thoughts. In a moment he looked down again at his sister, and that was how Scott remembered him the next day when everyone was asking questions: David with his dark head tilted and looking down at Claudia, engrossed in his thoughts of the responsibility he didn't have, and ought perhaps to take.

Mr. Mancini reached across to the bedside table and pulled another grape from the stalk with his strong fingers. His hand was on the plump side, though not soft-looking; there were black hairs growing profusely on the back, as there were on his chest. He was a hairy man, and it pleased him, because he was short and without much grace; and since he'd been a boy he had taught himself that a man's greatest attribute was strength, and the evidence of strength in his appearance was a matter of pride in him. He had discovered long ago that he was attractive to women, and this was why he had never married; it would have been an embarrassment to him, and of course to his wife. Instead he had many women friends, not all of whom were attracted solely to his wealth.

These were the translucent seedless grapes from California, locally grown, which Patsy, the red-headed nurse, had brought in for him. They were very kind here, and he felt grateful to them.

But they were also an impediment, and as he sat by the window eating the grape he put his mind to what he had to do.

The situation with Fiorenzo Pharmaceutical's new broadspectrum drug Adrenon was at this time critical. It had been known within the company that there were certain problems connected with its final clearance tests at West Coast Research. These tests—now being conducted—were stringent. All tests at West Coast were stringent, and that was how Carl Heideker had established his reputation with the Food and Drug Administration. There had never, Mario Mancini had learned in his talks with the president of West Coast, been a case of a drug getting through final clearance tests and subsequently proving unsatisfactory in any way, as regards side effects or unexpected toxicity.

It had taken a great deal of persuasion on the part of Mario Mancini to convince Heideker of his case. There was of course no question that Adrenon was a *dangerous* drug, if used within the prescribed limits. It might conceivably have toxic effects, even dangerous toxic effects, on persons whose metabolism was so disbalanced that they were under prolonged and even indefinite nursing; and the moral consideration for Fiorenzo Pharmaceutical was whether to withdraw their new drug from final testing and do further work on it, or to proceed to marketing, with the help of West Coast Research, on the grounds that they would otherwise be depriving a multitude of people a potent means of combating their disease, for the sake of placing an infinitesimal number of patients at risk.

It had been decided at a closed-door session of the board to put the matter frankly to Carl Heideker, who had tested their products for several years and found them satisfactory; and Mario Mancini had been selected as emissary. Along with his physical strength he had an astute brain and the ability—shared by some of the greatest of mortals—to see the objective with clarity and reach it despite all opposition.

After several talks Carl Heideker had agreed with their point of view. He was aware of the immense power wielded by Fiorenzo Pharmaceutical, and of the fact that their allies in Washington would become his own allies if he were to cooperate in the Adrenon project, particularly at a time when he was seeking to enter state politics. It was also understood that the equivalent of one million dollars in

Fiorenzo convertible stock would be offered him as a token of the company's good faith and esteem.

The grape was sweet in Mario Mancini's mouth. From force of habit he kept rooting with the tip of his tongue for the pits, before remembering it was seedless. It was remarkable, he thought, how man had learned to manipulate nature and produce such a fruit. But then, manipulation was part of the machinery—of *all* machinery. It provided the checks and balances of government, industry and commerce, the world over.

Carl Heideker had recognized this when he had telephoned Mr. Mancini early on the morning of the fifth. Mancini had not been in bed, but at a private party at which considerable Arab money was looking around for a corner in the drug market; and the call had been put through to him via the telephone in his car and the parking attendant.

Heideker had told him briefly that immediate action was now required in the matter concerning the Phase C and Biopsy X5-79 trials at West Coast. It had been in effect a prearranged signal, since there had been earlier indications that the trials had come under suspicion from one of the young biochemists, and Mancini had told Heideker that if any "definitive action" were considered necessary he would take it personally.

It was not the first time Mario had been approached with a request to take effective action in situations inconvenient to Fiorenzo. He was aware that more than one member of the board regarded him as a hit man, and this he found pleasing, since a hit man was essentially possessed of strength—a quality he prized above all others. It was the first time, however, that he had failed to make his action effective, though of course it was only a temporary holdup. The summons from Heideker had been urgent and the means had perhaps been clumsy and inconclusive: the driver of the dark green sports car should have suffered terminal injuries but had chanced not to do so.

For the following twenty-four hours there had been the hope that no further action would need to be taken, but the patient in Room 6 of the Intensive Care Unit had continued to survive by artificial means, and Mario Mancini had moved in. It had not been difficult: his family had carried a history of heart disease and his brother had died of it; he was overweight and held a responsible position that exposed him to stress; and he knew enough from his medical training and his researches into the pharmaceutical field to choose an experimental drug at present under testing at West Coast Research—suggested by Carl Heideker—to produce a change in his CPK and SGOT enzyme levels and substantiate a coronary diagnosis.

At that hour—eleven o'clock on the night of the fifth—he had caused only a minor traffic jam in the street just three blocks from Garden Grove Hospital when he had stopped his car in the middle of the roadway and slumped across the wheel. (It was not the smoke-gray Pontiac, which had been left in his garage at home for a minor repair to the body by a privately employed engineer. He had rented a Ford.) The ambulance had reached the scene within the calculated five minutes and the car had been driven by the police to the hospital parking lot.

Soon after his admission to the Cardiac Care Unit he had been obliged to effect a change in his heart rate, because Dr. Thayer had seemed surprised at his rapid recovery. He had swallowed a few cc's of soapy water, holding his breath and rinsing his mouth with orange juice from the bedside table. Within fifteen minutes the nurse Frieda had come in to look at him, having seen the change on the electrocardiograph screen at the station; and he had complained breathlessly of chest pains. Dr. Thayer had been paged immediately.

195

But Mario Mancini couldn't prolong his stay for more than was strictly necessary. He was needed at the office, and there was the risk of the patient in the ICU regaining consciousness and uttering the few words that would prevent—in the final analysis—the new broad-spectrum Adrenon from ever reaching the vast market awaiting it.

He pulled another grape from the cluster on the side table and put it into his small fleshy mouth, gazing from the window at the line of traffic along the freeway, his dark glasses protecting his eyes from the glare. He had learned that the optimum time for going into the Intensive Care Unit was in the early hours of the morning, when there usually remained only one nurse at the station. She would frequently visit the various rooms in turn, remaining for several minutes to make routine checks or talk to a patient needing reassurance. He had seen this for himself, standing outside his room and looking along the corridor; and he had once gone as far as the nurses' station, saying he couldn't find his way to the bathroom. From there he had seen all that was necessary: Room 6 was the first on the left, and the second bed was empty.

He had rehearsed what he had to do, once he was in Room 6. It would take fifteen seconds. The total time for the operation, from his own room to the ICU and back, was an estimated one minute and twenty seconds. Two minutes would be sufficient to leave a wide margin of error.

At some time tonight he must avail himself of those two minutes. There would be no question later of an inquiry: the actual extermination would require only 10 cubic centimeters of air.

His teeth closed on the grape and it burst, releasing its delightful juices.

Chapter 13

Dr. Fineman, please. Dr. Fineman—Code 1.

The two nurses at the central desk raised their heads and looked at each other. They didn't want any more Code 1's—the CCU was now full and the ICU would have to take the spillover cases.

"We should dry his lungs," Scott Rand said in Room 2, and pulled down the blinds another inch: the sun was making a glare off the windowsill. "Start him on nasotracheal suctioning and check his blood gases every hour." He looked down again at Mr. Cohen. "See if you can get him to cough."

Half an hour ago Sonny Cohen had responded to his name, and the delirium had passed; but they were still having a problem oxygenating his bloodstream and Scott had called for a consult with the respiratory unit. At noon they'd had the new set of enzyme values and found everything had increased: SGOT 590, LDH 1180, CPK very high at 312. But at least the cultures back from the labs were all negative.

"How do you feel, Mr. Cohen?"

Something like "Yes" came from the puffy lips. It might have meant anything, but it was a response.

Scott went to his office and called the Police Department again just before two o'clock. Detective Cody was out, but would call him back. Did he have any information? Scott said he didn't. All he wanted to know was what Cody was

197

doing, what he'd found out, how much closer he was to the man who was evoking the "continuing scream" inside the head of Claudia Terman.

The phone began ringing but he ignored it, and after a while it stopped. He was sitting behind his desk staring at the picture of Eve in her leotards, not seeing it.

"We had a workout," Patrick Terman had told him an hour ago, "in the gym. Without gloves, just for the hell of it." The raw blue bruise on his jaw gave him a lopsided look.

"I didn't ask what happened," Scott said indifferently.

In the last two days he'd begun speaking straight out of his mind, sometimes hurting people. He felt he didn't have time any more for protecting their feelings. He didn't have any time for anything at all, while the scream was going on.

"There isn't any question of surgery," he told Terman, "until her condition improves."

This was what Terman had come for, to suggest calling in someone else.

"How long will it be?" he asked Scott.

"I don't have the slightest idea. Nobody has."

"But Jesus Christ"—bouncing on the balls of his blue-and-white sneakers, the bright blue eyes coming wide open —"it could go on like this indefinitely. Right?"

"Right," said Scott with emphasis.

"I'm not talking about—you know—her getting back up on her feet." He spoke as if he could persuade Scott to bring about a recovery, like you could persuade people to buy a dishwasher. "I just want to know when you think she'll be able to talk again."

Scott couldn't remember whether in California both parties of the marriage were required to attend the court, or only one. It looked like it was only one. All Terman needed was her oral agreement, and maybe a signature to confirm it.

"In this place," he told him, "we spend our lives wanting to know things, and most of the time we never get to succeed." He came around from behind the desk. "We'll keep you informed of Mrs. Terman's progress."

"So we just go on waiting?"

"We just go on waiting."

He had to open the door for Terman before he got the message. The phone was ringing and he was glad of the excuse; the more he saw of this buster, the more he understood David Pryor's longing for responsibility.

Terman went out while Scott was on the phone, leaving the door open and standing for a moment in the corridor looking toward the Intensive Care Unit, then turning suddenly and heading for the elevator.

It was the last time Scott Rand ever saw him.

The tip of the ball-point ripped into the top sheet halfway down and she tore the paper off and began again, her hand moving in feverish jerks and the pain in her head hammering and hammering until the light began going on and off as if the sun were on a switch.

Someone was calling out but it was far away and at the same time inside her head where the hammering was, dark and light, dark and light, while the pen stabbed across the top sheet of the scratch pad and she sat crouched over the desk with her body hooked in a kind of spasm, her breath coming in shivers, long and slow and regular like the pulsing of a ventilator.

"It's all right," someone said, but not to her.

The words came stringing out from the tip of the striped blue pen, line after line of them, tangling like wool and straightening out again, tangling and straightening, none of them with any meaning.

I'm hurrying, she said, *I'm hurrying,* because that was what they wanted her to do.

"No," someone said, "there's no problem."

Her head was clearing now and she felt lighter, easier. The paper was ripped again and she started a new sheet, trying to write slower but not managing—this was a kind of torrent and it was whirling her along and she couldn't stop.

For God's sake help me, she said.

A phone was ringing and someone answered it.

The words writhed and tangled, scoring the soft white paper. She couldn't stop. She could only look at her white knuckles and the blue stringing of the words while she tried to keep on breathing, slow and regular, like a machine.

Dr. Glezen, please. Dr. Glezen to ICU.

Drops had begun falling, coming away from her face. Her whole head burned. The drops fell onto the paper, distorting the long writhing lines she was making.

Over, she said, it's over.

"That's good."

"Thirsty," she said.

Her hand slowed and the pen stood upright and then skittered away somewhere.

"Jean, get some water to drink."

"Yes, Miss Dean."

Dr. Glezen to ICU, please. Dr. Glezen.

"All right now?"

"What?"

"Are you all right now?"

"Oh God, I'm so thirsty."

She wiped her face with her hand, feeling the perspiration stinging her lips, salty and warm. She took deep breaths, again and again as if she'd been diving and had come up for air.

"Deep breaths," Miss Dean said. "Dee-eep breaths."

"Yes."

Her head was perfectly clear now, the migraine completely gone; but she didn't feel relieved, as she normally did after it had happened. She just felt scared as hell.

He wants to kill me soon. Can't anyone stop him?
They had to study four sheets of close nonstop writing before they could come up with these two phrases. They were a distillation of a whole stream of indecipherable words and half-words with many repetitions, but no one felt any doubt that the two phrases carried the theme of this, the sixth message to reach them from Claudia.

Don Glezen had got to the ICU by the time Arlene was drinking cup after cup of water, Miss Dean looking after her. It had been almost an hour before she could go back on duty, and even then her face was still white and her eyes nervous. Don talked to Scott in his office and they called Ernst Stein, but he wasn't in.

"It's nothing new," Scott said.

"Just more urgent," Don told him. "That word 'soon.'"

They called the police and left a message for Detective Cody.

Scott went to see Charles Jordan, the Administrator, to ask for a police guard to be mounted in the ICU at night, and after fifteen minutes' tussling the answer was no. The unit was "more than adequately staffed," according to Jordan, for the protection of the patients; and there was still some doubt in his mind as to whether these "wild messages" were any more than an expression of a damaged mind.

Bill Brickman was in the unit when Scott got back from seeing the Administrator. He'd visited Room 6 twice during the day; it was generally believed that Claudia's elevated blood pressure and heart rate were at least partially a reaction to the preoperative anesthesia, and this was Bill's field.

"What happened?" Scott asked him right away.

"Happened?"

"Sure. You look as if something—" He shrugged.

201

"Oh." They came out of Room 6 and stood by the fire exit, where no one could hear them clearly. "Look, Scott, can you do something for me? I'd like Arlene transferred back to Recovery."

"Just like that?"

"Have you seen her?"

"How d'you mean, 'seen'?"

This was Scott's unit and he was running it and he resented Bill's making this kind of request. It didn't occur to him that a few days ago he would have listened a lot more patiently, if only because Bill Brickman was a working associate and a personal friend. "A few days ago" didn't have much meaning any more: time had telescoped and he was running headlong through a tunnel and couldn't stop—until the screaming stopped.

"This thing's taking it out of her," Bill said quietly. "You know that."

"This isn't a rest home for retired nurses."

Bill drew a breath. "Okay. She has to work and she has to take it as it comes like we all do." He brought his tone down a little. "But you're using her for an experiment, Scott, and I don't think there's anything about that in the hospital employees' charter." From where they were standing he could see Arlene going into Room 2 with a nasotracheal set, looking just the same as usual except for the slight differences that maybe only he would notice: her walk less quick, her blond head held less high, her eyes narrowed with strain as she turned to say something to the aide carrying the towels.

"She can go back to Recovery," Scott said briefly, "just as soon as she wants to."

"She wants to, but she doesn't know how."

"Oh come on, she has a mind of her own, hasn't she?"

"No."

Scott stared at him. "What does that mean?"

202

"It means she's being taken over."

Bill's eyes had slow-burn anger in them but his voice was soft.

"That's putting it a little dramatically," Scott said.

He could see Miss Dean coming toward him, but she looked at him and turned away. A telephone was ringing faintly somewhere.

"I don't think so," Bill said, and Scott looked back at him. "You're being taken over too, but not quite so obviously. You can still help yourself, but Arlene can't, because she's under the direct influence of that"—he turned to look in the direction of Room 6, his eyes hostile now—"of that mind in there. It's all it is. It—"

"Stop," Scott said quickly.

"What?"

Bill was staring at him and the hostility was still in his eyes; but his voice was soft and Scott could hardly hear it. He didn't want to hear it.

Stop, he said again, but his own voice didn't have any sound to it: he just knew he was saying it.

"It's just a mind you've got cooped up in there, Scott. Switch that thing off and the body goes. That'd be okay if the mind was whole—but it's damaged. It's desperate and it's got a hold on Arlene and I'm going to break it."

Don't you go in there.

"What?"

"I said don't you go in there."

Scott felt his hands tightening into fists.

"I've got to go in there sometimes," Bill said. "The levels are still too high." But Scott didn't catch all of it because his voice was too far away.

I'm warning you, Scott said, but he could tell his own voice was too quiet, because Bill wasn't listening, wasn't registering anything. I'm warning you.

"Either you tell her she can go back to Recovery, or I'll

203

have to ask Charles Jordan." Bill was looking at him steadily. "And I don't want to do that."

"You'll have to."

"Okay."

"She's helping a patient, Bill. She's a nurse and she's helping to heal, and that's all I can think about. Claudia—"

"I can see—"

"Claudia *needs* her, don't you understand? Arlene's her *only* link with the outside world—the only way she can communicate. If it—"

"I'm not thinking about Claudia. I'm thinking about—"

"If she didn't have Arlene she couldn't tell us anything. We wouldn't know, any of us—Don, Ernst Stein, me—we wouldn't know what was happening." He put his hand on Bill's arm, urgently. *"We wouldn't know she's screaming in there."*

"Dr. Rand?"

It was someone else.

"Don't you see what I mean?"

"Sure, Scott. But I told you—it's not her I'm thinking about. She—"

"Dr. Rand, could you please come quickly? It's Mr. Cohen."

"All right." He turned away and Bill came with him because they were getting the crash cart and running with it into Room 2. There wasn't time to talk any more.

At six o'clock in the evening the sun touched the tallest of the palm trees that stood beside Memorial Grove, across the street in the next block. During the afternoon there'd been another Code 1 alert to deal with a coronary, and the patient had been transferred from the Emergency Room to the ICU. He was given the last vacant bed except for the one in Room 6.

Candystriper to Outpatients, please.

A few minutes ago Mrs. Cohen had called again and been told that her husband was rallying after his relapse and that she'd be welcome to visit him at any time, but mustn't talk to him.

Arlene was at this time in Room 6, checking Claudia for a suspected edema along her left thigh. She had assisted with the crisis in Room 2 and seen Mr. Cohen respond to the fibrillator within fifteen seconds; from the moment his heart had begun beating again he had continued to rally, and everyone had felt good about it. There weren't any statistics for the success/failure ratio with the fibrillator but the hits weren't high.

And here in Room 6 there was no edema. She left the patient turned on her other side and drew the sheet up as far as the tracheal tube, looking for a moment at the quiet face of Claudia. She had to make herself do it, because she knew now that behind this face there was the nightmare raging inside the skull. In the first few days after the messages had started she hadn't been able to relate the face with the brain, or the brain with the intangible influence that had slowly taken a hold on her. Now she could look down at Claudia and know who she was. She wasn't the girl in the photographs on Dr. Rand's desk, the girl with the white smile and the tan limbs and the flying hair; she was the migraine, the spiraling inwards of alarm and the need to snatch the pen and jerk at the paper with it while she crouched with her body hooked over the task and her breath coming in long slow sobs like the ventilator in here. She was all that Arlene had ever been afraid of, in all her life.

But she couldn't quit.

Dr. Rand had spoken to her after the crisis with Mr. Cohen was over.

"Dr. Brickman feels you should go back to Recovery,"

he'd said. But his tone was casual, as if he knew she'd refuse.

"I'm all right here. She needs me."

He hadn't said anything more.

She couldn't quit.

She wanted to help Claudia but she didn't want to be *made* to help. She'd begun living in fear that it was going to come on again, the feeling, any next minute when she wasn't ready for it. It sounded crazy, but if she could only be *asked*, by a thought kind of put quietly into her head, it would be okay—there wouldn't be that scary feeling of helplessness, of being caught up and flung across the room and made to write as if it was the last thing she must do before she died.

Dr. Gomez to Pathology, please. Dr. Gomez.

Everything else was going on just the same as always, and people were doing just the same, all over the hospital, leaving her alone with this waking nightmare till she was so scared that even Don couldn't help her, even Bill. She was alone.

No. Worse than alone. She was with Claudia.

She was *in* Claudia.

She *was* Claudia.

Claudia.

"She okay?"

"What?"

"No edema?"

"No."

Tracy went away.

She turned for the door to follow her out but stopped, without meaning to stop. There was nothing else to do: she'd finished the routine checks and there wasn't any edema, so she didn't have to feel the hammering begin again inside her head as she caught her breath and swung

206

around to the door but turned back again because this time she was going to refuse.

I refuse, but the air was growing cool against her face and she wanted to run because of the strength she felt that wasn't her own but someone else's, hammering inside her head and spinning her around to look for a pen, *but not this time because I'm Arlene and not you, I can do things on my own and you can't stop me if I fight back hard enough.* Spinning and whirling but holding on with the air cold and the scream coming, faint at first and then getting louder, *I can't stand it any more,* getting louder till it filled the room and the whole room screamed and she saw the machine and saw the switch and reached for it, falling, and the scream stopped.

At midnight Garden Grove was quiet under the waning moon, its white tiered structure riding in the night like a ship becalmed, with only its pilot lights burning.

Half an hour ago a Code 1 alert had been announced and Dr. Matheson had been summoned, reaching the operating room within twenty minutes and starting work as soon as the anesthesiologist was satisfied. He would still be working when dawn came: it was a traffic case with multiple injuries.

Now it was quiet again, but for the small night sounds that told those patients who were awake that they were not alone, whatever happened they were not alone.

In the children's ward a nurse sat by the desk, her back to the green-shaded reading lamp and her shadow—small though she was—covering half the beds in here. For ten minutes no one had called to her. In the children's ward ten minutes was a record, even alarming: there should be at least one small voice demanding something, if only comfort; but the ward was quiet, and she savored the respite.

Five beds along on the other side, Sheila Baron was sitting up, as she was permitted; the nurse could see her shape in the low light but not the coloring book that was propped on her knees, or what she was drawing with her crayons.

Higher in the building, in the terminal ward, a man lay complaining in soft monotones, saying he had the thing half finished and now he wouldn't be able to do the rest, and they'd get all over the place again and annoy the woman next door. He was talking about the hens. Don Glezen sat on the end of his bed and listened, letting him worry without trying to console him; it was a good thing when they fixed their minds on something trivial to complain about in their last hours: in this case there could be a lot of things more worrying than a hen run.

In the Intensive Care Unit on the fifth floor Tracy was alone for the moment: Diana was helping out in the CCU—which was now at full-ward status—and Arlene had been taken home soon after seven o'clock this evening and wouldn't be back for a while.

Tracy wasn't sure what had happened, exactly; they'd found Arlene on the floor in an odd position, her arms out like she'd been kind of flung down against the wall opposite the MA1 ventilator. They'd checked her thoroughly in a treatment room but there wasn't anything wrong; she said she'd just fainted. There'd been some kind of a row—someone had told Tracy—between Dr. Rand and Dr. Brickman, and Dr. Brickman had driven Arlene home himself, leaving a candystriper there in case she had a relapse.

The phone rang again and she picked it up.

"ICU, this is Tracy."

"Is everything all right?"

It was the third time he'd called inside an hour.

"Everything's fine, Dr. Rand. Mr. Cohen is sleeping now, and Mrs. Graham was actually asking for something to read." She gave a little laugh. "I guess all we have is her chart."

"What are the readings for Mrs. Terman?"

She glanced up. "Ninety-eight bpm on the EKG, five cps on the EEG."

After a pause he said: "Call me if there's any change." He hung up.

Shortly after 12:30 Tracy checked Mrs. Terman again but didn't turn her, because by that time the electroencephalograph was displaying 3.5 cycles per second in the delta region of deep sleep. She slept very infrequently, and the instructions were to let her do so unless it was essential to disturb her. In a normal patient in coma the brain would register delta cycles the whole time, but with Mrs. Terman the EEG hookup showed that her coma varied from "sleeping" to "waking."

Tracy left Room 6 the moment she had finished her routine checks; she was uneasy there, as most of them were. Nothing had been said officially but apparently there'd been some pretty odd things happening, and even the police were involved.

At 12:52 she checked Mr. Cohen again in Room 2 and stayed with him for ten minutes: he was awake and needed reassurance. Going back to the nurses' station she thought she heard the sound of a buzzer, and glanced quickly around the unit, at once noticing that the door of Room 6 was closed, not open as she'd left it. She hurried across to it and went inside.

At the Rand home in Seal Beach the telephone rang at ten minutes past one in the morning and Scott picked it up at the second ring. It was a respiratory therapist on the line, reporting that the MA1 ventilator in Room 6 had been found switched off for an unknown period of time and that emergency procedures had been started in the hope of saving Claudia Terman's life.

209

Chapter 14

"What are the levels now?"

"They're coming down, Dr. Rand."

"Check them again."

Someone asked: "Do we still need this on?"

"No."

The big lamp went out.

"She's not taking it, Dr. Rand."

"Try again. Can we increase the oxygen?"

"Not much," the anesthetist said. "We can do it a little."

"Do it, then. As much as you can."

The ventilator pulsed.

There hadn't been any kind of breakdown, the technicians had said. The switch had been thrown.

"Can we raise her a bit more? I want to get her head higher."

Two of the nurses brought more pillows, working cautiously among the tubes and electrode wires. A supervisor helped them.

There were still seven people in here; an hour ago at 2 A.M. there'd been ten. Some of them had nothing to do, but they were here because at any next second they might be needed. Miss Dean had come in from her home and the two respiratory therapists had got here within a half minute of the code alert because they'd been on standby since the CCU had become full. The crash cart was still near the

doorway, where they could swing it around in one movement and start work again if they had to.

"We'll do it again," Scott said in a monotone. "Two and
a half percent dextrose, 0.45 percent sodium chloride. And
someone open that window."

He looked up again at the electrocardiograph and saw
another wild fluctuation beginning, the heart rate swinging
up from 50 beats per minute, where it had plunged from
106 a few minutes ago. The electroencephalograph hadn't
moved from 4 cycles per second since the crisis: Claudia's
brain rhythm was at the lowest ebb in the theta region, just
above deep sleep.

The body temperature was down again to 97.

Her face had the pallor of the dead.

"Get some more blankets," Scott said.

He went outside and drank from the water fountain, trying to think what else they could do. There was nothing
else.

Detective Cody came again soon after 3:30 A.M. and
Scott was able to talk to him this time: when he'd been
called in a few minutes after the MA1 had been found
switched off there'd been no chance for anyone in the ICU
to see him because they were already fighting for Claudia's
life. Cody had talked to the staff in the CCU and one of the
respiratory therapists, who had shown him an MA1 ventilator in operation.

He was now able to talk to Scott Rand in one of the treatment rooms on the floor below, where no one would inter-
rupt them.

"How's it going up there, Doc?"

"She's still alive."

Cody looked away from the strained, crumpled face.
When people were having a rough time they didn't want
some bright cop staring at them: it made them shut up, instead of talking.

"She going to stay that way, Doc?"

"What the *hell* d'you think we're trying to do up there?"

"I guess I have the message," Cody said quietly.

"Have you talked to anyone? Any of the staff?" Scott heard his voice was still sharp and didn't care.

"I haven't talked to the staff who were on duty when the respirator was switched off. When can I do that?"

"I'll take you up there in a minute." He realized he'd missed something, and went out and along the corridor to the nurses' station on the gastroenterology ward. "If you get a call from the ICU, I'm along here in your treatment room D and I don't want you to waste any time."

"Very well, Dr. Rand."

He went back along the corridor.

"Do you have any ideas about this thing, Doc?" Cody asked him.

"You know the situation. We think someone's trying to kill Mrs. Terman and now it looks as though they got to her —for the second time. What exactly do you mean by 'ideas'?"

Cody looked at him deadpan. "On who might have done it."

"That's your job."

"Okay, but you know more about her than we do. You're—"

"We've told you all we know ourselves. You need more?" He ripped a Kleenex out of the box on the treatment cabinet and wiped his face again. "We'll go upstairs. I thought there was something to talk about—I hoped you'd found a lead."

"We're looking, Doc." As they went into the corridor he asked casually: "Do you have any thoughts on the husband? Patrick Terman?"

"Certainly. If you're looking for a motive, he has one. So have a lot of other people." He didn't say any more because

212

there didn't seem any point in throwing suspicion around at random; it wouldn't get them anywhere.

In the elevator Frank Cody looked obliquely at the haunted face of the man beside him and said: "It'd be a little misguided, Dr. Rand, if you chose not to tell me the name of anyone you suspect. Professional ethics can involve loyalties, I realize, but you—"

"My only loyalty in this case," Scott told him sharply, "is to my patient." Going through the CCU to Intensive Care he said more reasonably: "The fact is that I don't suspect anyone who's known to me, simply because the second message we had from Mrs. Terman implied someone had tried to kill her before she was brought into this hospital. I certainly don't suspect any of the staff."

"It doesn't," Cody told him as they went into the ICU, "have to be the same person. Someone may have tried, and someone else may have tried again."

Scott Rand stopped and they stood together in the doorway. He kept his voice low. "All right: Patrick Terman wants a divorce and can't get it until his wife either regains consciousness or dies. Her brother David has been hit pretty hard by this thing and he's upset that he doesn't have any responsibility for decision-making on behalf of his sister; it could be that he feels she'd prefer to die than go on living as what he calls a guinea pig." He saw Amy Dean going across to the nurses' station from Room 6 and knew she wouldn't leave there unless the situation was stable. "Those are the only ideas I have, since you asked."

"Yes, we're checking on them," Cody said.

"Already?"

"We try, Doc. We really try."

Scott took him into the ICU without saying anything more. The police had been told that Arlene had been found unconscious on the floor of Room 6 last evening and had questioned her, and in any case it didn't seem conceivable that she could have any motive for harming Claudia. Bill Brickman had been worried on her behalf and had spoken his mind about it, but Scott couldn't see a man like Brickman trying to kill a comatose patient in order to relieve Arlene of stress.

There had to be someone else.

He told Cody he wanted a plainclothes police guard mounted in the ICU and the detective said he'd arrange it, though he would need to ask the Administrator's formal permission retroactively tomorrow morning.

"If you find him difficult," Scott told him brusquely, "get back to me about it. I assume you can say right now that you're investigating a case of attempted murder?"

Cody looked at him in slight surprise.

"Oh, yes."

Scott nodded. "If that's official, we'll have less trouble with the Administrator."

After Cody had left the unit he went back into Room 6, where two nurses and a respiratory therapist were still monitoring the patient. An electric blanket was now covering her and the body temperature was rising gradually through 98.1.

"We're still getting those swings on the EEG, Dr. Rand."

He looked at the printout.

"We'll just have to stay with it."

Sitting down wearily on the spare bed, he checked his watch with the clock on the wall; they both showed 3:46 but he had to think for a moment before realizing it was A.M. and not P.M.

For ten minutes nobody had anything to do except wait to give the next injection of vitamins to complement the IV delivery. They sat, the four of them, in the quiet room, listening to the rough hiss of the ventilator and watching the monitor screens.

Somewhere inside the figure on the bed, Scott found him-

214

self thinking, was a spark; and they were blowing on it; and they would go on blowing on it till it took flame, or went out.

Before leaving the hospital Detective Cody questioned some of the key personnel, particularly the night clerk at the reception desk, who told him she had noticed a man coming in through the main doors some time around midnight.

"Did you know him?"

"I didn't see his face, just his back, so—"

"How far away?"

"Huh? Well, he walked past that wall over there."

"Did you call out to him?"

"I was going to," she said, a little worried now, "but the phone rang and I had to answer it."

"Where did the man go?"

"I didn't see, because I—"

"Which way was he going when you saw him?"

"Toward the elevators, through those—"

"You didn't see him actually get into an elevator?"

"No. I hope I—"

"Everything's okay. Can anyone walk in here at night without someone here at the desk seeing him?"

"I guess. If they waited till we were busy, answering the phone or doing something in the inside office, things like that. We often—"

"Would you recognize this man again?"

"Gee." She looked at the wall opposite, as if he might be there again. He wasn't. "I guess not. I mean he was just— just a guy in pants and a jacket."

"No hat, cap, headband, anything?"

"No. He was bareheaded."

Cody questioned her for another five minutes, having to drag the answers out of her one by one: a heavy man, or thin? Young or old? Quick or slow? Short or tall? The clerk

215

chewed on her gum and gave a little breathy laugh sometimes, like it was a guessing game they were playing—which,
godammit, thought Cody, was usually the case when he was
grilling a witness.

"Okay," he said at last, "if you can remember anything
else about him, call me. Anything at all, okay?"

She said she would.

But he didn't think so. He went down the steps to the
parking lot and decided he'd drawn blank pretty well all
round. As soon as he could he'd put a guard up there in the
IC Unit: that was where the action had been and that was
where, maybe, they'd pick up the lead they wanted. Maybe.

Mr. Mancini sat propped against his pillows, thinking.

Frieda Hoff, his capable night nurse with the Austrian
accent and the rather strict approach to her patients, had
broken a rule and stayed talking to him for five minutes a
short while ago. He had already heard the news that had
been spreading throughout the Cardiac Care Unit since one
o'clock this morning—that one of the MA1 ventilators in the
ICU had been found switched off behind a closed door—and
had heard for himself the initiation of emergency measures
triggered by a code alert on the paging system; and now
Frieda Hoff had told him the name of the patient whose life
was still in the balance.

She was Mrs. Terman, in Room 6.

But such a thing was impossible, Mario Mancini had told
Frieda, in a hospital like Garden Grove.

Such a thing had indeed happened, Frieda had told him.
But it would not happen again, she had added severely,
since there was now a policeman on guard in the unit.

Mr. Mancini sat thinking. His temperature was up
slightly and he was sweating. He had begun sweating when
his nurse had told him she believed Mrs. Terman would
recover, thanks to the efforts the staff were making. Last

216

evening he had planned his immediate future with fore-thought and precision and it had now been blown apart and he wanted badly to know by whom. But nobody could tell him. Nobody knew.

It would of course be convenient if Mrs. Terman were to succumb to this attempt on her life, but Mancini never laid his bets on uncertainties and he must assume without any doubt whatsoever that she would survive it. That would not be so very inconvenient if all others things had remained equal. They had not. There was now a police guard on Room 6.

He was also deeply disturbed by the discovery that some-one else wished Mrs. Terman dead. It might of course have nothing to do with her involvement in the Adrenon research trials, but again he never relied on uncertainties, and it was safer to assume there was a connection. It occurred to him in passing that Mrs. Terman was a fortunate young person: two people had so far attempted to kill her, and she was still alive. But the worst aspect of the affair was that his own plans for a final and successful attempt had now been com-promised by a bungler, and he could see no way of getting through a police guard and reaching the patient in Room 6.

Mario Mancini sat very still, propped on his pillows, his strong hairy hands lying on the coverlet and his dark glasses turned toward the blank wall. By this time tomorrow the death of Mrs. Terman must have taken place, by whatever means and in whatever manner. To this he would hold him-self dedicated.

It was already noon the following day when Scott came out of Room 6 and asked for some coffee and sat alone in his office with his feet on the desk and the reflected sunlight revealing the dark blue stubble on his face. His eyes re-mained closed until one of the nurses' aides brought his coffee in and put it hesitantly on the desk beside his feet.

217

"Thank you."

"You're welcome, Dr. Rand."

Don Glezen found him there five minutes later.

"How is she, Scott?"

"She's out of immediate danger."

Don sat on the edge of the desk and looked down at him. "Now you need some sleep."

"Yes." His face was itching and he put his hand to it, feeling the stubble in surprise. "You want some coffee?"

"No," Don said.

"Can't you find something better to look at?" Scott asked him irritably. "What do you think I put pictures on the wall for?"

He knew what Don was thinking: he could have got Thayer or Gomez or Fineman to take over the supervision for him in Room 6 at intervals to give him a break, but he'd had to go it alone for twelve hours nonstop because he was obsessed—everyone thought so. All right, he was obsessed. He didn't want Claudia to die and he wouldn't trust anyone else with that spark in there they'd been blowing on since midnight last night, hour after hour until they'd got a flame.

"Don," he said in a moment, "you know what's on my mind. You know what we're up against now."

"Yes." Don got off the desk and stood looking out of the window instead of at Scott's hollowed face. "We don't have to doubt any more that she's functioning in the paranormal. That last message said: *He wants to kill me soon.* 'Soon' being the significant word. And now he's got so close to her that she's in subliminal shock—and she can't express it."

"Because Arlene's gone." He wanted to make quite sure that Don had the point.

"But of course." Don turned to look at him. "And you want me to think of a way we can reach her—or she can reach us. And I can't."

Scott closed his eyes again, as if by shutting them he

could shut his mind to the scream that was still going on, though they couldn't any longer hear it.

"We think she killed Neil Kistner," he said. "So why didn't she kill whoever it was who switched that ventilator off?"

"Their heart was probably stronger. Or she didn't have a sufficient degree of psychic energy. I've been talking to Ernst Stein, and he agrees with that: we both think the terror she feels is draining her resources—physically it's producing the symptoms of brain damage that doesn't exist, and psychically it's leaving her more and more vulnerable. You've seen the brain rhythm—it's settled at just half a point above deep sleep, at almost zero potential."

He would have liked to say something more hopeful and give Scott the lift he needed; but there wasn't anything he could think of that wouldn't sound specious.

"If we could only get Arlene back," Scott was saying, "we might get a message from Claudia, something that would give us a clue to the man we're looking for. She—"

"Bill wouldn't let her come back," Don said quickly. "And of course he'd be right." He left it at that, because he had a theory about Arlene's fainting last evening in Room 6 and it mustn't ever be passed on, even to Scott or Ernst Stein. Or anyone. "Are you going home now?"

"No." Scott shook his head. "I'll sack out in a treatment room, where I'll be close." He got to his feet clumsily.

"Till when?" Don asked him.

"What?"

"How long are you going to drive yourself?"

"For as long as I have to. Till they find the man, and she can stop screaming."

Don turned to the door with him. "It may take a little time."

"Okay. So it may take a little time."

He stood in the doorway, looking in. It was as far as they'd let him go. The police guard had checked his list and just said: "Okay, Mr. Newby, but you have to stay outside."

So that was where he was standing: outside. And it occurred to him at last that where Claudia was concerned he'd been standing outside all along, looking in but never going near, never touching.

He listened to the steady pulse of the machine that was keeping her alive; it sounded like someone breathing, but there was no one in there breathing: she was being *breathed for,* which kind of narrowed the difference between life and death to the difference between the active and the passive voice.

His thumb still hurt from the bruise, and sometimes he was aware of it when he came to see her. It seemed such an *awful* long time ago when it had happened—when she'd hit wild and the ball had come curving out to bruise his thumb; but it wasn't really so long; he hadn't bothered to count the days but if his thumb still hurt it could only be pretty recent. Standing outside the door looking in at Claudia, he didn't believe it had been this year, even, when it had happened; and he knew this was because the *difference* was so unbelievably great—not the difference between then and now, but between what *she* had been and what she was.

All that vitality.

Where did a flame go when it went out?

But it hadn't gone right out. Doc Rand said there was still a chance. There was always still a chance, he thought, if you hoped for it hard enough, believed in it, wished it, willed it, yearned for it, yelled for it till someone would hear. Maybe if he went on yelling hard enough, and long enough, she'd hear, and somewhere inside of all the tubes and wires and whiteness and silence, somewhere deeper inside the quietly lying head that was most of what Claudia really was, she would respond.

220

That would be something. And if it ever happened, if ever he saw her eyes open again, he'd begin from there. He'd go near at last, and talk to her, and touch, and finally make the bid he'd have to make before she started looking around and saw some other muscle-bound beach bum like the last one and did it all over again.

Just after she came on duty at 11 P.M. Denise Ross took a call from Patient Allocation and was asked to confirm that since the Cardiac Care Unit was now full the ICU would have to take any spillover cases.

There were two beds available, she said: the one just vacated by Mrs. Graham, and the second bed in Room 6, which Dr. Rand didn't want used until it was essential. She didn't anticipate any of her patients leaving the ICU tonight, unless Mr. Cohen had a terminal relapse. (This was not put into so many words over the phone.)

Denise was hanging up when Fran Engel came past the nurses' station and dropped a copy of the evening paper on the desk.

"Did you see this? I took it from the coffee shop and they want it back."

She had left the paper open to page 2 and Denise saw the headline immediately because the name of the hospital was there.

ENIGMA AT GARDEN GROVE
Brainwatch Maintained
Over Accident Victim

A minute-by-minute brainwatch is being maintained in the Intensive Care Unit of Garden Grove Hospital, where a team of doctors is working around the clock to bring a patient back to consciousness.

The object of the vigil is an attractive young woman—

221

whose name is being withheld—who was seriously injured in a freeway smashup six nights ago. She is presently in the state technically describe as coma 4, which indicates total unresponsiveness to any stimuli.

As the fight for her life continues and her breathing is maintained by artificial respiration, the specialists attending her—who include a psychologist and a psychiatrist—are striving to establish whether or not she is accidentally a psychic link with the paranormal, due to her brain injuries sustained in the crash.

The police have found no explanation for the crash itself, and are pursuing their inquiries in the light of certain "information" said to have been given by the comatose patient through the medium of a nurse at the hospital.

A "mysterious occurrence" was mentioned further on in the story, described only as "a disquieting indication that the patient's life may still be in danger." The police were stated to be receptive to the idea that "something very unusual" was going on, and a twenty-four-hour guard had been mounted in the Intensive Care Unit. Detective Frank Cody, in charge of the investigation, was said to be "actively searching" for any person who might bear a grudge of some kind against the young woman in coma.

Denise folded the paper and looked up into the face of David Pryor, his sudden appearance making her jump. To-night they were all nervous and trying not to show it, particularly Fran Engel, who'd taken up whistling under her breath.

"Well hello, Mr. Pryor!"

"Can I go in?" He stood there looking like a sleepwalker, his hands dug into his jacket pockets as if he were cold.

From the chair outside the door of Room 6 the police guard watched him.

"We have some new instructions," Denise told him. "Nobody can go in unless Dr. Rand or Miss Dean is with them. Nobody outside of the staff, that is."

David was already moving toward Room 6 before she'd finished. The guard sat straighter in his chair, watching him as he came. He was a square-bodied man with a crew cut and a perfectly blank face, his eyes leveled as if they were aimed at whatever they saw. His name was Brady.

"I'm her brother," David said.

"Mr. Pryor?" Brady was looking down now at a list in his hand.

"Yes." He began going through the doorway, but was swung half around as Brady's hand came out.

"Sorry, Mr. Pryor. You have to look at her from here, okay?"

David stared at him dully. "She's my sister. My *kid* sister."

"Sure. But you can't go in. Sorry."

He didn't take his hand away.

"People keep trying to kill her," David said. "Don't you understand?"

"Sure, we understand. That's why I'm here."

"Mr. Pryor," Denise said as she came over from the nurses' station, "I can't let you disturb Mrs. Terman." She took his other arm. "And I want you to do something for me—it'll help her too." He was looking at her now, his eyes trying to focus. "If I give you something to help you sleep, will you go and lie down? We have a room you can use, on the floor just below."

He felt their hands on his arms, one on each side of him. His sister was in there and he wasn't allowed to go see her. They were keeping Claudia in there, *Claudia,* and he wasn't allowed to do *anything,* however he tried. Because they said he didn't have the responsibility.

"What do you think you're doing?" He said it in a shout and jerked his arms free and took a step into the doorway,

but the man with the crew cut was very quick and his fingers felt like they were clamped around the bone this time, just above the elbow.

"Sorry, Mr. Pryor." His voice was very quiet.

"I tell you I'm her brother—" And he tried to jerk free again but the cop had both arms now and was moving him away from the door, walking him like he was a big stuffed toy that didn't have any strength, while the nurse kept on saying she'd look after him if only he'd be reasonable. Another girl was here now and he recognized her because he'd seen her so many times: it was all he'd seen that he could remember now—nurses and the machine in there and Claudia lying so still that every time he saw her he thought *oh Christ it's happened, oh Christ she's dead,* till he had to steel himself to come inside this place where they were keeping his kid sister.

"When you lose sleep," someone was saying in the tone of a mother, "you lose your sense of proportion."

But he began struggling again because they surely couldn't realize who he was, but the man was too strong for him and they took him into an elevator and down to a bare narrow room where there was a bed with a blanket, and a young guy in a white coat came in and started talking to him while another voice sounded from outside somewhere, saying *Dr. Glezen, please. Dr. Glezen to Gastroenterology Room A.*

At midnight Fran Engel checked the patient in Room 6 again, recording her temperature, blood pressure, heart rate and brain rhythm on the chart, even though they'd been running a constant printout of the two monitors since this time last night on Dr. Rand's orders.

After she had gone out there was no sound in the room except for the regular pulsing of the spirometer as the diaphragm rose and fell inside the glass cylinder.

Claudia lay slightly on her left side, perfectly still, her arms under the blankets and her dark head turned against the pillows; in the window the three-quarter moon had cleared the foothills behind the city and was lifting through the haze, some of its yellow light coming into the room and lying across Claudia's face, to leave on her cheek the faint crescent shadow of her lashes.

By one o'clock the moon had moved higher than the heads of the palms along the boulevard and its light was whiter now, its beams entering the windows of the children's ward lower in the building, where one of the nurses was sitting with a boy who couldn't sleep.

On the other side of the ward, in the fifth bed along, the eight-year-old Sheila was sitting up again, as she often did during the dark hours. Her coloring book was open on her knees and she was using a red crayon; in the past few minutes she had covered three whole pages, not filling in the printed figures as she was meant to do but drawing over them, her crayon moving very quickly, almost as if it were running away with her.

Most of the sketches were of the same three scenes, and though they were crudely drawn because she was in a hurry they were still quite recognizable: one was some kind of animal in a cage, and another looked like a small automobile, but upside down with the bodywork very jagged. The one she was doing now was a person's head—a woman's, because the hair was long—with blobs against her temples and thin lines coming away from them.

The crayon was moving in fierce little jerks, staining the paper with its crimson.

Chapter 15

Shortly before 2 A.M. a Code 1 alert was announced over the speakers and Dr. Thayer went down to the Emergency Room as the ambulance paramedics were bringing in the patient: a middle-aged janitor from the Green Shield Insurance offices three blocks west of the hospital. He was in the throes of a massive coronary and Thayer put him straight under shock therapy with the fibrillator and started him on oxygen.

By 2:15 the man's heart was beating regularly enough to permit his being transferred to the Intensive Care Unit on the fifth floor with the oxygen and an IV running and a telemetric monitor taped to his chest ready for scanning as soon as he reached there.

The staff of the ICU took over the work on him and Scott Rand came along from the treatment room where he'd been sleeping. Thayer had the situation in hand and Scott went into Room 6 and looked at Claudia, talking to Denise Ross as she finished a periodic check. The patient's temperature was now normal and the electric blanket had been removed. The heart rate was satisfactory at 78 beats per minute, but the chart and printouts showed that the brain rhythm had remained constant at 4 cycles per second in the theta region just above deep sleep.

Scott had never experienced this condition before, in any of his patients. As Don Glezen had told him earlier tonight, it was as if Claudia's brain had been numbed by the attempt made on her life and was now unable to change its wave rhythm.

As he left Room 6 he talked for a moment to the police guard.

"You've nothing to report, Brady?"

"Not really, Dr. Rand." With his leveled gaze he noted the area of stubble the shaver had missed, the tension in the mouth and the eyes as Scott stood watching the monitor screens at the central station. "We had her brother in here a while back, that's all."

"David Pryor?"

"That's right. He wanted to go in there but we didn't let him. They're looking after him somewhere."

"Denise."

"Yes, Doctor?"

"Where did you put David Pryor?"

"In Room A, down in Gastro. He's under light sedation."

"Why?"

"I guess he was a little wild," Brady said.

"Because you wouldn't let him in there?"

"I guess."

Scott nodded. "Have you been in touch with Mr. Cody?"

"A half hour ago."

"Are there any developments?"

"Patrick Terman's been arrested, and—"

"Oh really?" Scott swung to look at him.

"Right. He's not standing up too well to questioning, and he can't produce an alibi."

Scott looked back at the monitor screens. "When was he arrested, do you know?"

"I think it was around midnight."

Scott went across to the nurses' station and checked the printout for the EEG. There hadn't been the slightest change during the past three hours. If it was fear of Terman that was keeping Claudia traumatized she might have

227

reacted at the time of his arrest, since he'd no longer be a danger to her. The EEG printout would have shown a shift of at least a few cycles per second, but it hadn't. Perhaps Terman had been too far away, and out of Claudia's limited telepathic range; but Scott didn't believe that. He didn't believe it was Terman.

There was still someone else at large; and inside her head she was still screaming.

"Let me know," he told Brady, "if you notice anything unusual or suspicious. Anything at all. And let me know if you get any further news from your department."

Mr. Mancini was on the floor.

The sudden increase in his heart rate had been seen on the slave monitor in the CCU and Fran Engel was the first to reach his room. Julie Sears followed her, her stethoscope swinging as she ran.

He had fallen between the bed and the window and was lying in the fetal position, his legs drawn up in agony; his face shone with moisture and his eyes were screwed shut behind the dark glasses.

"Crash cart," Fran said, and Julie ran back to the nurses' station, calling for Denise to page Dr. Thayer, who was on duty tonight in both units.

This was at 2:46 A.M.

Fifteen minutes later Mr. Mancini was placed on a trolley and taken into the Intensive Care Unit and wheeled past the police guard at the door of Room 6, where the last available bed in the unit had been readied for him. His heart had not at any time stopped beating, but he managed to tell the staff that he had severe chest pains extending along his left arm. He seemed desperately frightened of a further attack, and resisted any efforts made to alter him from the fetal position.

Dr. Thayer ordered 100 mg of Demerol intramuscularly,

and an immediate enzyme analysis. Both the Cardio-Pulmonary units were now full and calls were made to other departments in the hope of reinforcing the overworked night staff.

The paging alert for Dr. Thayer had wakened Scott some twenty-five minutes ago and he had helped them transfer the patient to Room 6. He told Thayer he'd remain in the unit at least until dawn and would be available for assistance in the event of an emergency.

By 3:15 Mr. Mancini was lying quietly in his bed with the EKG screen at the nurses' station recording a gradually decreasing heart rate through the high nineties. His CPK and SGOT enzyme levels had been found normal, and it was Dr. Thayer's opinion that the patient's fear of a further heart attack had probably aggravated his physical condition psychosomatically, which was not untypical in nervous persons.

At about four o'clock Mario Mancini opened his eyes and looked at the ceiling, where the streetlights threw the shadows of the palm trees.

The curtain had been drawn between the two beds, but he could hear the MA1 ventilator breathing for Mrs. Terman on the other side of the room. For a few minutes he lay listening to it.

The stimulant he had used for increasing his heart rate was a 10 gr capsule of Virinol C that he had taken from the trolley in the corridor of the CCU last evening for this purpose. A few moments before the two nurses had come running to his room he had splashed his face with water, and had considered it unnecessary to use any more elaborate methods to simulate the attack; the rest was a matter of appropriate and realistic acting.

He had waited until now to make his killing because it had required time for the effects of the Virinol to wear off:

229

he had wanted the nursing staff to become reassured about his condition, so that their visits would become less frequent. They had checked his blood pressure and temperature twenty minutes ago, and soon afterwards they had visited Mrs. Terman. In the normal course of events he would be alone with his fellow patient for the next fifteen minutes, and he was now ready to act.

Listening to the rough hiss of the spirometer on the other side of the curtain, he went over the immediate situation. The MA1 would continue pulsing when the young woman died, and the alarm signal would not be triggered: the machine would simply continue breathing into a dead body. This would give him ample time to return to his bed.

The first indication of crisis would appear on the EKG monitor screen at the nurses' station, when the heart stopped beating. They would take immediate emergency measures but would not succeed in resuscitating the patient, because of the air present within the heart. The syringe was already in his hand, its plunger drawn back to the 10-cubic-centimeter mark and the cylinder already containing the required material: air. Injected into the median cubital vein of the arm, it would reach the heart within a few moments and cause an embolism, the effect of which would be terminal. There would of course be no evidence of any interference with the patient.

Turning his head, he saw through the slats of the window blind the thin figure of Nurse Sears at the central station; her head was held low and she appeared to be writing. The other nurses were busy in the rooms on the far side, and he could hear one of them talking quietly. He could also see the outline of the policeman sitting not far from the door, his back half turned to Room 6. The lighting in here was very low, and the pulsing of the MA1 would cover any slight sound he might make with his bare feet.

The time was now right, and Mancini drew down the

sheets and left his bed, moving around the end of the curtain in the dim light and looking down at the patient, the syringe in his hand.

Sheila was screaming.

A few minutes ago the children's ward had been quiet, but now its peace was destroyed as the screaming went on and the nurses hurried to the fifth bed along the row on the right.

"*Sheila!*"

"We're coming, darling, it's all right!"

But she couldn't stop. She sat crouched in her bed with the coloring-book lying open on the floor where it had fallen, the images bright on its pages in red crayon—a caged rat, an overturned automobile, a woman's face.

Dr. Glezen, please. Dr. Glezen to Children's Ward—Code 1.

Sheila could not stop.

The sound of her screams was frightening in itself for the other children, and some began crying; it was as if a fever were spreading through the ward. One of the nurses was readying a needle in case sedation was necessary.

Spasms began shaking the child now, and as the first nurse reached the bed Sheila sprang from it, cowering away as if in terror, her bare feet pattering as she darted aside to stop them catching her. The scream was changing now, becoming stronger, till it was no longer a child's, but a woman's. As the nurses dodged and turned, trying to hold her, she put her small head down and charged through them, racing for the doors and swerving as Don Glezen came in, opening his arms to catch her but in vain.

She ran toward the emergency stairs, her hair flying.

Scott Rand was coming out of his office on the corridor above when Sheila's small figure came scampering from the emergency stairs, squirming out of his reach as he tried to

231

stop her; he began running after her, but she was quicker. Wild-eyed and with her hands flung out, she made headlong for the Intensive Care Unit at the end of the corridor, her screams primitive and terror-stricken, and as powerful as a grown woman's.

Seconds later as Scott reached the ICU at a run he received a medley of images: the child sobbing in the arms of a nurse who had managed to seize her and hold her safe, a patient in dark glasses swinging his body around in Room 6 and hurling something at the police guard, the guard pulling his gun as a glitter of blades and glass flew against him from the instrument case that Mancini had thrown, and then the bloodied face of the guard as he staggered against the wall, bouncing and pitching forward as Mancini broke for the fire exit beyond the nurses' station.

Brady was too slow to reach the man before he'd burst through the exit door but kept on after him and caught him on the emergency staircase between the fourth and third floors, not using his gun because the man wasn't armed and he could get at him now, plunging half across the guardrail and groping for him. But Mancini was quick, taking a last chance and going over the rail, his hand clawing out as he went down, catching the rail again but too late to close his fingers on it as he went down again, went down, his legs flying out and his arms reaching for the rail more than once as his short strong body turned and jerked, bouncing away from the banisters and striking them again, till he reached the concrete basement.

Some sort of calm had returned to the Intensive Care Unit a few moments later. A nurse was picking up the litter of instruments and glass fragments; a telephone rang and was answered; and by the doors Don Glezen was cradling the child in his arms, soothing away the last of her sobbing as she clung to him, exhausted.

In Room 6 Scott Rand stood watching the monitor

232

screens above Claudia's bed. A moment ago the electroen-cephalograph had begun showing an increase in the brain-wave rhythm, and it was now fluctuating at seven cycles per second, crossing from the theta region into alpha.

"Dr. Rand, should I—"

"Wait," he said.

The neon-green band of light was still quickening as the brain began functioning in the higher reaches of the alpha range of light meditation, then crossed gradually into the conscious field of beta as the mind of Claudia surfaced at last.

Scott watched the screen, for a moment unable to move; then he looked down as he heard a change of tone in the ventilator.

"Doctor, she's—"

"Yes." He checked the gauges and saw the patient had started assisting the machine. Over the next sixty seconds he adjusted its controls by careful degrees, until he could move the main switch, turning the ventilator off.

They listened to Claudia breathing.

On the EEG screen the brain rhythm was now steadying in the conscious field, and Scott looked down again as she opened her eyes.